The
Islanders

The
Islanders

F. J. Campbell

Matador
9 Priory Business Park,
Wistow Road, Kibworth Beauchamp,
Leicestershire. LE8 0RX
Tel: 0116 279 2299
Email: books@troubador.co.uk
Web: www.troubador.co.uk/matador
Twitter: @matadorbooks

ISBN 978 1789014 426

British Library Cataloguing in Publication Data.
A catalogue record for this book is available from the British Library.

Printed and bound in Great Britain by 4edge Limited
Typeset in 11pt Minion Pro by Troubador Publishing Ltd, Leicester, UK

Matador is an imprint of Troubador Publishing Ltd

To R.C., O.C. and T.C.

Island (ˈaɪlənd), n.

1. *A mass of land that is surrounded by water and is smaller than a continent.*
2. *Something resembling this: a traffic island.*
3. *Anatomy: a part, structure or group of cells distinct in constitution from its immediate surroundings.*
4. *A boarding school in the countryside of south-west England that's so remote and cut off on all sides, its pupils have nicknamed it The Island.*

Chapter One

1988

Early morning, the earlier the better, was Milo's favourite time of day by far. When he was walking alone to school he was something close to happy, despite everything. He blinked in the autumn sunshine as he stepped out of the woods, his eyes adjusting to the view that he knew so well. No need to stop and take it in; he'd seen it a thousand times before. His feet pounded the tarmac as he strode on, down the hill past the sports hall and the boarding houses towards school.

He was especially glad to be early that day, because it meant he saw her first. These things were crucial to his best mate Guy: Milo never would've heard the end of it, if Guy had seen her first. It was a matter of minutes, seconds even. If he'd stopped to tie his shoelaces or had an extra piece of toast for breakfast, it would have been a different story.

A car swooshed around the circle of grass in front of the main school building and he only caught a glimpse of the girl in the passenger seat, but it was enough, that glimpse, to make him stop and look again. It parked facing away from him. Inside the car he saw her arm reach up to the mirror, into which she stared for a longer time than necessary for someone so pretty. It was funny to see her staring like that, completely still, lost in herself. She didn't even fiddle with her hair or put on make-up or anything. Milo thought he saw her eyes in the mirror and he looked away quickly. Had she seen him watching her? He turned to go, but heard the car door open and glanced back again.

Oh.

Her legs unfolded, like in a film, and they were long and slim and he thought he might be dreaming them. Miniskirt, shabby red coat, dark, shiny hair falling over her shoulders, clear, pale skin, a smile on her red lips. She was breathtaking. Milo actually stopped breathing. He didn't know that was a thing that happened. Admittedly, his basis for comparison was limited, but she had to be the most beautiful girl in the history of the world. Easily.

Next thing he knew, the car had driven away and she was at the main entrance, trying the big iron handles on the double doors.

'Those doors aren't usually open. Well, sometimes they are. But not... umm... today.' *Nice one, Milo. Very slick.*

She turned and glared at him. For a long time. Her perfect mouth curled up, disbelief in her eyes. Disbelief at how anyone could be this much of a pathetic loser. 'Any chance you're going to tell me which doors *are* open? Before I die of boredom.'

Her voice nearly brought him to his knees. It curled around his brain, squeezing any last vestige of sense out of him. It was all he could do to point in the vague direction of the side door. She gave him one more frightening glare and flounced away, leaving him standing alone.

That's where Guy found him a few moments later.

'Hey, big man, I've just met the girl of my dreams. Well, when

I say, "met", I mean I saw her. In the corridor. What a babe.' Guy waved a hand in front of Milo's dazed face and then stopped. 'Oh, I know what this is. You saw her first. Didn't you?'

Milo nodded twice.

'That is just my bastard luck. Who is she? What did she say to you? I can't believe you saw her before I did. I think I might love her.'

But Milo pulled himself together enough to remember how she'd stared at her reflection and that self-satisfied smile, and said, 'Not quite as much as she loves herself.'

Milo slid into a seat at the back of the room, just as the headmaster started talking. He counted the other scholarship candidates: three boys, five girls. Including the girl with the red coat. Of course. He tried not to stare at her too much, in case she could feel it through the back of her head. Mr Toms' usual speech about the school drifted over him. He'd heard it before.

'Weatherbury Hall... fantastic opportunities... develop talent... give something back to the school... utmost dedication... Springer's Scholarship.'

That made Milo switch back on.

'Applicants for this scholarship must have been born and brought up in Wessex and will have to display excellence in a number of areas: academia, sport, art, drama or music. They will need to be motivated and enthusiastic. They will need to be good team members and leaders. This award is worth one hundred per cent of the sixth-form fees.'

That was the one for Milo; the only way he could stay at The Island after fifth form. His dad couldn't afford the fees, even with his staff reduction, and Milo didn't want to think about what he'd do if he had to leave. He'd been living here for all of his almost seventeen years, and in the next three days it would all be on the line. His shoulders tightened and a sensation spread through his stomach, fear mixed with doubt. *No. Forget my nerves. Forget the girl.* He shifted in his seat and planted his feet firmly on the ground, willing himself to concentrate.

After the speech, Milo returned to normal lessons while the other candidates had the school tour. He'd been excused due to the fact that he knew the place like the back of his hand. Still, he would've gladly gone too, if it meant he could have spoken to the girl again. In double maths he had to stop himself daydreaming about walking around the school grounds with her, showing her the woods, the river, the sports fields. He would have shown her all the places that meant something to him – the hill with the view of the sea where he'd had picnics with his mum, where his dad had taught him how to ride a bike, the rugby pitches, his cottage, the adjacent farmland his grandparents used to own. She would love it all as much as he did – how could she not?

The rest of the day was exams and interviews, one after another. By the evening, he was done in and ready to go home to the quiet cottage, to another silent evening with his dad. It was dark and way past curfew when he hurried up the hill towards the woods. The road was deserted and silent, except for the sound of muted voices and music coming from the boarding houses.

A sash window at the side of Norcombe House opened and a girl climbed out and sprang to the ground. Milo drew back into the shadows out of sight. He was pretty sure it was Olivia Rose's room, but it wasn't Livvy who had climbed out: this girl was taller than Livvy, athletic and graceful. She was wearing a sweatshirt with a hood, underneath which was a woollen hat. To a whisper from inside the room, the girl outside replied, 'Trust me, I don't need it.'

The window was closed from the inside and she turned from it and ran in the opposite direction from where Milo was standing, towards the sports hall. Now would have been a good

4

time to forget all this, go home and get some rest. Milo wasn't normally very adept at breaking rules and nobody could ever call him stealthy. And yet, he was curious; there were no teachers about and he told himself it was on his way home anyway. So he followed her.

Around Norcombe House, to the sports-hall doors. But she was nowhere to be seen. The doors were normally locked at this time of night (Milo knew full well, since his dad did the evening lock-up), but he tried one of them anyway and it opened. *Huh.* The surprise made him draw back and at this point, sense won over curiosity and he decided to go home. As he looked one last time through the doors, he saw the girl's hat lying on the foyer floor. Before he knew it, he'd pushed open the door, grabbed it and stuffed it in his pocket. *Right, that's it – out of here.* A quick look over his shoulder – still no teachers – and he skirted around the side of the swimming pool building towards the woods and home.

He heard a faint splash as he passed under a high window and stopped in his tracks. It had to be her. There was a steep grass bank, the top of which was level with the window, and he scrambled up it, but what he saw made him wish he hadn't.

The girl was swimming in the water.

There were no lights on in the pool.

She was far away.

But.

It was clear to Milo that she had no clothes on.

He had never seen a naked girl before. Her skin shimmered as she moved through the water and her long, dark hair fanned out behind her. That skin, that hair, he knew who she was – the girl in the red coat from that morning, except now she wasn't wearing her red coat. Milo couldn't help himself; he laughed out loud. Afraid that she'd heard him, he ducked and slid to the bottom of the bank. He ran, crashing and slipping through the dark woods, the picture of her burnt onto his eyes. All the way home, out of the school gates, along the overgrown path to the cottage. He opened the door, called to his dad, 'I'm home, I'm going to bed', ran two stairs at a time up to his room and collapsed onto his bed. He had to get a good night's sleep.

After one of the worst night's sleeps of his life, he woke with his alarm. He showered before his dad had even woken up and left a note to say he'd have breakfast at school. Milo thought it would probably be a relief for his dad to avoid the strained atmosphere between them, for once.

On the way to school, Milo was buzzing. If he saw her again, he might manage to say something less unbelievably boring – or at the very least a full sentence in coherent English. They were after all doing the same scholarship exams, so it wasn't beyond the realms of imagination that they might be on the same intellectual level. He wasn't thick, although he looked it – as Guy constantly reminded him – and he was a year older and about a head bigger than all the other fifth-formers, so that didn't help. Farmer West, they called him, on account of his size and strength, the former occupation of his grandparents and the total lack of wit and originality of the typical boy at his school.

He didn't mind, though: he wasn't proud. He'd failed his GCSEs in the summer, might as well not have turned up, but the school had given him another chance, and that wasn't something they did very often. 'Exceptional circumstances', they'd called it. He had gritted his teeth and sworn never to mess up like that again, no matter what happened.

There was an ache he had, when he thought about his mum, and he became very good at swallowing it, ignoring it. Milo never spoke about her, not even to his dad. Especially not to his dad. Every day, he took his place in class, he spoke when spoken to, he kept his head down. It worked, because it had to. It wasn't like anyone noticed much of a difference in him anyway: he was hardly the world's greatest talker, hardly the coolest kid in school. He was just the boy from The Island with no idea about music or clubs or parties.

But this girl, she wouldn't care that he wasn't cool. He would talk to her. Impress her. He could do that. There's always a first time for everything. *Hello, yes, nice to meet you, my name's Milo West, and you are...?*

Jesus, I sound like such a plank. He started to panic as he left the woods. He felt the hat in his pocket and for the life of him couldn't remember how it had got there. As he turned the corner past the sports hall, there she was, alone; a miracle if ever he saw one.

'I found a hat,' he said, without any other greeting. *Way to go, Milo.*

'You, again. That's my hat.' She reached out her hand towards it, her hand was right there, next to his, and then she paused. 'Wait. Where did you find it?'

'In the sports-hall foyer, last night.' He registered, too late, the surprise on her face.

She looked at him through narrowed eyes. 'What's your name?'

'Milo. West.' He took his eyes off her face. *Oh God, I hope she doesn't think I'm a pervert.*

'Well, Milo West, what are you, some kind of pervert?'

'No, I...' He was looking at his dirty old boots; the laces were undone. He couldn't meet her eyes. 'I just wanted to...' He glanced up finally and saw that she had walked away from him. He still didn't know her name.

'Elizabeth Atkinson,' Guy whispered, triumphant but red-faced, glasses askew, shirt untucked, slamming his books down on the table next to Milo in the library and earning a hard stare from the teacher on duty. 'She's called Elizabeth Atkinson.' He sat down and grinned from ear to ear.

'Mmm? What's that? Who?'

'The girl, big man, the girl. Keep up, will you?'

'Oh, right.' Milo sighed and shrugged. 'You mean the one that's been ignoring me all day?' Milo had decided not to tell Guy about the swimming pool, since he'd been gutted enough that Milo had seen her first, let alone seen her *naked* first. And Elizabeth had blanked him at breakfast and again at lunch, but he couldn't blame her for that – he'd not only been spying on her, which made him weird, but he'd also admitted to doing it, which made him gormless. All things considered, he would've thought less of her if she *had* taken any notice of him.

'That's the one. Now, listen, there's no time to lose. You can't get close to her with all these other soppy wazzocks hanging around her. You've got to get her alone. What's your plan?'

'Soppy wazzocks?'

'Yes, haven't you noticed? "Elizabeth, can I carry your bag for you? Elizabeth, can we sit together at lunch? Elizabeth, can I stare at your tits a bit more?" So, you've got to formulate a plan. You can't mess this up, or you will profoundly regret it for the rest of your long, unhappy and lonely life.'

Milo shook his head wordlessly and turned back to his book.

That evening, after the second day of exams and sneaking furtive looks at Elizabeth Atkinson, Milo arrived home. He'd lost his key. He had forgotten to eat lunch, had a maths exam and the headmaster's interview the following day, and now this. Where the hell was his dad?

He stomped round to the back of the cottage with a ladder, aiming to climb up to the bathroom window, which had a loose latch he thought he might be able to wrench open. As he reached up to the window, he heard a noise in the woods. His foot slipped off the top rung, plunging into only air, his other knee buckled and the ladder seemed to fall away from him. He made a desperate grab at it, grazing his hand against the rough wood, knocked his head on something hard and everything went black.

Milo opened his eyes and was sure he was still dreaming. The girl, Elizabeth, was right there, right above him, almost smiling as she peered down at him. He closed his eyes again. If this was a dream, he didn't want it to end. But she wasn't having any of that.

'Milo? Wake up. Are you OK? Wake up, would you? Say something, or I'll have to call an ambulance.'

'Whatsappening?'

'Whatsappening is that you've fallen off a ladder, you brain donor. You could have broken your neck. What are you doing here anyway – are you trying to do over this house?'

'Smyhouse. Lossmykey.'

'Ah, I can help you there, Sleeping Beauty. I found this on the path in the woods.' She held up the key in front of her, and when he reached out towards her hand, she dropped it into his. He closed his fingers around the warm metal. He didn't want to move again; he was so comfortable, and it occurred to him that, for the very first time ever, she wasn't angry with him. That was worth falling off a ladder for.

He watched her pull out a pack of cigarettes from the pocket of her red coat. She tilted the pack towards him, but he shook his head.

'Good boy. They'll kill you. If you don't manage it yourself first.' She put one in her mouth – *lucky, lucky cigarette* – lit it and stayed next to him on the mossy grass, looking around her as she smoked. Taking a last drag, stubbing it out on the ground, she helped him sit up and peered at him.

'Are you sure you're going to be OK? You're not bleeding, but you've got an impressive lump on your head. You should see a doctor.'

He raised his hand to his head and felt the lump, trying not to wince. 'I'll be fine. Thanks to you.'

'Yes, well, it's quite all right. It's not like I saved your life or anything. Did you say you live here?'

'Uh-huh. Would you... would you like to come in? For a cup of tea?'

She paused, looked at the cottage and then at him again. 'You know what, another time maybe. I should get back to school.'

'What if I black out again?'

'Don't milk it.'

He sort of laughed, but because he was so nervous, it came out more like a cough. 'Sorry. Thanks. Umm... see you tomorrow?'

'Yes, no doubt you will.' She stood up, brushed off her coat, and walked backwards to the cottage gate. 'If the last few days are anything to go by.'

Milo wondered if he could've played that better. She might have been flirting with him, just a bit, but he wasn't sure. He racked his brains about what every word and look had meant. She'd called him Sleeping Beauty. But also a brain donor. What he could remember most was a blurry feeling of being warm and close to her. He was no good at this. It was making his head ache. Or maybe that was the lump.

Anyway, she'd only be at school for one more day, and after that, if either of them didn't get a scholarship, they'd never see each other again. He had one day, then.

First up on Friday he had the interview with Mr Toms, the headmaster. Candidates were supposed to talk about their future ambitions: Milo wanted to discuss applying to Bristol University to study veterinary science. But Mr Toms was a big rugby fan, so he rushed through that and all the other questions and they talked about rugby for the rest of the time. Mr Toms told Milo that Mr Shepherd, the coach, would appoint him 1st XV captain for next year, but to keep it quiet until the summer announcement. He praised Milo's leadership qualities, and said he'd been impressed with how he'd coped with school this year. Actually, when Milo shook hands at the end of the interview, he had the feeling that Mr Toms had done most of the talking. *Is that a good sign? Not sure.*

As he was leaving, Mr Toms asked him to hand out tickets to the fifth-form party that night. And there he had it – one more chance to speak to Elizabeth alone. He distributed the tickets in the different houses, leaving Norcombe House until last. Rugby practice started in twenty minutes, so he changed into his kit and hoped it would impress her, show her that he could do something other than spy on her and fall off ladders. Clutching the tickets in his hot hand, rehearsing what he would say, he walked up the hill to Norcombe House after lunch, hoping she'd be in Livvy's room.

She wasn't, but Livvy was. She was lying on her bed, reading a letter on a large piece of paper, each line of which was written in a different coloured pen. The girls' bedrooms in the school boarding houses were very similar to the boys' – big enough for two beds, two desks and a wardrobe to share. Livvy had decorated hers with African printed scarves and photos of herself and her friends on beaches and ski slopes, and a large poster of John Lennon and Yoko Ono in bed. Milo liked Livvy, she was always friendly to him; mind you, she was friendly to everyone. She was that girl – every school has one – who knows everyone, and also what their parents do, especially the famous and the rich ones. Milo couldn't remember stuff like that and wasn't interested in it anyway, and despite her friendliness, he wouldn't have trusted her to keep a secret – had he been interesting enough to have one.

When he walked into her room, she put down the letter and swung her legs over the side of the bed, turning to face him. He handed the tickets to her and sat down on her desk chair. He took a deep breath. She smiled at him, a knowing smile, and raised an eyebrow, waiting. Milo looked around the room and his eyes fastened on the other bed. He looked away again.

'I just wanted to ask you, you know, do you—?'

'About Beth Atkinson? What do you want to know? She's fifteen, lives in Melchester with her aunt, likes films and books, very brainy, a virgin—'

'Whoa. Stop. No, nothing like that. I just wanted to know... if anyone has asked her to the party yet. Do you know if she's going with anyone?'

'Ah, OK, that. I don't know if she's decided yet, but Nate asked her, also Sam, and Golo, and Matt—'

'Big Matt or Little Matt?'

'Both. But I don't know who she said yes to yet. Or she might just be going alone, with me, you know.'

He stood up to go, regretting that he'd said anything to Livvy. It'd be round the school before the day was out and probably she and Elizabeth would have a good laugh about him. He muttered something about rugby and turned to the door. But as he opened it, there stood Elizabeth.

'Hi. How's your head?'

'Fine. Thanks. Thanks again.'

'You don't have to keep saying thank you.'

'Oh, right. OK.'

She gave him a questioning look. 'Did you come to see me?'

'What? Oh, yes – I mean no. Doesn't matter. Got to go. Pugby ractice. Rugby. Um. Thanks. Sorry.'

She moved sideways, but stayed in the doorway so that when he stepped past her, no part of him touched her, but every part of him almost did. He couldn't get out of there quickly enough. Down the steep path, through the trees towards the rugby pitches, and only one thought: *Elizabeth*. At least now he knew he had zero chance with her. She had the pick of the boys at school – why would she choose him?

Then he heard footsteps behind him. A small hand slapped him on the shoulder and he stopped. Elizabeth was panting, waving her hand while she caught her breath. She rushed out the words.

'I've just heard from Livvy you came to ask me to some party or other and she thought it was a great joke because she told you loads of boys had already asked me. It's not true. Nobody's asked me.' She stopped and the colour rose in her cheeks. Was it from running after him, or from embarrassment? He wondered. And waited.

'It was a bit harsh of her. I don't know why she did it, just to tease you I think, because you... I mean... Well.' She shrugged.

Milo blushed and grinned at her. He didn't know why he grinned, but perhaps he did stand a chance after all. According to Guy, Milo looked like a village idiot when he smiled; his mouth was too wide and his eyes crinkled up and his dimples took over everything. Guy's theory was that boys should never smile at girls; they prefer the brooding bastard look anyway. But Milo couldn't help it – that was the effect she had on him. He looked in her eyes and she was smiling right back at him.

'So... if nobody else has asked you, would you, umm, like to go with me?'

The smile disappeared.

'Oh. Um. Well, I didn't mean that I want to go with you; I only meant to tell you that Livvy was teasing you. I'm not even going to the party, you see. I don't... it's not really my thing to go to parties with boys. I think you got the wrong idea.'

OK, so now he was really confused. Livvy's stupid joke was one thing, but now Elizabeth was saying that she'd rather not go to the party at all than with him. *Huh*, he thought, *she can't stand me.* Or perhaps this was part of the joke. Perhaps she would go back to her room and the two of them would snigger over it all. But that didn't seem right; they wouldn't be that cruel. Would they? There was no getting round it: Milo West knew nothing whatsoever about girls. He sat down on a tree stump next to the path and, before he knew what he was doing, he took her hand and pulled her down to sit next to him. Her hand was small and felt cool and smooth next to his.

He took a deep breath and rushed out the words before he could change his mind. 'I don't care about the party and whatever Livvy said. I just... ever since I saw you I can't stop thinking about you. I mean, ever since I saw you on Wednesday morning, not in the pool, you know... sorry. I know I'm not good enough for you, but—'

She wriggled her hand out of his and interrupted, but her voice was kind.

'Honestly, you don't even know anything about me and if you did, you wouldn't be saying all this stuff. It's you who's too good for me. Anyway, I'm not interested in boyfriends and that sort of thing. You've got to stop all this now, it's absurd.'

She was so close to him and he could see her eyes, dark and clear. Her body was rigid, her hands clenched in white fists. She edged away from him.

'OK,' he answered dully. 'I understand. It won't happen again.'

And that was the last time he saw her before everything fell apart.

Chapter Two

'**O**i, you, oi! Your Majesty. Slow down.'

Beth sped up. Crap. This was all she needed. *He* was all she needed.

He caught up with her. 'Did you not hear me? I said wait.'

'I heard you,' said Beth. She glared at the boy. His name was Steve Dean, but everyone at her school in Melchester called him Bueller, or rather, she suspected he made everyone call him Bueller because he reckoned he looked like Matthew Broderick. But his eyes were too piggy and he had a mean, thin mouth. 'What do you want?'

'I think we should walk home together, babe,' said Bueller. To her endless annoyance, he lived on the same estate as her and tried as often as possible to escort her home from school.

'You can think? That is an astonishing development.'

'Oooh, an astonishing development. La-di-da, aren't you, Your Majesty?'

Beth shrugged and walked on.

He shouted after her, 'I know a secret about you.'

Beth's insides went cold, but she forced herself to carry on walking. He couldn't… how? It wasn't possible. He was bluffing. Bueller was full of shit, end of story. She heard his feet on the tarmac as he pulled level with her again. Her upper lip twitched but she turned it into a scowl.

''Cause I know where you were last week,' he said with a triumphant smile on his face.

Oh, that. Thank Christ it's only that. 'Yeah?'

'Yeah,' he said. 'You were doing exams at that posh school in the middle of nowhere. Waterbury, Wankerbury or whatever. Want to know how I know?'

'Not really,' sighed Beth. Try as she might – and she didn't try very hard – she couldn't get used to this half-aggressive, half-amorous attention she received from the boys at her school, the illustrious academic institution of Melchester Comprehensive. Bueller was displaying all the usual signs: puffed-out chest, overconfident leer, nervous shuffling and standing so close to her that she could see his dilated pupils. She took a step backwards.

It hadn't always been like this. She had spent most of her life trying to be normal so that nobody would notice her. But when she was twelve, her body had decided that being ordinary was no longer the modus operandi – it had grown up and up, like a beanpole, like a long streak of piss, to quote two of the special nicknames she acquired at that time. She was teased for being clever too, and spent her time at school alone, shoulders hunched, face down – still trying, but failing, to be invisible.

Then last summer, her fourteen-year-old body had rebelled again. She was minding her own business that summer, reading *The Count of Monte Cristo* in the shade of a tree in the park near her house, and while Edmond Dantès languished in the Château d'If, Beth was filling out a little, in some places a lot. While he planned his escape and swam to freedom, her hair became shiny and her skin flawless. When he took his revenge on those who had betrayed him, Beth's dentist took off her train-track braces. In the space of that summer, she became extraordinary.

Now, when she walked down the street, open-mouthed men would watch her as she passed by. The boys at her school harassed her for a different reason than before and the girls, jealous of her new beauty, were bitchy and suspicious that she would steal their boyfriends. But she didn't know anything about boys and didn't care about the ones at her school. She grew a thick skin, concentrated on her schoolwork and told herself that friends were overrated. Or just plain unwanted, e.g. Steve Bloody Bueller Dean.

'My old man's a teacher there,' he persisted.

'Really, Steven? A teacher? What of?'

'Well, not a teacher as such. He's… he's a…'

Beth watched as Bueller searched in the furthermost corners of his tiny brain. Didn't take him long.

'He's the groundsman.'

'Bullshit. The groundsman's name is Mr West. If your dad works there, which I seriously doubt, then stop fannying about and admit that he's a cleaner or a skivvy or whatever he is. And yes, I did go to Weatherbury Hall to take the scholarship exams and I can't wait to escape from this execrable dump and hope never to lay eyes on you abysmal bunch of tossers again.'

Bueller un-puffed himself and the leer disappeared, replaced by terrified piggy eye-flicks to check no one else was listening. He waited until she'd finished and then muttered, 'Fuck off, you stuck-up bitch.'

She leaned in close to him, noticing with great pleasure that he flinched, and said, 'Consider it done.'

Just before Christmas, Beth and her Aunt Anne, who was her guardian, had a surprise visit from her Uncle James, Anne's brother, who was a teacher and lived in London. He'd been writing a book for the past three years, a biography, and he had a letter from the publisher with a contract to sign.

'It's make-our-minds-up time,' he said. 'We all have to be one hundred per cent sure about signing, otherwise it's not fair. Anne, you first.'

'I vote yes. It would be so lovely to be rich, for once.'

'I think "rich" is pushing it a bit. We're talking pocket money, a holiday every now and then, maybe some new clothes, nothing big. Don't get your hopes up.'

'I still vote yes.'

James turned to Beth with a worried look. 'I'm sure we can arrange it so that none of this comes back to you, at least until you finish school, or even university. You know I think that eventually, someone will figure out who you are. But this way we get to control the story, at least to some extent, and make *some…*' he gave his sister a pointed look, 'money out of it. So I vote yes, too.'

They both looked at Beth, waiting. She remembered how she'd felt when she thought Bueller had known. She thought with apprehension about how her life would change if anyone found out about her connection to the book. But extra money, some control, more time – it all sounded so sensible. Didn't it? And she loved Anne and James so much, after all they'd done for her.

'Yes. I vote yes.'

Beth received her own letter, congratulating her on winning the Springer's Scholarship and inviting her to attend Weatherbury Hall School in September 1989. She started crossing off the days on a calendar and she daydreamed about her new school. The thought of it made her heart lift. *Weatherbury Hall. My new school.*

That first day of the scholarship visit, when Anne had driven her there and they'd turned a corner at the end of the long, tree-lined driveway, Beth had stared in wonder at the main building. It didn't look like a school, it looked like a French chateau: three storeys of red brick with tall white-framed windows and red-and-white chimneys surrounded by pristine green lawns. *So this is what it feels like to be out of your depth*, she thought. *Well, there's a first time for everything.* She checked her face in the mirror to give herself a little time to recover her nerves.

When Milo West spoke to her as she wrestled with the locked doors, he made her jump, which made her angry. Good thing too – she was on the verge of running after Anne's car, but pulled herself together and glared at him. The first thing she noticed about him was how tall and wide he was. He had a mop of curly blond hair and dark blue eyes and wasn't exactly good-looking, but wasn't hideous either. He sort of mumbled at her and so she summoned up a hostile glare, one of her medium-petrifiers – after all, he was trying to help – and that shut him up.

Beth didn't think about Milo for the rest of that day, because she only had eyes for Weatherbury Hall. She never knew schools like this existed. They were taken on a tour of the grounds by a sixth-former: there were libraries (plural), a computer room, a room in the art block that was *only* for sculpture, a post office, a tuck shop, music rooms, each with its own piano – she counted twenty pianos. There was a photography darkroom, there were squash courts, grass tennis courts, stables for horses, a boathouse by the river, a fleet of minibuses for sports teams, a twenty-five-metre swimming pool, and best of all, a theatre. It had eight hundred tiered seats, proper lighting and sound equipment, everything to professional standard.

But it wasn't just all that, although that would have been enough. What astounded Beth the most was how she fitted in. She felt right away that she belonged here. She wasn't the tallest girl, she wasn't the prettiest or the cleverest and she certainly wasn't the richest. There was nothing out of the ordinary about

Beth Atkinson when she was at Weatherbury Hall. There were people who looked at her and some – like Milo – who even stared. But she thought that people liked her, for whatever reason. She made friends. This was new for her, and she liked it. She couldn't get enough of it.

She called Livvy with the good news about the scholarship and they arranged to meet up the next day, when Livvy was in Melchester for Christmas shopping. They sat together at a table near the window in McDonald's, watching the other shoppers struggling with huge bags and grim expressions through the driving rain.

'I think I'll just get Our Price vouchers for my whole family. Job done,' said Livvy. 'It's going to be fantasmagorical, next year at school. Dibs we share a room, pretty please, say you will?'

Beth smiled. 'Who else would I share with?'

'And you're so brainy, you'll help me with my homework—'

'We're not going to do the same A Levels, Livs,' Beth pointed out.

'Oh. Ah well, never mind, you can help me anyway.' Livvy giggled. 'I can't wait. We can share all our clothes.'

Beth raised her eyebrows.

'Fair enough, you're right, I'll never fit into your stuff.' Livvy sighed as she looked Beth up and down. 'Those poor defenceless boys won't know what's hit them.'

'Sounds painful, when you say it like that.'

'Oh, speaking of poor defenceless boys, do you remember Milo West?'

'The big gentle one, with the curly hair?'

Livvy's lips flickered into a smile before she straightened out her mouth. 'That's the one. Word on the street is, he has to leave our school because he didn't get the scholarship, and go to the local comp.'

Beth frowned. 'In Melchester?'

'Not sure.'

Beth shuddered at the thought.

Livvy said, 'I feel sorry for him, he's been living in Weatherbury village all his life. His mum and dad worked there—'

'Worked, past tense? Why not any more? Thought you said his dad was the groundsman?'

'Yes, but did I not tell you this? I can't believe I didn't tell you. I must be getting sloppy. Milo's mum was our music teacher, but she died two years ago last spring. It was so sad. She was lovely, she was my fave teacher, and then she got ill with cancer, and she died.'

Beth swallowed a lump in her throat. She remembered Milo all right: with his face up close to hers, a sprinkling of freckles on his nose, the sweat on the line of his upper lip, the blond stubble on his jaw. She had liked the way he'd smelt, a boy-sweat smell, it had taken her by surprise and she'd realised she'd never been that close to a boy before. And his smile was so adorable – she hadn't been able to resist smiling back at him.

Livvy interrupted her thoughts. 'And now his dad has gone all bizarre, you know?'

'Not really. How d'you mean, bizarre?' Beth liked Livvy, but she was often baffled by her unique turn of phrase.

'He hardly turns up to work any more – I heard some of the other ground staff talking about it. I asked Milo and he said he's ill. A lot. When he is there, he's like a zombie, and once I saw him down by the grass tennis courts, just staring off into the woods, so I said hello and he was crying. Bizarre. And what's even bizarrer—'

'More bizarre.'

Livvy pulled a face. 'Yes, that. When Mrs West died, that's exactly how Milo was. I mean, he didn't disappear, he was still at school, but all that summer, if you talked to him he just blanked you. Stared off into space. He screwed up big time with his GCSEs, even though he's no thicko. Unlike moi. He's OK now, he's really brave; I expect Mr West will muddle through too.'

But Beth thought that Livvy didn't look convinced. 'Do you really think Milo's OK?'

'Yes, maybe, not sure. He seems better these days. Why do you ask?'

Beth breathed in and out. 'I just think, you know, he's this great hulking rugby player and he looks so tough and… I dunno, strong. And then you talk to him and he's actually really sensitive and… his eyes. He just looks a bit lost. Like a lost puppy.'

'Yeah? I think that might be something else.'

Beth frowned and thought about the way he had looked at her after he'd fallen off the ladder, his hair crushed down on one side like a huge, messy child woken from a deep sleep; how his big, brown hand had trembled as he held hers when they sat together on the tree stump. She had been so silly with him, unkind really, flirting with him a bit. Or a lot? She felt bad about it now, but what could she do? Should she write to him, or ask Livvy if she had his phone number? But what good would that do? No, it was best to let it go. He would leave Weatherbury Hall and she would start the following term and they'd never even meet again.

Beth didn't see Livvy again for a while. James' publishers kept calling with updates about the biography and it was becoming clear that there would be more money than they had ever dreamed of. Anne put down a deposit on a house in a better part of town and they moved in just before Easter. The new house was away from the estate and there were only a few weeks to go until Beth would be finished with the comp. They were going away in the summer holidays, somewhere swish, the three of them, and there were new clothes in her wardrobe for once, and she could buy all the books she wanted. The future, with money, glowed in her mind with so much promise: escape, freedom, fun, never-ending skies to be discovered, everything hers for the taking. So all in all, she had to convince herself less and less that it had been a seriously bad decision to let James write the book.

At the start of the summer term, Livvy called her in tears.

'It's Milo,' she said, and Beth heard a great sob at the other end of the phone.

'Who?' *Oh, Milo West*, she thought. 'What? What is it?' Livvy sounded so upset, and a dread feeling crept into Beth's mind. *Surely Milo wasn't...*

'His dad. His dad committed suicide.'

Beth's first thought was, *Thank God*. But what kind of a thought was that? Milo's dad had committed suicide? She couldn't bear the thought of what Milo must be going through. She managed to stammer, 'How is he?'

'He's dead, Beth. Did you not hear?'

Beth waited until Livvy's howls had calmed into sniffling. 'No, I mean, how's Milo?'

'Oh. I see. He's a mess. Totally flaking out. We've had a massive lecture about it from our housemistress. Apparently, Mr West disappeared on the anniversary of Mrs West's death. Two days later, they found his... body up on a hill near the school; he'd taken pills.'

'Who? Who found him?' Beth felt sick.

'Some random hiker. He – Mr West, not the hiker – left a letter, saying he couldn't cope.'

'Couldn't cope? What the hell?' After the initial shock, Beth felt only anger that he could have done something so monumentally selfish. 'How could he do that – leave Milo alone in the world? What kind of a shite father was he?'

'He was depressed. Desperate. No one saw it coming, but he hasn't been right since his wife died.'

'Still. How will Milo... what will he do now? Does he have any other family?'

'Nope, I asked Mrs Toms. He's all alone now. He's seventeen, so he doesn't have to go into care, he can live independently. He's boarding this term; they've given him a room in Casterbridge House so he's not living by himself during exams. After that, he's got his parents' house to live in.'

'Shit.' Something else occurred to Beth. 'Never mind the Weatherbury Hall school fees – how can he afford to go to school at all? Surely he'll have to get a job?'

'Gosh, hadn't thought of that. I'll have to ask him.'

'No, don't. Don't bother him. Poor Milo. Last thing he needs, after all this, is for you to give him the third degree.'

Beth said goodbye to Livvy, having arranged to meet after exams were finished. She thought about Milo a lot that summer, about what a nightmare his life had turned into, and whether he was going to be able to 'muddle through' all over again, or not. Before term ended, she made a decision, discussed it with James and Anne, checked her fat bank account, and dialled the number for the headmaster's office at Weatherbury Hall.

'Mr Toms? It's Beth Atkinson here.'

'Beth?' His voice sounded strained. 'What can I do for you?'

'I… um. I heard about Milo. Milo West. Mr West,' she gabbled.

'Yes. Very unfortunate. A sad business.'

'I… it's about Milo…'

There was silence at the other end of the phone.

She took a deep breath. 'I want him to have my scholarship.'

More silence.

'Pardon me?'

'I want him to have my scholarship.'

'Excuse me, sorry, do I understand you correctly – you are not taking up the scholarship? You're not coming to Weatherbury Hall?'

'No, Mr Toms, that's not what I meant. I would still like to come to Weatherbury Hall – very much. I just don't want – I mean, I don't need – the scholarship any more. I'll pay the fees. Would it be possible… is it allowed… can Milo have the scholarship?'

'Goodness gracious. Have you considered this fully?'

'Yes, I have.'

'Are your parents – your guardian – is your aunt aware of this?'

'Yes, she is.'

'Are you serious?'

'Yes, I am.'

There was a whoosh of breath on the line. Beth was expecting complications and objections but to her surprise, Mr Toms said, 'Wonderful. Marvellous. Yes. What a simply... I can't tell you... just a moment, please...'

She waited.

'I can't tell you how much this will mean to Milo, and how much it means to me. Milo is a very deserving young man who, as you are aware, has suffered enormously in the last few years. You are doing a remarkable thing, Beth.'

'Thank you.'

'No, thank *you*. I'd like to clear this with the board of governors immediately, and then notify Milo as soon as possible. Goodbye, Beth, I look forward to seeing you in September. And Beth?'

'Yes, Mr Toms?'

'We were right to award you that scholarship.'

Chapter Three

Milo had spent every waking moment of the summer term revising for his GCSEs, never allowing himself to think about his mum or his dad, only leaving his desk to eat in the dining hall or go for a run in the woods. Even at night, in his new room, he pushed them out of his head. He listened instead to the noises of the boarding house that kept him wide awake – creaking floorboards, flushing toilets, faint voices in the hallways. And the strange smells too, of damp socks and furniture polish and sweat. He stared at the walls of his small room, bare except for his revision timetable, a photo of his mum and dad and a poster of Winona Ryder that Guy had lent him. His new home. But it didn't feel like home. Nothing felt like anything. He was a robot, a 'Milo Machine' according to Guy, the only person who could raise a faint smile on Milo's face. Others tried: Mrs Toms insisted he ate dinner with her and the headmaster once a week, and she fussed about whether he was eating enough and worried that he'd lost some weight.

And then, out of nowhere, Elizabeth Atkinson. Again. The girl in the red coat, the girl who had told him to forget about her. Milo was stunned by what she had done for him. She liked him; or at least, she didn't hate him; or at the very least, she didn't mind him. That was something. And what was more than something: he could stay at The Island. He could keep his room in Casterbridge House, and the cottage for weekends and the holidays. He would still have Guy and his other friends from the rugby team. But he wouldn't be captain next year – Mr Toms had explained with regret that the captaincy had been given to an upper-sixth-former, Justin Ravensdale, when they'd thought Milo was leaving Weatherbury Hall. Milo accepted it with good grace; it seemed churlish to do otherwise.

At last, GCSEs finished and the whole summer stretched before him. It would be lonely without his mum and dad, but after that he'd be back at school again, all thanks to Elizabeth. When he thought about her and how he'd chased after her, it almost made him laugh, it was so – what was the word she'd used? – absurd. She was way out of his league, as she'd proved beyond all doubt by not only being spectacularly hot, but also a winner of scholarships, so minted that she could pay her own way through the sixth form, and philanthropic to boot. What a girl.

He, on the other hand, wasn't ever going to get a girl like that. He refused to feel sorry for himself, but her charitable act marked out the difference between them: *I have everything, so here, have it; I don't need it, but* you *do.* He had been reduced to nothing, that was the brutal truth about his dad's suicide that he had to face up to. And not just financially. His dad was supposed to have looked after him, at least until he turned eighteen or left school. But he hadn't managed it. Milo had meant nothing to him. There was a void where his mum used to be and Milo could never fill it; he was invisible, not special enough to his dad, who hadn't been able to summon up even a speck of love for him.

He didn't want to talk about it, not with anyone. How would that conversation even go?

Milo West: 'I believe I am so irrelevant to the human race that my own father topped himself rather than spend any time with me.'

Guy Revel: 'Wow that is an epic headfuck. Want to watch TV?'

And if Milo said it out loud, it would make it worse, more real. He didn't know much, but he knew this: whatever had happened to him up until now was over. As of now everything was up to him; he had to ignore the ache again, make sure he didn't let it do to him what it had done to his dad. He had to swallow his pride and accept charity. He had to fight, or everything would turn to shit. No self-pity. No sob stories. Starting now.

After Speech Day, the pupils were taken home from The Island by their parents, cheerfully discussing their summer plans: holidays to the Med, the Cayman Islands, Hong Kong, sailing, surfing, parties at their parents' beach houses. Milo wasn't going anywhere this summer – he needed every day of the holidays to earn money to live on. The new groundsman had given him a month's work and he had picked up two weeks at Melchester Racecourse, as a waiter and barman. The restaurant and bar manager had turned a blind eye to the fact that he was not yet eighteen – he looked so much older, nobody would question it. Milo accepted Mrs Toms' offer of driving lessons, and they practised on the miles of school driveway until he passed his test. She also insisted on showing him how to cook a few basic recipes. He thought, with immense gratitude, *She's teaching me how to survive.*

Melchester Racecourse was thirty miles from The Island. Milo knew the way there because it was close to Melchester hospital, where his mum had spent the last few weeks of her life in the Macmillan Ward. Milo borrowed Mrs Toms' battered old

Ford Fiesta for the two weeks, while she and Mr Toms were on holiday. He had to be at work at eight o'clock every morning and worked until midnight, clearing up after the guests in the bars and hospitality marquees had gone home. It was loud, hot and busy in the marquees, and the days were long and tedious, but it was well paid.

On the final Friday of the races, Milo was working in the champagne marquee, when Livvy and a group of friends he didn't know sat at a table at the far end of the tent. Milo went over to take their order.

'Hi, Livvy,' he said quietly, pad poised.

'Milo,' she squeaked, and stood up to hug him. She was already drunk, and so was everyone else at the table, their cheeks flushed and their eyes glittering.

'Who's your friend, Livs?' asked a red-faced boy with floppy blond hair and a posh voice.

'Everyone, this is Milo. He's at my school. And he's here too. He's everywhere.' She collapsed into giggles and sat down as he took their orders.

'I say, Miles, you couldn't sneak us a couple of bottles of champers on the q.t. could you?' asked Floppy. 'I'm seriously low on funds at the moment.'

'Milo. No, I'm sorry, I can't do that.'

Behind Floppy's back, Livvy was mouthing *Tosser* at him as Milo tried to keep a straight face.

'I'll just… get these drinks. Bye.'

He brought the bottles and glasses to the table and listened as he poured.

Someone was asking Livvy, 'Is that other school friend of yours coming? Beth?'

Milo kept his eyes on what he was doing.

Livvy answered, 'Yes, supposedly, but she's late as usual.'

'Oh goody, she's not spoken for, is she? Didn't you say there was some fellow at your school who was mad for her?'

Milo flicked up his eyes to meet Livvy's and his hand slipped as he twisted the next bottle. The cork banged out and hit the ceiling of the marquee, champagne fizzing out of the bottle and soaking his trousers.

'Shit. Sorry.' Milo hoped his boss hadn't seen: the waiters were bollocked if they wasted the champagne. Only the punters were allowed to spray it around. He wiped his hands on his shirt and grinned ruefully at Livvy, who was giggling again.

Elizabeth arrived after lunch and Milo hardly recognised her. She looked more confident and grown-up, in a white sundress with a green-and-pink flower pattern. She must have been on holiday; her long legs and slim arms were tanned. At each table she passed, Milo saw heads turning: lazy, drunken smiles from the men; whispers and nudges from the women. Milo steeled himself and kept his eyes focused on the work he was supposed to be doing: uncorking bottle after bottle of Veuve Clicquot.

Out of the corner of his eye, he saw her joining in with the raucous behaviour of the group at her table. That was where she belonged now, with that sort of person. Floppy was trying his best to get off with her, filling up her glass and draping his arm over the back of her chair. Once, she glanced over to Milo and he thought she smiled at him. Apart from that she ignored him. So he took the hint and kept his distance.

Later that night, when the marquees and bars were closing, Livvy and Elizabeth's group were still hanging around. Milo kept an eye on them as he cleared the glasses, bottles and plastic cups from his area. It seemed that the game was to be moved on from every area of the racecourse until the whole place was shut down. By that time the staff were thoroughly annoyed with these obnoxious poshos, and Milo was told to get them to clear off, since he knew them.

Without bothering to deny it, he wandered over, his mind scrambling at the thought of finally speaking to Elizabeth after all this time, and after what she'd done for him. The group had finally decided to leave – there were about six of them left now, gathered around a new, shiny jeep, discussing who was going to drive them to Livvy's place for the next party. One of them leant his hand on the bonnet of the car and was sick on the ground. *Jesus*, thought Milo, *she can't possibly get into a car with one of these cretins driving.*

'Hey, do you lot need me to call you a taxi?'

'No thanks, Milo,' said Livvy, trying to keep a straight face. 'Beth's driving – she's an accomplished automobilist. One of her many talents.'

Milo watched in alarm as Floppy gripped Elizabeth's arm to guide her to the jeep door. He seriously doubted that she could drive; she wasn't even seventeen yet, so she didn't have a licence, and she couldn't even walk in a straight line. She was staring at Floppy's hand and then she looked at Milo – was that a flicker of anxiety in her eyes?

He tried to give her a meaningful look. She didn't react. He shook his head quickly, so only she could see. He was frightened now, and angry – if Floppy took one more step towards the jeep, he'd have to rugby-tackle him. He gestured to her to come over.

'What's up, Milo West?' she drawled. But she loosened herself from the boy's grip and walked towards him. Her face was half scared, half defiant. 'Don't bloody lecture me, it's just a dare. Can't resist a dare.'

He stepped closer to her and bent his mouth to her ear, careful not to touch her. 'Why don't you let me drive you back home? Or I could drive you to the party? If you get caught drink-driving, you'll be in trouble. They always have extra cops on the road into town after race days – they'll be waiting for you.'

'Shit. Is that true? You're not just saying it to make me go home with you?'

Milo couldn't believe she was flirting with him. He blushed. Floppy had noticed too, and he climbed into the driver's seat and revved the engine of the ludicrous jeep. Livvy and the others were calling to Elizabeth, but she ignored them and the jeep roared off.

'Oh, for fuck's sake, that's charming, isn't it? Now I'll have to come with you.' But she looked relieved. 'Why don't you come to the party too? Come and have some fun. You look like you need it.'

Milo led her to Mrs Toms' car, opened the door for her and wound down the window on her side. He drove out of the now-dark racecourse car park and as he turned onto the road to Melchester, he asked her for her address. She didn't answer, and he glanced over, only to discover she was asleep.

Milo chuckled, despite himself. All the tension from seeing her again disappeared. She had fallen asleep in his car. Unbelievable girl. Also, her language was appalling. He pulled over and reached for her bag, to find her address. He rummaged around for a minute before he found a fake ID card with her name and an address in Melchester on it.

He headed towards the Cathedral Close and found the street, no problem. He rang the doorbell, keeping his fingers crossed that it was a real address and that Elizabeth's aunt, with whom Livvy had said she lived, wouldn't be home tonight. There was no answer. Good. Her keys were in her bag too, so he opened the door of the house before going back to the car. He gave her a gentle shake but she was fast asleep, so – taking a few deep breaths to calm his nerves – he picked her up in his arms and carried her into the house. His heart was thumping so loudly, he was certain it would wake her any second.

Inside, he didn't know where to take her: up the stairs to her bedroom, the thought of which nearly made his legs buckle under him; or through a half-open doorway to the left into a living room. He thought that would be the safer option, and so pushed open the door with his elbow and managed to get her through the narrow doorway without banging her head on the frame. There were two sofas facing each other and a low table between them, covered with books, newspapers and old coffee mugs, overflowing ashtrays and something that might have been a pizza last week. He laid her down as gently as he could on one of the sofas and spread a blanket from the back of the sofa over her. He plonked down on the other sofa, exhausted, and gazed at her.

He must have fallen asleep because when he jolted awake, the clock on the mantelpiece said three o'clock. He didn't feel like leaving her yet; if she woke up she might be confused, or she might need him if she was sick in the night. It was the responsible thing to do, to stay with her.

He peered back into the hallway and found his way to the kitchen, to make himself a cup of instant coffee. The living room and kitchen were small and the hallway was narrow. He felt too large for it all. There were some unpacked removal boxes lying about; he stubbed his toe on one and splashed coffee on his jeans. There wasn't much furniture, and the kitchen was pretty much empty, except for some more dirty coffee cups and a loaf of bread on what looked like a garden table. Milo looked in the fridge – the milk was off. He decided to drink his coffee black.

Back at the sofa, he started looking through the books on the table. There was one underneath a pile of last week's newspapers, a new hardback called *Ten Lives* by James Hurst. He opened it with mild curiosity and a letter fell out of the first page. He wasn't meaning to read it, but somehow the word 'Beth' caught his eye and he couldn't help himself.

Dear Anne,
So, here it is at last. I hope it's something we can all be proud of, because without your help and Beth's agreement, I couldn't have done it.
The publishers are on board with all our ideas about

how to protect both of your anonymity; you can see that all of the pictures they used were the ones we agreed showed the family resemblance least. I think we can get away with this, I really do.

I'm still waiting to hear from the agent in LA about when I need to be there, but I'll plan to stay for at least two years. After that, Beth will be in a better position to protect herself, or at least make her own choices about her future.

See you on the 13th.

Big kisses for my favourite sister and niece,

James

Milo was confused. Why did Elizabeth need protecting? Who were Anne and James? Her aunt and uncle? What about LA? Feeling sure the answers must be in *Ten Lives*, Milo started reading, turning page after page, speed-reading, in case she woke up. The book was a biography of the Sauveterres, a mega-famous couple in the 1960s; he was a successful fashion designer, everyone in the world knew who he was. He married a stunningly beautiful young model, and they were a sort of mad party couple who lived in hotels, knew rock stars, partied with royalty and never stopped working and being talented and beautiful and cool. They basically were on a bender that lasted for about a decade.

And then suddenly that stopped. They stopped. They apparently decided one day to have a baby. Crazy decision, crazy people. But with the news of the baby, they changed. They did an interview together on a TV chat show, saying that the baby was the best thing that would ever happen to them, and they were going to settle down and give it a stable, normal life. They did some charity work, gave away all their money, moved to the countryside, stopped modelling, stopped designing – they became Mr and Mrs Ordinary. They did another interview when the baby was born, saying she was a miracle and that they had decided to live a new life full of good deeds.

That carried on for another year or so, and people lapped it up. They loved this ex-glamorous couple and their new virtuous life and their sweet baby, and yet people said how incredible it was that they had got away with all the drugs and the parties, their life of sin. And then the Sauveterres went and got themselves killed in a car crash.

That was August 1974. Their deaths made the front cover of every newspaper in every country in the world, and the world mourned the loss of their darlings. The book ended with the funeral, attended by hundreds of film stars, models, fashion people, royalty and anyone who was anyone.

Milo closed the book and knew without doubt what this meant: James Hurst was Elizabeth's uncle, Anne was her aunt, their sister was the famous model, and the baby, the little girl who everyone assumed had died in the car crash, that had to be Elizabeth. Adopted by Anne, who changed her surname to Atkinson to protect her from being exposed to the press. Milo had never heard of the Sauveterres before now, but he knew about *Ten Lives* because he'd seen it in all the bookshop windows and the bestseller lists in W. H. Smith's.

Milo closed the book and let it sink in. His mind whirling, thoughts whizzing in and out of his head, he tried to make sense of it. This girl, this miraculous girl who, let's face it, he was madly in love with, was something like royalty. Even now, he could feel her drifting away from him as she lay there on the sofa, looking like a sleeping angel, and his heart ached because he knew for sure she would never want him. What was he? The son of teachers and grandson of farmers. He was nothing special, not jet set like her; he had never even been abroad, except to Jersey, which he thought didn't count.

Time passed, the ticking of the clock moving him forwards to the moment when she would wake and he would be faced with this new Elizabeth, who would always be out of his reach. He wanted to stop time right there, freeze this night so that he would never have to face up to that. But he couldn't, and around nine o'clock she stirred and opened her eyes.

'Milo?' She stretched and sat up on the sofa, looked around, wrinkling her forehead in confusion and pain. 'The thing is, I have a shocking headache and I'm going to need a coffee before I can work out what's going on here... would you...? No milk please...'

Milo, dark circles under his eyes, his frayed and dirty shirt stinking of yesterday's work at the racecourse, his back aching and his heart as good as broken, stood up, rubbed his eyes and turned away from her towards the kitchen. When he returned with two coffees, they sat opposite each other and sipped in silence. Her eyes fell on the book, lying face down on top of the newspapers. She looked quickly from the book to him and he couldn't hide from her that he knew. *Here it comes*, thought Milo. *She's going to tell me to leave, shout at me, give me one of her evil glares.* But she didn't. She let out a long sigh and flopped back against the sofa cushions.

'Shit. Crap. I just need to think.' She rubbed the base of her palm on her forehead and closed her eyes briefly. 'OK, listen, you can't tell anyone about this. I dread the life I'd have to live if anyone knew who I was.' She shuddered. 'I have to be able to... just be me. Can you do this for me? Can you keep this secret?' She joined him on his sofa. 'Look at me, Milo, this is important.'

He looked at her and saw that she was serious and there was a fierce determination in her eyes.

'You stepped up for me last night when I needed you. Now I need you to do it again. You brought me back here, I was drunk, you didn't take advantage of me—'

'God, no, I would never—'

'Relax. The question is, can I trust you? What I need you to be is my friend. Not boyfriend, friend. Do you understand?'

He swallowed and paused, knowing that this was all she could offer him now, and it made him feel grey and empty to think that this was all it could ever be.

'Yes. You can trust me, I can be your friend.'

Chapter Four

It was almost lunchtime when Milo left her house. She closed the door and leant against it for a moment, before wandering through the living room towards the garden. She picked up *Ten Lives* and flicked through its pages, stopping to look at the photos of her mum and dad. With the book in her hand, she settled herself into a deckchair and closed her eyes, the remnants of her hangover making her feel lethargic.

She smiled as she thought about Milo. What a nice, solid guy he was. She barely knew him, but she had an instinct she could trust him. It was the strangest feeling – when she'd realised he'd read the book and put two and two together, instead of anger or fear, she'd felt only relief. Then she'd spilled everything. For the very first time in her life, she had told someone about her parents, just as Anne and James had told her when she was a little girl.

'Why did they tell you when you were so young? Didn't it upset you?' Milo had asked. He looked exhausted, he reeked of stale alcohol (yesterday Livvy had said something funny about an exploding champagne bottle; she hadn't made much sense, she'd been wasted), his hair was tousled and dirty and his eyes were half closed. But he insisted he was fine. Beth felt sorry for him, so she plied him with coffee and toast and he beamed at her. Easy to please.

'Not so much, really. I was too young, I suppose, to know what it meant. I just accepted it. Like you do. I thought it was quite exciting, to have a real name and a made-up name. I used to… umm…'

'What?'

'No, nothing. It was so silly.'

'Go on. You can tell me.'

'No, I really can't.'

'It can't be that bad. When I was young, my best friend was also an only child, and we used to pretend we were brothers. We thought we had it all worked out – my mum, his dad, they must have "done sex" together.' Milo wiggled his fingers in the air. 'So one day we accused them of it and, let me tell you, they were not at all impressed. We got into so much trouble.'

'They didn't see the funny side of it?'

'Might have been something to do with the fact that we made the accusation in front of about a hundred people, all of whom knew my parents, at the village fete.'

Beth smiled.

'And once, when I was about nine, I tried to run away, to go to his house. I had a map of England, a compass, all my *Beano* comics and a bar of Kendal mint cake. Suffice it to say, I didn't get there.'

'There? Where did he live?'

'London.'

Beth burst out laughing. 'OK, well, I suppose it's not that bad. I'll tell you mine. But it goes no further than this room, agreed?'

Milo nodded, with a serious look on his face.

'I used to pretend I was this girl called Elizabeth de Sauveterre – please note the addition of the pretentious "de" – and that I was a heroic soldier lifting the siege at Orleans and burning at the stake.'

'Ouch.'

'Or that I was a doomed but plucky princess languishing in the Bastille.' Beth felt safe; she liked telling Milo all this stuff. 'Or an ingenious Resistance spy caught by the Gestapo.'

'Not that ingenious, then.'

'Exactly.' She grinned. 'I just always had to be French and I always died young. Read into that what you will.'

Milo looked like he was about to fall asleep. More coffee required.

She continued, 'It was a good plan, to change my name. I didn't know it at the time, but all Anne and James ever wanted for me was to have an ordinary childhood. A normal life. Not like my mum.'

'How come nobody ever tried to look for the baby – for you? The press, I mean. Didn't anyone ever suss out that you weren't in the car on the night of the crash?'

'Don't know. Anne and James reckon it was a complete fluke. There were a couple of reports and questions in some newspapers, but it never came to much. Then, two weeks after the funeral, Watergate happened and Nixon resigned. Our story was forgotten. Anne and James used to do this toast at Christmas to Tricky Dick and then pour wine down their Deep Throats.' She shrugged. 'I guess you had to be there.'

'So then, what made your uncle write the book if you were all so happy being ordinary? If you thought you'd got away with it?'

Beth hesitated. She'd been asking herself the same question this whole time. 'I know. It seems stupid, doesn't it? But we thought about it for ages and there were loads of reasons to do it. We knew that the story would come out anyway, sooner or later, and we thought this way would give us more control over it. We also… I know it's greedy, but we've never had any money. We had enough to get by, but never more than that, do you know what I mean?'

Milo nodded like he knew exactly what she meant.

'And we thought it would be cool to have a bit of extra pocket money; it was too much to resist. But then it all got out of hand. The publisher's pissing his pants because it's selling like hot cakes and James' agent is talking about Hollywood, and then these cheques start turning up and… I dunno, it was all so exciting and we just couldn't stop it, or didn't want to. I suppose we thought we deserved it, anyway. Anne and James never got a penny from my parents; they gave away all their money or snorted it up their noses. *Ten Lives* is payback.'

Beth tried not to sound bitter, but she had always had a measure of contempt for her parents, no matter how much Anne and James had adored them, because in her opinion they'd been spoilt and selfish. Their decision to bring her into the world had seemingly been made while they were having some sort of drug-addled mental fit. Not a thought of how it might be for her: a life of being stared at and talked about, simply because of who they were. But Anne had given her as normal a childhood as possible, and for that she was eternally grateful.

Milo said, 'And why did you choose The Island?'

'The what?'

'The Island – Weatherbury Hall. Didn't you know everyone calls it that?'

'No, it wasn't in the official speech.'

'It's been called that for as long as I've been around. It's so cut off, you see – the river to the south, all the farmland to the west and north, and the hills to the east. It's so remote, one road in, one road out – it may as well be an island.'

'Huh. Well, I think that was kind of the point for us. We

wanted somewhere that was out of the way, so that I could just kind of disappear again for a couple of years. James had to go to LA to write the screenplay and if there was no connection between us, we thought we'd stay anonymous for another few years. So The Island is a perfect hideout.'

Milo shuffled in his seat and rubbed his hands on his jeans absent-mindedly. 'I... I don't know how to thank you for what you did. The scholarship. I couldn't believe that someone would do that... be so generous.' He raised his eyes to hers. 'One day I'll pay you back.'

She shook her head. 'No you won't. Don't think of it that way – that I gave you money. Even if you hadn't needed that scholarship, I still would've given it up. It would have been unfair for me to take it when someone else could use the financial help.' She saw his shoulders slump. 'Don't get me wrong, I'm glad it was you who benefited. But for me, it was more about the principle,' Beth lied smoothly. Milo didn't need to know how much she would have pushed to ensure he got her scholarship.

Milo stood up, unfurling himself and easing up to his full height. 'I'd better go,' he said. 'I'll see you at school next week.'

She fell asleep on her deckchair and awoke to the sound of the phone ringing.

'Hi, it's me, Livvy. We lost you last night. What happened?'

'You didn't *lose* me, you *left* me at the racecourse, remember?'

'Ah, but we left you in good hands. Milo take you home?'

'Yes.'

'And...?'

'And what? I hope you're not suggesting, Miss Rose, that anything happened with me and Milo last night?'

'When did he leave?'

'Mmm? Pardon?' Beth cursed to herself.

'At what hour did the gentleman leave, Miss Atkinson?'

Bloody Livvy. 'About half an hour ago,' she mumbled as quietly as she could.

'Oooh. Whathappened, whathappened, whathappened? Shall I come over? Tell me everything.'

Beth sighed. 'There's nothing to tell. He was worried, I passed out in the car, he just brought me in and stayed on the sofa to check I was OK.'

'And this morning?'

'This morning we just talked. He's really nice, I like him.'

'Like him or like-him like him?'

'I just like him. Like a friend. Don't you? He's a nice guy, don't you think? What's he like at school?'

'Ha, you said it – twice. He's "nice". Nobody has anything bad to say about him. Milo's just... he's not really... well, he's just sort of... there. Do you know what I mean?'

'I do, actually. He keeps turning up.'

'Like a bad penny,' agreed Livvy.

'No, like a good penny. Definitely good. Perhaps there's more to him than you know.'

'Hidden depths? Maybe. He's been through a lot recently. God. I can't even begin to think. But... Beth?'

'Yes, Livvy?'

'It's probably none of my business... but you seem awfully pally with Milo. Because you also said you weren't interested in boys.' Livvy paused. 'I still don't get that.'

'I... I just think they make everything... complicated. And not in a good way. You're right, no boys. And definitely not Milo. He's all wrong for me.'

She couldn't let it happen again – all those times when they'd been alone, that had to stop. She needed him to be on her side and she couldn't risk hurting his feelings, not now he knew her secret.

Beth said goodbye to Livvy and hung up, stretching out on the deckchair in the garden, feeling the warmth of the sun seeping through her skin and enjoying the vague memory of being held in strong arms. She decided to think about the matter of Milo West another day and then she fell asleep.

A week later, term started and Beth piled her suitcases into a taxi. This was what she'd been waiting for: a new beginning, new friends, a new Beth Atkinson. She rolled down the window and smoked her last legal cigarette for a while, thinking about the list of rules that had arrived in the holidays. No smoking, obviously. No alcohol or drugs, no cars – but horses were fine, what was that all about? Curfews, times when you couldn't play music, times when you couldn't visit anyone of the opposite sex's room. There was a list of punishments too: pre-breakfast runs, extra cleaning duties, Saturday night detention, suspension, expulsion. That she could do without. She wasn't used to so many rules; Anne was pretty relaxed, and Beth wasn't going to find it easy to remember what she could and couldn't do. Tough shit, then; she'd just have to not get caught.

The taxi turned into the front of the school and there it was again, the view of the main building that she'd found so daunting last year. This time, the taxi turned sharp right and followed the hill up to Norcombe House. Beth had been gutted that the single room she'd been allocated as a scholar had been reallocated when she gave up the scholarship. Never mind, at least she was in a double with Livvy; that wouldn't be so bad. Livvy wasn't there yet, so she dumped her suitcases on the single bed next to the window. Livvy would understand why she wanted that bed. She couldn't be bothered to unpack and there was nobody else about, so she thought she'd explore and maybe run into Milo.

Great minds think alike – he was waiting in the courtyard outside the house.

'Walk in the woods?' he said.

Beth eyed him, ready to put him back in his place, but he was smiling normally at her, no sign of the gawky kid who looked like he was in pain. Good. She had a pack of fags with her and wanted Milo to show her where the best places were to smoke without getting caught. May as well start now. They trudged through the woods and down to the river, Milo pointing out shortcuts and good hiding places. He was a mine of information about the school and its grounds, but when she asked him about the other pupils, he just shrugged.

'Best ask Livvy about that, that's her area of expertise.'

They chatted about her old school and Anne and James, and about Milo's parents.

'We're kind of the same now – orphans. I'm sorry about your mum and dad. That was really tough. At least I never knew mine.'

There was an awkward silence. Beth looked at him, expecting him to say something about how his dad had really landed him in the shit, or about how he missed him or hated him or anything.

But he looked the other way and his mouth tightened; then he said in a low, controlled voice, 'I'm fine. I'll survive.'

Beth didn't know if she'd said the wrong thing, or how to unsay it. *Quick, change the subject.* 'Um. D'you remember when you fell off the ladder? When can I come for that cup of tea?'

Milo smiled. 'Sorry, you're not allowed; nobody from school is allowed to visit without a permission form and they'll never give you one—'

'What, because I'm a girl? What do they think you're going to do to me?'

She could see him trying not to blush, scuffing his boot into the earth, his hand rubbing the back of his neck.

'OK, so I'm not allowed to come to your lair. But tell me, is it filthy? Do you live on takeaways and beer?'

'I'll have you know, I'm very domesticated.'

'Well, well. Is that a fact?'

They were back at Norcombe House by now and there were cars and trunks and parents and children milling about the courtyard. As Milo said goodbye, he paused for a moment and looked worried.

'I shouldn't really be telling you this, but… when you go to the dining hall for dinner tonight, there's this sort of lame tradition that the new sixth-form girls are given marks out of ten. It's so stupid – it's mostly the rugby boys; they sit on a table near the entrance, like a panel of judges. I just wanted to warn you. There's a different entrance at the back; if you want I can show you, or ask Livvy…' He tailed off and made an apologetic face. 'What's so funny? Aren't you pissed off?'

Beth was grinning. 'Are you on the panel of judges? You're a rugby boy, aren't you?'

'Yes… no… I mean, I am but… I just think it's stupid, don't you?'

'Well…' She tucked a stray bit of hair behind her ear. 'It's just that, if you were judging, I might stand more of a chance of getting a ten.'

She found Livvy and later they walked to dinner together. Beth noted that Livvy hadn't told her about the judging; lucky Milo had come through for her again so she'd had time to check her hair and put on a bit of lipstick. It was a stupid tradition, totally sexist, Milo was right, but still, she wanted to get a good score.

There were twelve of them, lined up at the first table opposite the serving hatch. Beth put on a convincing stony face, made sure she was standing up straight and ignored them. As she turned with her tray of food from the hatch, she glanced over at a row of nines, and as she and Livvy made their way up the aisle to find a table, the boys rose from their chairs and gave her a special round of applause, which made them both giggle and ruin the act.

Livvy found them two places at a table with some other lower-sixth-formers. She introduced them all to Beth, who instantly forgot all their names. They were all talking about their summer holidays – jet-skiing, sailing; one of them had even learnt to play polo. She zoned them out; it was too much at once. Someone was buzzing about a rumour she'd heard concerning a girl called Bonnie Markham. She asked Beth if she knew her.

'What, me? No, who is she?'

'She's the little sis of Edward Markham, you know, the head boy? She was in the fourth form last year and she's been taken out of school by her parents; she's at a day school in Truro now, that's what I heard.'

Beth made an effort to seem interested. 'Why have her parents taken her out of the school?'

'That's the mystery. Nobody's seen her all summer, except for once at a party in London, when she turned up late, had a massive argument with someone and left after about five minutes. She looked really ill, so I heard.'

'So, why don't you just ask Edward?' Beth suggested.

'God, no, no way, he'd never tell, not likely. Blood out of a stone.'

Now she was intrigued and asked the girl, Melanie, to point out which one was Edward Markham. He was sat at a table towards the back entrance of the dining room with a tray of food in front of him, bolt upright, talking seriously and nodding politely. Tall, with neat, dark hair, dressed in an impeccably clean white shirt, with an expensive watch, Beth thought he was incredibly handsome, like a statue of a Roman god. For a couple of seconds she stared openly at him. She'd never seen anyone that looked like him before.

Her reverie was interrupted by the arrival of two very red-faced, very blond, identical giants: Livvy's twin brothers, Billy and Jake Rose. She'd met them over the summer at a party at their house. They were collectively known as 'BJ'; were boisterous and lively, like large, friendly dogs; constantly told Beth how much they adored her; and only called people by their surnames.

'You will *never* guess what we've just heard,' they shouted at their sister in unison and then, not waiting to hear what her guess would be, 'Ravensdale has been busted for bringing in a bottle of vodka and three hundred duty-free fags. He's been suspended for a week and he's not 1st XV captain any more.'

Beth's eye was caught by a hulking teacher in a Weatherbury Hall tracksuit approaching a table at the back of the dining hall, and she watched him whilst vaguely listening to the twins' roaring. He stopped at the table where Milo was sitting and put his hand on Milo's shoulder. Milo stood up and shook the teacher's hand and as they chatted, she saw his face break out in a grin, as happy as she'd ever seen him.

She jumped as a voice boomed in her ear, 'Atkinson, my darling girl, that'll be West, our new 1st XV captain.'

Chapter Five

The weeks passed and summer turned into autumn, the woods around the school bursting into colour. Beth received a postcard from James every week, signed each time from a different James Bond character, and she pinned them up on the wall above her bed. Goldfinger told her he'd grown a beard; Rosa Klebb was into yoga; Blofeld hated the city, but loved the mountains and forests and the California coast; Holly Goodhead wrote to her about the earthquake that had hit San Francisco in October.

Beth made a point never to spend time alone with Milo, after that first afternoon of term. He needed to understand that's how things had to be. No more flirting or being alone all night with him. It was easy – they didn't have the same classes and he was busy with rugby and whatever else he got up to.

What she found more difficult was the day-to-day regime of The Island. All the rules and deadlines and curfews. She couldn't get the hang of having to be in certain places at certain times and her housemistress was forever handing her punishments for being late. When she compared it to living with Anne, it felt claustrophobic. Anne was such an unfit mother – her words, not Beth's – but they had a laugh together and she let Beth get away with anything. When James had visited from London, or when they'd stayed at his flat there, he took a dim view of how they lived and reminded Beth that being spoilt and beautiful hadn't helped her mother, in the end. That was when she'd realised: it was up to her, and her alone, to make great things happen in her life.

One October day, Livvy, Melanie and Beth were walking to their house after morning lessons. They passed the fork in the road that led to the boys' houses and Beth caught sight of Edward Markham heading towards them. Ever since she'd seen him on that first day in the dining hall, she'd found herself looking out for him around school and whenever he appeared, she felt a thrill spreading through her. He always looked the same: spotless white shirt, dark trousers ironed razor-sharp, gleaming shoes. And he was always so serious and aloof. She was sure that underneath that proud exterior, he'd be so romantic and fascinating. That day, Beth cursed to herself because she knew she wasn't looking her best; she hadn't had time to wash her hair that morning and her shirt sleeve was spotted with ink. It turned out not to matter – he showed no sign of noticing that they even existed as he passed by.

'Livs, what's the story with Edward?' Beth asked when he was out of earshot. 'Has anyone heard about his sister – Bonnie, wasn't it?'

'It's as if she's disappeared,' said Livvy conspiratorially. 'Nobody has seen her; she doesn't return letters or phone calls. I reckon her parents are keeping her prisoner. She must of done something really awful and they need to hush it up.'

'Must *have* done something,' Beth corrected, to general eye-rolling. 'Who are her parents and why do they need to hush up their awful daughter?'

'Her dad is a politician, quite senior I think. Minister of Foreigners and Secretaries or something...'

'*That* Markham? Edward is the son of the Foreign Secretary?' *Crikey. Also, can't these girls ever read a newspaper?*

Livvy was in her element now. 'So, he's really gorgeous, am I right? But he has never, not ever, been out with a girl, not from our school or out of school, because my cousin lives in Truro, near where the Markhams live, and she told me. She even tried calling him, asking him to a couple of parties, but he wasn't interested. Point-blank refused, quite rudely actually. A friend of my cousin, she's soooo pretty, she and her family went with the Markhams on a skiing holiday to Val-d'Isère. Every single night she tried to chat him up. Nada.'

Beth half listened as they prattled on and on. Anything and anyone was fair game for the well-oiled gossip machine of Livvy and Melanie. She was fond of the two of them, but they also drove her crazy with their childishness and their sheltered and privileged view of life. She could picture them in a few years from now, married to rich stockbrokers or bankers, with a litter of children and a fleet of servants, lunching at the tennis club and gossiping all the livelong day.

Livvy said to Beth, 'Do you have a crush on Edward Markham, then?'

'What's a "crush" when it's at home? Sounds painful.'

Livvy peered at her. 'You're so funny. Do you like him? Do you luurve him? Do you want to f—'

'OK, I get the picture,' said Beth. 'So what if I do?'

'Good luck with that. Anyway, I thought you weren't interested in having a boyfriend? And what about your biggest fan? Farmer West isn't going to take this lying down...'

'Oh, give it a rest, will you?' Beth snapped. 'You know Milo and I are just friends.'

'He's not good enough for you anyway. You could have any boy in the school you chose.'

Except Edward Markham. Beth frowned.

They were interrupted in their cerebral ruminations by the sound of twenty pairs of feet pounding on the tarmac behind them. They turned around to see the entire rugby squad bearing down upon them, and they jumped out of the way in the nick of time. There were BJ and Milo and Justin and the rest, on a training run. The girls let them pass by and carried on up to their house, hearing distant voices singing:

'I don't know, but I've been told, Atkinson is made of gold.
I don't know, but it's been said, I wouldn't kick her out of bed.'

After lunch every day, everyone met in the sixth-form common room, down in the cellar corridor of the school, to watch *Neighbours* on TV and catch up on the important news of the day – meaning The Island news, since nobody was interested in the actual news in the real world. Billy Rose had a letter from another cousin, or it could have been the same one who'd been so keen on Edward. The Rose network of cousins was so extensive and so efficient at newsmongering, they gave Rupert Murdoch a run for his money. The latest revelation was that Bonnie Markham had been removed from The Island by her parents, who had been concerned about a relationship with a boy that was 'too intense'. The boy's identity was as yet unknown.

That set off a flurry of questions between Livvy, Billy and the rest of the group, punctuated by loud shushes from the crowd watching TV. Beth wasn't paying much attention. Could it be true? Could anyone find out who the boy was? *Could I give less of a shit?*

'It is true; it came from something Bonnie's mum said. It sounds right, anyway. Bonnie's so pretty, she doesn't look fourteen. As long as I could get past Markham, I'd definitely be interested in getting intense with her.' Billy winked at Beth. 'Since you're not interested, Atkinson. Or… are you?'

At that moment, Milo walked in with Guy Revel and Jake,

changed for rugby training. Beth watched Justin Ravensdale get up and leave, a sour look in his eyes under their thick, dark brows. Justin resented the fact that Milo had been given his captaincy after he'd been suspended. He didn't know, because Milo refused to tell him, that Milo had been first choice as captain, before they knew about the scholarships and before Mr West had died. But Milo was too decent to take Justin down a peg; that was the kind of person he was. Beth would have done it in a second. Justin gave her the shivers.

Milo had just come from a meeting with the careers advisor. He and Guy were talking about university and he had some brochures in his hand. He sat down opposite Beth on the sofas and asked her what she wanted to study and to do for a job. She'd never talked to anyone about this before. But when Milo asked, she found she wanted to talk to him about it.

'I don't know what I have to study, but I know what I want to do.'

Everyone stopped talking to each other and she could almost see their ears wagging. *Oh well, here we go.*

'I want to be a film director.' It was so private, and she'd just shared it with the whole room. She braced herself for the inevitable teasing or dismissal of her unrealistic ambition.

'Cool,' said Guy. 'Sounds great. Can I have a part in your first film? Only, not if it's a porno, I can't do porno; my dick's too small.'

'Oh, man, shut up, will you? You are so gross.'

Guy rolled his eyes. 'Just saying.'

But they all ignored him. 'Seriously, that sounds brilliant, Beth, you'd be so good at that.'

Relieved that they hadn't laughed her out of town, she went on, 'Actually, I wanted to ask if it would be possible to direct a play here. How would I do that? Is that something I can do? I'd really like to.'

Livvy and Henry told her how to go about it, and the others

all said they'd audition. Their voices were enthusiastic, their faces eager to help. Beth glanced at Milo. He rubbed his hand over the back of his neck and she thought she saw him sigh. He stood up and left with BJ and Guy for rugby training.

She didn't waste any time with her plans for the play. She went to see Mr Gifford, the head of English, who gave her a slot in the theatre at the end of the Easter term. She had to choose a play by Christmas, organise auditions in January, and rehearsals would be weekly at set times through the Easter term. Mr Gifford was her English teacher, so he knew she could handle the directing, but he dropped some heavy hints about her timekeeping and suggested she co-direct with someone a little more punctual. She said she'd think about it.

So she started reading plays and trying to decide which one to put on. Shakespeare might be a bit much; she wasn't into musicals; last year they'd done *The Crucible* so that was Arthur Miller out of the running. She considered something from Eastern Europe, Václav Havel perhaps, what with the Berlin Wall falling a few days before. She couldn't decide.

In the end it was Milo who gave her the best idea. She found him one day, sitting alone in the main corridor, reading a book by Stella Gibbons that she'd loved when she'd read it a few years ago – *Cold Comfort Farm*.

'Give me that,' she said as she crashed down on the seat next to him and shoulder-bumped him. 'This is perfect, Milo, we have to do this – we have to adapt it into a play.'

'You could ask your uncle to help,' he suggested in a quiet voice.

'I don't need his help, I can manage quite well alone, thanks. It can't be that difficult, adapting a book into a play. If the dialogue's good enough, and funny enough, and the actors know what they're doing, it's a cinch.'

Milo's face was doubtful, but he said, 'I could read it through if you want? Or if you need someone to do rehearsals or whatnot?'

'Don't you want to be in the play?'

'I can't act to save my life. Must be because I'm too honest or something.'

'And so modest, too.' Beth thought about it. She had wanted to do this by herself, but maybe Mr Gifford was right; maybe she needed someone to assist. And Milo would be perfect, actually; he wouldn't try and take over. 'OK, you're in. First thing we have to do is get this book written into a script. Let's meet every week and I'll have a few scenes ready for you to check. You'll be my editor. Let's see…' She flicked through the pages to the back of the book. 'Twenty-three chapters. I'll write it in three acts: the first in London; the second at the farm, ending with Aunt Ada Doom's appearance; and the third from there until the end. Piece of cake.'

'It's a lot to do before Christmas.' The voice of reason.

'Well, I'm sure I can do it. In the meantime, you carry on looking for plays if you like. We won't find anything better than this. I can already imagine some of it. I wonder who'll audition for the main parts?'

'You'll have a lot of trouble finding anyone in the school who doesn't want to audition.'

'Except you.'

He laughed. 'Especially me.'

But all the while that she was dreaming up ideas and writing and meeting with Milo, Beth was thinking, *There's another person who won't audition*, and it was bothering her. To everyone else in the school she was Somebody; it was flattering and she lapped it up. They were like sheep, copying the way she dressed and wore her hair. She couldn't help noticing how some of the girls had been shopping during half-term and had come back with new clothes exactly like hers, and was relieved that she'd been shopping too, to stay one step ahead of them. But the more attention she received from everyone else, the more noticeable was Edward's lack of interest in her. She couldn't understand it at all. Maybe it was an act, or was he gay, or did he have a secret girlfriend? The more she thought about it, the more important it became, and she was determined to find out the reason if it was the last thing she did.

Milo and Beth spent all their spare hours together, working on the play. Through November, as the days grew shorter and darker, they huddled together in the library or the common room or wherever they could find a quiet corner. She was right about one thing: Milo was the perfect person to help with the play. She wrote and wrote all week and whenever he wanted to suggest changing something, it always made sense and, because it was Milo, she never felt like it was a criticism. Beth hated criticism.

Most afternoons, she had squash and Milo rugby practice, so they met afterwards. Beth wouldn't have been seen dead without showering after sport, but Milo couldn't care less. Sometimes he showered, but mostly he just turned up in his old tracksuit, smeared with mud or blood, bruises on his face and arms, his hair sticking up in all directions. Despite the battering he was taking at the hands of his so-called teammates, he was at his most mellow and cheerful after rugby.

'What's the big deal about rugby, anyway?' she asked him one day as they were on their way back from the tuck shop with Coke and crisps. 'What's so great about it?'

Milo did his usual thing, taking his time to consider his answer. 'Umm, I suppose I like the rhythm of the game, you know, how it flows, sometimes slowly when we're in the scrum, and then the speed when the ball is up or when the wingers have it. It's really exhilarating, the power and the speed and the skill. You should come and watch sometime. But I guess what I really like the best is the feeling of belonging to a team – we all rely on each other; we're nothing without each other. When all fifteen of us are playing well together, when it clicks, it's a great feeling.'

They were walking along the main corridor, where old photos of sports teams lined the wood-panelled walls. The faces stared out at them and Beth looked at them sceptically.

'You see, that's the bit I don't get. Why would you want to be reliant on all these other people? It's not real, is it? In real life, it doesn't work that way. After school, you'll all go your separate ways and you'll never see half of them again. You're always on your own, in the end. I never want to feel that I have to be responsible for anyone else. I want to be alone and take care of myself.'

'Like an island?'

'Yeah, I suppose so.'

'But no man is an island, as someone once said.'

'Well, it's lucky I'm not a man then, isn't it?'

Livvy and Henry were organising the sixth-form Christmas party and by the end of November it was all Livvy could talk about. The party, Henry, Henry, the party. They had all sorts of outlandish plans to decorate the dining hall, and someone's older brother was coming from London to DJ. It was Livvy who came up with an idea to get Edward's attention.

'Let's make it a proper ball, where you have to invite someone. Then we'll give out the tickets in pairs and you have to be collected from your house by the boy and you come together.' She saw Beth's frown and added hastily, 'Or the other way round, the girl collects the boy, but the point is you have to have a partner. You invite Edward, he'll have to say yes. Nobody else will dare to ask him.'

It was a stupid idea, Beth thought right away; typical of Livvy to dream up something like that. But she hadn't had any other ideas up until then about how to approach him without making a fool of herself. Could Beth pull off what nobody else in the school had managed? Edward was head boy, a scholar, the most handsome boy she'd ever seen. He – and only he – was the one she'd made up her mind that she wanted. So they wrote a poem to Edward and put it in an envelope, planning to leave it in his house postbox. But then Beth had second thoughts.

'I don't know, I'm not sure about this… it seems so silly. I don't like the idea of it.'

Livvy sighed. 'What idea don't you like? It's fun, it's a laugh. I think it's perfect.'

'But it's not really my style.'

'What, fun? Fun is not your style? Look, just relax. This is meant to be – you and Edward are meant to be together. It's fate.'

'Livs, do you even know what fate is?'

She looked hurt. 'Of course I do. Fate is the predetermined power that controls all of us, independent of our will or actions.'

Beth blinked, taken aback by the sudden outburst of philosophy from her friend. 'Ahem, OK, well, thanks for that. But wouldn't you say then that – if you believe in fate – I shouldn't send this letter? Surely that would be trying to change my fate?'

'No, you don't get it, do you? You and I were meant to be friends, I was meant to organise the party, I was meant to have the idea to invite partners – so you and Edward can be together. It's fate, see?'

Beth still wasn't convinced. Livvy was so full of shit. Beth's will was stronger than any pre-bloody-determined power, and there was no way Livvy would ever convince her otherwise.

'OK, I'll prove it to you,' Livvy pressed. 'Let's flip a coin. Heads you send the poem, tails you don't. I know it's going to land on heads, because it's predetermined. Agreed?'

By this time Beth was thoroughly fed up with the whole conversation and so she agreed. She fetched a coin from her drawer and threw it up in the air.

It landed on heads.

Chapter Six

The following day, on his way to breakfast, Edward checked the post table by the front entrance of Shottsford House. He saw two letters addressed to him. The first was in Bonnie's scrawl; the second had no stamp and the writing was unfamiliar to him. He tucked it into his pocket for later, eager to hear from Bonnie. As he walked down the hill towards the dining hall, he opened her letter and began to read. It was, as usual, a mundane letter about the news from home, his parents, their jobs, Bonnie's new school. Nothing about her own feelings. Nothing about what had happened last year. So he was still in the dark.

Bonnie had enclosed another letter this time; she had addressed it to Milo West and had asked her brother to pass it along to him. He paused on the road in surprise. He would have immediately suspected Milo to be the boy with whom Bonnie had been involved, but somehow it was unlikely. Edward knew Milo and liked him – he was a decent, honest bloke, trustworthy, and shy with girls. Plus, he'd had a tough few years and Edward couldn't imagine that he'd have been chasing girls while his mum lay dying of cancer. Unless he had made a substantial error of judgement about Milo West, he couldn't possibly be Bonnie's boyfriend.

Edward continued towards the main school. It was Saturday, so either Milo would be at breakfast, or Edward could walk down to his cottage this morning and give him the letter. He could ask Milo for a quick game of chess; he liked to play before a rugby game, it took his mind off his nerves. After lunch, Edward's father was collecting him in his car on the way home from Westminster to take him home to Cornwall for the night. He remembered the other letter and pulled it out of his pocket. It was a small, square envelope and inside was a folded letter. He read it, turned the paper over and frowned. Was this really for him? He read it again, and a third time. What a strange little note.

> *I think about you all the time*
> *I am in your thrall*
> *I'd like to ask you to be mine*
> *And to take me to the ball*
> *B. A.*

Edward couldn't see Milo at breakfast, so he found a table that was reasonably empty, sat alone at the end of it and wondered about the poem. He only knew one sixth-former with those initials – a new girl in the year below him, Beth Atkinson, Norcombe House, long dark hair. Other than those details, he didn't have a clear picture of her in his mind. But why would she send him this poem? Was it some sort of a joke?

He ate his breakfast more quickly than usual, returned to his room in Shottsford House and sat at his desk. He opened the poem and read it out loud. '*I think about you all the time… be mine.*' The words twisted themselves around in his head, making no sense at all. His hand trembled as he checked the envelope again, in case he had missed something important. It affected him more than he could have imagined. It was the first time that he had ever received something like that; a love letter, he supposed it was.

Edward glanced out of his window and then remembered Milo. He reached into his wardrobe to find a coat and saw his reflection in the mirror on the inside door. He stared at himself, curious to see what others saw, and felt a familiar sensation of everything slipping away from him. His eyes were dark like bruises as they glared back at him, his mouth tense, a thin line. He blinked, frightened to look deeper inside himself and find nothing real there. He slammed the wardrobe door and left the room.

His housemaster was in his office, and Edward asked him to sign a permission form to visit Milo, which was no problem as his housemaster was also Milo's rugby coach. Edward knew where the cottage was because the headmaster had briefed him about Milo's situation in their start-of-term meeting.

The walk lasted half an hour and Edward took his time, enjoying the peace of the morning, weak November sunshine filtering through the tall trees, a sharp edge to the cold that he found refreshing after his stuffy room and his oppressive thoughts. The damp leaves that he kicked through smelt musty and earthy, and reminded him of walking the dogs at home.

Home. His attention strayed from the mystery of the poem to the mystery of his sister, as it often did. He loved Bonnie so much, they were very close, but he felt her beauty was too dangerous. She was only fifteen years old and yet she looked a lot older, and he hated the way that the boys in the school had ogled her. He had overheard some indecent remarks last year and had ticked off the boys so badly, they still cowered every time he came near. She was a lovely girl, very sweet and kind, with a mane of blonde hair and blue eyes. It pained him to think that one of these crude boys had got his filthy hands on her, and things had gone so far that it had made Bonnie ill.

When Edward and Bonnie had been collected from school at the end of the summer term, not by the family's driver but by their father, there had been a meeting between Mr Markham and the headmaster, his father uncharacteristically ruffled and angry. He drove them back to Cornwall in silence and they waited, Bonnie trembling and pale-faced, as he spoke in hushed tones to their mother upstairs.

When their parents finally reappeared, they had made a decision. Bonnie would not be returning to Weatherbury Hall after the summer holidays; they would find another school for her, a day school, so she could live at home. Bonnie broke down in tears and was whisked away by her mother. The family holiday to their cottage in Scotland was cancelled – instead, Bonnie went with her mother to an aunt in Stockholm, and Edward spent a long, lonely summer at home, walking the dogs and reading books, occasionally going with his father up to London to an art gallery and to see *Hamlet* at the National Theatre.

He had had mixed feelings about school. He was head boy now, and had finished his university application to study law at Cambridge University; Corpus Christi College, like his father. He loved The Island, but without Bonnie there, it would be different. The light she brought to his life, every day when they greeted each other at breakfast, and the other times they managed to spend together, walking, talking; he cherished them and he knew she was a good influence on him, calming him and grounding him, teasing him if he got too pompous, reminding him of their mother, so sweet and lovely.

But neither his parents nor his sister had told Edward the details of Bonnie's romance. He had never seen her with one boy in particular, and what was the illness that presumably they were treating in Sweden? Edward dreaded to think that Bonnie might have been pregnant; the thought wouldn't focus in his brain because he found it so horrifying. She was so small and young. Whoever could it be? He had racked his memory, and had made a list of all the boys in the fourth, fifth and sixth years, keeping it in his desk drawer, crossing each name off the list when he was sure that it couldn't be them. Milo's name was crossed off.

Without noticing where the time had gone, Edward had reached the school gates. There was Milo's cottage, set back from the path along the wall, with a well-tended garden, a vegetable patch, a small lawn and some fruit trees. Milo's bike leant against the wall near the front door. Edward knocked and Milo, dressed already in his rugby tracksuit, his hair still messy from sleep, opened it and looked rather startled to see Edward standing there.

'Hi, Edward, everything OK?'

'Yes, good morning, may I come in? I've brought you some breakfast, in case you hadn't had any yet.' He held up two croissants, wrapped in a paper napkin he'd saved from the dining hall.

'Wow, thanks, I'm starving. I've got the kettle on. Um… would you like a cup of tea?'

Edward sat down at the small pine kitchen table, waiting for Milo to make the tea. He served it in a white teapot covered with delicate orange and yellow flowers, with proper cups, saucers and a matching sugar pot and milk jug. In Milo's hands, it looked like a girl's toy tea set, and Milo saw him staring.

'It was my grandmother's,' he mumbled.

When Milo sat down, Edward brought out the letters from Bonnie; the one to him and the other addressed to Milo. He handed over Milo's letter with a quizzical look on his face, but he saw that Milo was as surprised as he was. Milo considered the envelope, turned it over in his large hands, bent it backwards and forwards a little.

'There's something hard in here, a card.' He carefully slit open the top of the envelope and upturned it onto the table. A letter, and a phonecard. A light dawned in Milo's face. 'Mystery solved. I lent her a phonecard last term. She promised she'd pay me back. I'd forgotten all about it.'

'But what's in the letter? She says I have to give it to you and we have to read it together. What does she say in the letter?'

Milo opened it up and read aloud to Edward.

Dear Milo,

Enclosed is the phonecard I promised you. Thanks so much, you saved my life that day! You were so kind. I'm sorry if I gave you a shock, looking so bedraggled and weepy.

I wanted to give you both an explanation as to what happened to me in the summer term. Edward deserves to know the truth, even though Mummy doesn't agree, and you... well, you might be wondering why I'm involving you... I know, from that day by the phones, and also from what Edward has told me about you, that you are a lovely, kind person and also very sensible and trustworthy. My brother is absolutely the most wonderful person in the world, but he has a terrible temper. So I wanted to tell him the truth, but also ensure that he has a friend at school who can perhaps look out for him a bit, stop him losing it completely and doing something he'll regret later. Milo, will you do this for us, please?

I was together with a boy from your year, Milo, he's called Zachary Smythe. I think you know him, he's in the rugby team too. He and I are in love (I know you'll say I'm too young to use a word like that, but it's true). We want to spend our lives together, and however people try to keep us apart, we won't accept it, we'll find a way.

We did, however, make a terrible mistake, which I have since paid the price for. I found out at the end of the summer term that I was pregnant. Zack was so lovely, he helped me to make some difficult decisions, and Mummy was in agreement with him, hence the trip to Sweden, where we went to terminate the pregnancy, far away from anyone who might know Daddy. I was terrified and so upset, but I knew it was the right thing to do.

Darling Milo, darling Edward, I feel so much better now you know. Edward, we have never had any secrets, and I hope that you understand why I wanted to tell you but couldn't. It has been the most difficult time of my life. And being apart from Zack is making it worse.

And now, my final request to you both – you cannot mention this to anyone! Please listen to me. Zack must continue at The Island, he must be allowed to get his A Levels and succeed at school. You must leave him be, both of you. And nobody should know about us, because if they do, he'll probably be expelled. I have to be able to rely on you two, otherwise every dream he and I had about our future will be wrecked.

Please consider what I've asked, and Milo, Edward can tell me your decision at the weekend when I see him at home.

Lots of love to you both,
Bonnie

Milo, faltering a few times, stumbling over some of the words, had read the letter from start to finish without looking up. Now Edward watched his hands fold the letter back into its envelope. He put it on the table and they both stared at it.

Edward's whole world collapsed. He supposed he'd known in his heart of hearts that Bonnie had been pregnant. But to have it in writing, black and white, from his sweetest, dearest sister – he felt as if someone had punched him in the stomach. His head fell forwards onto his hands.

And now he had a name: Zack Smythe.

Bonnie and Zack. Zack and Bonnie. *That* was the enigma: she'd been pregnant, had an abortion. Their parents keeping her close, keeping her apart from Zack. That was what everyone in the school wanted to know.

Edward was devastated. All of his life he had tried to do the right thing, for himself and for his family, and especially for Bonnie; to be a good older brother, a good son. The path that he had always taken, that he wanted to take for the rest of his life, through school, university, to the law, was carefully laid out for him. Now it felt threatened because of Bonnie, who was a child when she and Zack had had sex together. Because of Zack, who had ruined her innocence.

Edward looked up at Milo, trying to hold back the angry tears brimming in his eyes, his hands clenched into white fists. Their eyes met. He said, 'I'm going to beat the living daylights out of him.'

'I'm with you on that one. But… what about Bonnie? What's it going to do to her, if you ignore her request? Don't we have to at least try to do what she asks?'

Edward stared at him, trembling with anger. 'Do you seriously believe that he loves my sister? Is that likely, given that it's Zack Smythe we're talking about?'

'Not sure. It's true, he doesn't usually stick with the same girl for long. But Bonnie is special. Perhaps Zack is in love with her. Perhaps she's the one. I certainly haven't seen him with anyone else this term. He's been quieter than usual, less of a show-off. Perhaps he's just as much in love with her as she is with him. They say with guys like that, when they find the right one, they stop…' He tailed off. Edward wanted to believe him. Milo was a good man. He would always be honest.

They sat in silence. Milo thought Edward looked reassured by his speech. He couldn't lie outright to his friend, but he also couldn't bring himself to tell him all of the truth. Edward had probably heard the rumours about Zack, about all the girls he went through, how he charmed them, slept with them, then moved on to the next one. That was common knowledge. It was less likely that Edward knew the sordid details that Zack reserved for the rugby team, the really bad stuff. Milo hated to listen to it; it made him feel sick and he'd put a stop to it now that he was captain. But last year, Zack had boasted how he and a group of other boys were ticking off girls' names on the School List each time they had sex with one who was a virgin. Edward did not need to know about the Virgin List.

To break the silence, Milo made another pot of tea and fetched the chessboard, knowing that it would distract his friend from his grief. While they were playing, Milo told Edward what he knew about Zack's family, and also about how clever and talented he was, sticking to the positives. Edward finally agreed that if it was in Bonnie's best interests to keep the secret, he would do it. Milo could only agree.

Milo knew Zack well, not just from rugby, and of all the boys in the school he could have chosen for Edward's sister, this one would've been the last in line. What was Bonnie thinking, to get involved with someone like him? She surely must be mistaken to think he loved her. And how did Zack manage, time and time again, to hoodwink these girls? OK, so he was charming and charismatic. He was the most confident person Milo knew. And, when he wanted to be, he was totally focused. Sweet little Bonnie wouldn't have stood a chance.

Milo sighed.

They played and talked until lunchtime, when Milo was expected to eat with the team in the dining hall before the match began at two o'clock. As they walked back up the drive towards the school, Edward pulled out the other envelope, the one with the poem.

'This came for me today too. I think it's from Beth Atkinson. You're friends with her, aren't you – what's it all about, do you think? Is it a joke?'

Milo was startled at the sound of Elizabeth's name, but

opened the small note and read the poem. He felt the heat rise up in his face as he mumbled, 'Yes, it's her writing.' He tried to smile. 'Sounds like you've got a date for the ball.' He handed it back, and was relieved to see the red brick of the school through the trees in front of them. 'Sorry, I'm late, I've got to hurry. Bye.' He broke into a jog and didn't look back.

In the dining hall, the rugby boys were sitting, ready for the game in their Weatherbury Hall tracksuits, at the table nearest to the food hatch – the same one where they'd sat on the first evening of term to judge the new girls. Milo sat down at the opposite end to where Zack was sitting, next to Guy, and ate his pasta quickly, forcing a smile and joining in with the chatter and the banter as much as he could. He had to put this morning out of his mind, the Bonnie-and-Zack business and the idiotic poem from Elizabeth, if he was going to concentrate on the match.

The team left the dining hall together and made their way to the sports pavilion, a white wooden building next to the pitch, for a pre-match chat and warm-up. As they clattered along the driveway, they passed Elizabeth and Livvy. Elizabeth smiled at Milo and mouthed, *Good luck*, and immediately the rest of the team burst into laughter and wolf-whistles. She tossed her hair back and strode off haughtily. Milo blushed and told them all to shut up.

'What does Atkinson see in you, West?' shouted Billy or Jake. 'You're just some great fat farmer and she is a fucking gorgeous piece of arse.'

Someone else joined in, 'She is so fuckable. She's got the best legs in the school.'

'Are you gay? Forget her legs. Look at her tits. Milo, has she ever let you feel her tits?'

Milo, reddening again, this time in anger, warned them, 'Right, enough, stop it now. Stop talking about her like that. Shut up and stop being so fucking disgusting. Next person I hear talking like that about Elizabeth Atkinson can sit on the bench for the rest of the season.'

He was furious with these idiots. He would never talk about girls like that, especially someone like Elizabeth, who had never led any of them to believe she was interested. Ever since she'd arrived at the school, he'd heard what they said about her, and read the graffiti in the boys' loos and seen the odds that were being given for which boy (including him) would sleep with her first. He was furious with her too, but he couldn't figure out why. Why did she have to be so beautiful that she attracted the attention of boys like this? And in the back of his mind, he knew that she had written that note to Edward, who wasn't a boy like that, who wasn't an idiot or disgusting and who would treat her well. The Markhams were important people, Edward was rich and he was everything that Milo wasn't, and Milo was furious with himself too, because he was bitterly jealous of his friend Edward Markham.

Chapter Seven

That afternoon, Edward and his father avoided the subject of Bonnie on the drive down to Cornwall. At a tense family dinner, Bonnie talked too much and too quickly, and their parents listened, trying to hide their worries behind fake smiles, while Edward steered the conversation away from anything to do with Weatherbury Hall.

After dinner, Bonnie and Edward went upstairs to her room, and Edward told her that he and Milo would follow her wishes. He felt too tired to be angry. He couldn't even bear to tell her how much he disapproved of Zack. Bonnie thanked him with a hug and left her room to go and run a bath.

A few minutes later, the front doorbell rang, and Edward heard the muffled voice of his father answering it. A question, another question; it was too far away to hear what was being said. He felt uneasy and hurried through Bonnie's open bedroom door towards the stairs. His father was still standing at the front door, and beyond him, framed by the light at the doorway, was Zack.

His father was explaining, 'We've been through this on the phone; you're not to see her. She's too young, and she's been through so much, thanks to you. She needs some time away from you.'

'Sir, I'm awfully sorry not to have called first, only I was in Cornwall with friends this afternoon and I wanted to see her, very quickly, to say hello.'

Edward thought he saw his father relenting, moving backwards, as if to let Zack in.

'No, it's not possible, she's asleep,' Edward called out as he reached the hallway.

'Oh, hullo, Edward, I didn't see you there. Is she really asleep? It's only 9.30.' Edward thought he saw a flicker of annoyance in Zack's smooth face, his eyes hardening and then adjusting back to their cool, unflappable gaze. 'It's just, as I was explaining to your father, I was in the area and thought, what harm could it do to say hello? I know she'd be pleased to see me.'

Mr Markham looked at Zack and back to his son. Edward realised in that instant that his mother hadn't told his father about the pregnancy.

'I'll sort this out. Please leave us alone for a moment.'

His father nodded and returned to the living room. Edward waited until he was out of earshot. He stepped up to Zack.

'Bonnie's told me everything. She wants you to leave her alone. She's trying to forget you ever happened.'

'I don't believe you. She said on the phone she'd be here; we had an arrangement.'

'Well, she's changed her mind. She said to say goodbye and give you this.' From out of his jacket pocket he pulled a delicate silver watch with an inscription on the back – *You walk in beauty* – and dropped it into the silent air between them.

Zack caught it, a look of fury on his rigid face. 'You're lying, Markham.'

71

'You'd know, since you're so good at it. Leave my sister alone.'
Zack spat, 'This is not the end', and stalked away.

When Edward returned to school late on Sunday evening, he wanted to find Milo in the sixth-form common room. Along the cellar corridor, he stepped over pupils sitting on the floor, and passed more hanging around in doorways, chatting, playing cards, listening to a ghetto blaster that was hastily turned down when they saw him approach. The common room was packed, music blaring from the speakers, the sofas spilling over with people. He stopped at the doorway, scanning the faces for Milo in the semi-darkness.

He took a few steps into the room and stopped when he saw Beth sitting at the far end, next to two girls he didn't know. Edward moved away from the doorway and positioned himself half behind a pillar near the bar, unnoticed by most people in the room, all busy with their friends and their own conversations. He watched Beth intently for the first time: her dark, shining hair, her perfect profile, her long neck and pale throat. Before now, he hadn't put much thought into what was and wasn't attractive in a girl. But surely she was attractive? His eyes were glued to her, drinking her in.

Edward didn't know how long he stood there, staring at her, but in the distance a bell rang for everyone to return to their houses. He slipped out before the crowd, ashamed of his behaviour, but having made up his mind: tomorrow he would find Beth and accept her invitation to the ball.

Edward slept badly that night, thinking with sadness about Bonnie and anger about Zack, and in amongst those feelings was something new and confusing about Beth that he couldn't understand or put a name to. He dreamt about her and woke on Monday morning, unnerved by the strength of his reaction and ashamed of his lack of control. Sluggishly, he showered and dressed, breakfasted, and made his way through the day, half asleep, distracted, thrown out of his normal routine and unsettled by his conflicting emotions.

When he thought about Beth, he sensed a connection between them. She had felt it too, otherwise why would she have asked him to the ball? It would be easy to talk to her, just like talking to his sister. He was excited and nervous as he sought her out in the evening. She wasn't in the library or in the common room – where could she be?

It was dark outside, the rain pelting down on the windows, when he headed back upstairs to check the main corridor. There she was, sitting on a chair opposite Milo, who was writing while she talked. Milo's back was to Edward, but Beth saw Edward as soon as he saw her. *No going back now.* He took a deep breath and a step forward. Milo, who had finished what he was writing, glanced up at Beth and, seeing her staring over his shoulder, looked back too and saw Edward approaching.

Edward lost his nerve. He nodded at Beth and Milo and continued walking, almost tripping over his own shoes in his hurry to pass them. The time it took him to reach the stairs at the other end of the corridor was endless. He felt ridiculous. What a fool he was making of himself.

November turned into December and still Edward hadn't summoned up the courage to speak to Beth. He watched her from afar, never daring to approach her, never finding the right words. To him, she was a perfect girl – beautiful, vivacious and always in the centre of every circle. Now he was paying attention, he heard everyone speak about her, pupils and teachers, everyone interested in what she said and did.

It wasn't his fault – he was dazzled by her and he felt alive for the first time in his life, flooded with a light and warmth he hadn't felt since Bonnie had left school. These feelings were new to him, and he couldn't know that the object of his devotion was not always perfect. Sometimes, Beth was stubborn and moody. She always refused to apologise, even if she knew she was wrong. She could be condescending and nasty to Livvy, her best friend. Edward never saw that Beth. Nor did he see her when she woke up in the mornings, before she'd had time to wash her hair and put on her expensive and flattering clothes. Or squeeze and cover with make-up a spot that appeared on her forehead, without fail, every month, the day before her period started.

It worried him that he couldn't get close to her, to speak to her and also to make the arrangements for going to the ball together. It was going to be after the final rugby match of the season, the Saturday before school broke up for Christmas. But he knew she'd be at the match along with everyone else, watching Milo and the other boys, so he saw his chance and followed the crowd down towards the pitch after lunch that Saturday.

It was a bright, bitingly cold afternoon, everyone wrapped up in hats and scarves and as many layers as they could find. Edward saw her ahead of him, wearing brown boots, a long coat and a dark red hat. Her school scarf muffled her face, but she was easy to spot: taller than most of the others and her long, dark hair was in a loose pigtail down her back, swinging as she strolled along. He followed at a distance and, as everyone took their places around the edge of the pitch, stamping their feet and clapping their hands together, he found a gap on the opposite side, so he could watch her.

The teams jogged out onto the pitch, BJ making a big show of how cold it was to be playing in shorts. The game began and Weatherbury, Milo in particular, were annihilating the team from Sherton Abbas school. A minute before half-time the score was 23-0. Edward left his place and skirted unseen around the edge of the crowd, which was distracted by a winger speeding up to score another try for Weatherbury. Everyone was shouting and clapping in excitement and jumping up and down, trying to keep warm. Beth didn't see him until he was right behind her. The half-time whistle blew.

'Beth, may I speak to you please?'

'Oh, Edward. Hi, yes, of course.' She pointed away from the pavilion, where everyone was hurrying to get a cup of tea or cocoa to get warm. There was an unoccupied bench beside the tennis courts, facing away from the rugby pitch, where he waited until she had sat down, then sat down himself and cleared his throat. He saw her shiver.

'Would you like me to fetch you a cup of tea?' he asked, concerned.

'No, really, it's OK. Thanks, though.'

'I've been meaning to speak to you since you sent me that note. It was a bit of a surprise, but I'd really love to go with you to the ball. Would you still like to?' His voice was edged with anxiety. *Please say yes, please say—*

'Yes, of course, that would be fun, wouldn't it?'

His shoulders softened, his hands unclenched. 'Well, that's wonderful. What's the form? I can pick you up, or would you like to pick me up, since you asked me?'

They made arrangements to meet at the entrance of his house at seven o'clock. They chatted about the rugby match, how well Milo was playing, and about the *Cold Comfort Farm* play. They were so deep in conversation, neither of them noticed that the teams were already out for the second half.

Milo noticed, and Guy did too; he nudged Milo as they ran out. Beth and Edward were both so tall and striking, even as they sat some distance away from the pitch with their backs turned to the game, it was easy to see who they were. Milo looked away, trying to concentrate on the game and the instructions the coach had given them at half-time. It was no good. He was distracted and kept fluffing his passes, his heart not in the tackles; he couldn't see the openings or hear his teammates when they asked for the ball.

'Mate, what's up?' gasped Guy, twenty minutes into the second half. 'You need to get back into the game.' It was 29-19. The coach was roaring angrily on the sideline, and the home crowd had grown silent, aware that their team was losing their grip on the match. Milo shook his head, his hair dripping with sweat, to clear it. He ran off, searching for the ball, trying to find the flow of the game, but it was useless. His loyal teammates tried to shield him, but he was a complete dud in that half. The Sherton Abbas team sensed the weakness, pressed their advantage and won the match 29-31.

As the Weatherbury Hall team trudged into the changing room after the match, they all heard Mr Shepherd, their coach, a giant Yorkshireman, outside the door with Milo, berating him loudly. 'What the buggery do you think you were doing out there, lad?' They didn't hear Milo's reply, but the coach stormed off, bellowing, 'Somebody keep that ruddy wench away from my team next time.'

Edward and Beth didn't even stay until the end of the match. They were so engrossed in each other, they didn't hear or see anyone else. Edward saw she was shivering and her hands were turning blue. He had this aberrant urge to hold them and pull them to him, into the warmth of his coat, but instead he suggested that they walk back up to school. They passed the stables, where Edward and Bonnie's horses were kept.

'Would you like to say hello?' he said.

'Oh no, I don't like horses.'

'Are you allergic? Or frightened?'

She looked insulted. 'I just don't like horses. I've never had anything to do with them.'

'Why don't you come and say hello now? They're the most beautiful creatures, up close. And they won't hurt you, I promise.'

Beth shrugged her shoulders and followed him over the stile that led through the field to the stable door. Inside, it was warmer, the smell of the horses, straw and leather at once making Edward feel relaxed. He led her along a concrete path between two rows of stalls until the jet-black face of his horse appeared over the upper half of one of the doors.

'What's his name?' asked Beth, her voice more timid than he had ever heard it.

'This is Gilbert. And over there is Bonnie's horse, Caspar.'

'Gilbert and Caspar – like in *Portrait of a Lady*?' Her eyes lit up. God, she was beautiful.

'Yes, that's right – Bonnie named them. We both love that book.'

'Me too.'

'Here, look, you can touch his nose here and stroke him, he won't do anything. Like this.' He took her hand and placed it on the horse's face, drawing it down towards the nose. Gilbert moved his head to nuzzle them.

'He's lovely,' Beth said in a soft voice and Edward lifted his eyes from the horse, his heart thudding against his ribs, and dared to look at her. Her eyes were glowing now, her face turned to his. He swallowed, his mouth dry.

He broke eye contact and looked back to the horse. 'Shall I teach you to ride? Caspar could do with being ridden more regularly; I think he'd like to get to know you.'

'Mmm, yes, why not?' She took her hand off the horse and looked down at her coat. She picked a piece of straw from it and then said, 'Oh. What time is it? Shouldn't we…? I think we should go. I need to get ready for tonight.'

When they emerged from the stables, the playing fields were empty, a low mist settling all the way down to the trees by the river, obscuring the bottom half of the H-shaped rugby posts. *Strange how the time has gone*, thought Edward mildly. He was sure the game would still have been going on. The light was fading. He checked his watch; it was getting late. They wandered alone towards the school and parted at the turning to Norcombe House.

Beth hurried up to the courtyard and flung open the door, running in excitement to find Livvy. She was in their room with two similar-looking girls who were cousins, Tabitha and Savanna, swigging Coke from cans and doing each other's hair. Soul II Soul was blaring out of the stereo, and they were giggly, excited about the party. Beth showered and washed her hair, lounging on her bed while it dried, sipping from the Coke cans, which she now discovered had been filled up with generous shots of vodka.

They wriggled into their dresses. Beth had bought a new jade-green silk mandarin gown, with a high neck and delicate stitching along the edges, very tight-fitting and slashed from the knee right up her thigh. Everyone oohed and aahed over it. By virtue of her height and slimness, Beth was spared the usual clothes-swapping ritual that most of the girls, including Livvy, Tab and Sav, were so mad about. They were constantly wearing each other's clothes and even shoes, but Beth was relieved not to have to share her wardrobe with anyone.

'It's really nice that you two have each other,' she said to Tab and Sav. 'I wish I had a sister.'

'But we're not even sisters.' They chuckled and rolled their eyes.

'You can be my sister,' said Livvy.

Beth grinned and hugged her. 'I'd like that very, very much. But I'd have to marry your brother. Hey – which one?'

'Marry whichever one comes through the door first,' said Tab. 'They'll be here soon to pick us up.'

At that moment, there was a knock on the door. The four girls looked at each other and held their breath. Henry's head popped round the door and he started to say something to Livvy but was drowned out by their laughter. He looked confused, but managed to get the gist of the story and dragged Livvy out of the door so they could make a few final preparations at the party.

They waited a bit longer, but Beth said she had to go and

fetch Edward. The girls, light-headed, flushed and giggly, made their way out of Norcombe House, agreeing that getting ready for a party was invariably better than the actual party itself. Billy and Jake were late, running up the hill, but made it up to them by being so charming, bowing down low, exclaiming how beautiful the girls looked and presenting each of them with a white rose. At the turning to Shottsford House, they waved goodbye and wished good luck to Beth, who turned the corner and followed the road away from the school. Her heels had not, perhaps, been the best choice; she was unsure how to walk in them and wobbled a few times.

At the door to Shottsford House stood Edward, wearing a dark blue suit and looking take-your-breath-away handsome. He had a bunch of twelve red roses in his arms. His face lit up when he saw Beth teetering up to the door. She was nearly as tall as him. He brushed a shy kiss onto her cheek, gave her the flowers and offered her his arm without saying a word.

In the dining hall, there was a gigantic Christmas tree lit up with hundreds of candles. The room had been transformed with holly trees in pots, ivy hanging from the walls and an incredibly large amount of mistletoe from the ceiling. In the middle of the ceiling, a disco ball was rotating. The music was already pumping out, but nobody was dancing yet.

Livvy dashed up to them. 'So, what do you think?'

'It's awesome, it looks fantastic,' said Beth, and Edward smiled and nodded his agreement.

'Like the mistletoe?'

Edward stuttered, 'Very… yes. I'll just… um… drinks?'

He turned towards the bar and Beth shook her head at Livvy, mouthing, *Don't.*

Livvy hurried off again and Beth checked she wasn't under some mistletoe, leaning against an ivy-covered pillar. Edward walked slowly back to her with two glasses of white wine, and they stood awkwardly, sipping and not speaking above the roar of the disco. Now some of the couples were starting to dance. Beth turned her mouth towards Edward's ear and shouted, 'Can you dance?'

'Not really, I'm not very good. Can you?'

'Everyone dances differently here from my last school.' They both watched the dancers for a while, some shuffling from side to side, others flinging their legs and arms in the air.

'What was your old school like?' asked Edward, leaning close to her.

'Rough. It's not so cool to be clever there. I didn't have a lot of friends.'

The song finished and a slower one came on.

'Shall we?' asked Edward, with a sideways nod of his head. He held out his hand. Beth wasn't really that keen, but the shuffling looked like something she could manage, so she flattened down her dress, tucked her hair behind her ear, took his hand and followed him to the almost full dance floor. Nobody looked at them as they moved between the other couples in the shimmering light of the disco ball. *Last Christmas* was playing and Beth put her hands around Edward's neck as he hovered his hands near her waist, so she could barely feel them. They drifted around together and Edward spoke.

'I hate these things normally. But with you... I wanted to ask you if maybe you'd like to do this again? I mean, go out with me...? I mean, not to a party or perhaps... it... it, umm...' He swallowed and closed his eyes, sighed and opened them again. She could see he wasn't finding it easy to speak. 'Would you like to go out with me?'

She took a little breath and twitched her mouth upwards into what she hoped would look like a smile. 'Er, I, um... how do you mean? Go together out somewhere? Or do you mean...?'

'I'd like to spend time with you, get to know you, take you out on a date. I guess what I'm trying to say is, would you like to be my girlfriend?'

'Oh, OK, I see. Well, it's really nice of you to ask me, but I don't really want to have a boyfriend, you know, not now. Maybe we could be friends?' she babbled, the smile still fixed on her face.

'Friends?' He looked so downcast, and she felt so sorry for him. 'I was hoping, when you sent me that poem, that perhaps we could be more than friends? I thought that was what you wanted too.'

'Oh. I've been meaning to talk to you since I sent you that poem. I did want to ask you to the party, I thought it would be nice. But I didn't mean... um. I like you, but not in that way.' She felt awful for him. He was so glum.

The next song came on, one of her favourite U2 songs, *With or Without You*. Unfortunately it was still a slow one, so Edward continued to hold her, a little harder now, around her waist. She concentrated on the lyrics of the song, which everyone was joining in singing, but it wasn't helping her situation.

He tried again. 'If you need more time to think about it, I don't mind. I can wait. It's important. You're worth waiting for.'

'Really, I don't think it's going to happen, Edward.'

'But will you maybe think about it for a while? Over the Christmas holidays perhaps? You know what – we're going to France, skiing, at New Year. Why don't you come too? It would be good for us, maybe, to have some time together away from school. Will you come?'

'Won't your mum and dad mind, you asking me like this? Shouldn't you ask them first?' Beth stalled, taken aback by the offer.

'No, it's really fine, we're always allowed to ask someone. Come. Please. Val-d'Isère. Will you?'

'Seriously?' She couldn't concentrate, her mind was whirring. 'I... I don't know.'

'Please come.' His eyes were desperate, pleading with her to accept.

Beth couldn't think clearly. The vodka and the wine and the lights and the dancing were all making her confused. She scanned the room and her eyes lit on Milo, who was looking three sheets to the wind, head resting on his hand, sitting in a corner with a few other boys. She thought about what Milo would do, and about that day when Edward had passed them in the main corridor and he'd looked at her disapprovingly. She thought about his honesty and his straightforwardness.

'No, I can't, Edward. It's not going to happen.' She broke away from him and walked as best she could in her stupid shoes, grabbed her bag with her cigarettes in it and headed for the door. She barged past a boy with messy blond hair snogging a girl she didn't know up against the wall, nearly knocking the pair of them sideways.

Edward, head hanging, stood still for a few moments, gathered up the roses, which she'd left on a chair by the door, and left the party.

Chapter Eight

B eth wasn't proud of her behaviour. She liked Edward and wanted to be friends with him, but she felt uncomfortable, because her flirty poem had been a crappy joke to play on him. She'd underestimated – by a long shot – how 'romantic and fascinating' he'd become. On the day after the party, she went to his house to explain herself again, but he wasn't there. She left him a note to say that she'd enjoyed the party and that she still wanted to learn how to ride on Bonnie's horse, but that she definitely couldn't come skiing and she didn't want to be his girlfriend. Could he accept her friendship instead?

She had considered it, of course. There was an attraction to going out with someone like him. They looked good together (Livvy said they looked alike – both tall, dark and handsome). They had lots in common, and Beth knew she couldn't do much better than him.

But the truth was, it was much more fun to be single than to have a boyfriend. Who wanted to be tied down, spending every spare minute with the same person? She had watched some of the couples at school, sitting next to each other in the dining hall for every meal, walking arm in arm everywhere and finishing each other's sentences. Dull, duller, dullest. It was a strange thing about this school, she thought, that with no parents around and everyone living merely metres away from each other, couples progressed from magical first kiss to boring married bliss in a matter of weeks. Beth was the undisputed queen of the school, and she wasn't ready to give up that position to become someone's girlfriend, even if he was the head boy.

In that last week of term, Beth worked on the final draft of the play every spare minute she had. Milo had cajoled the headmaster's secretary into typing it out for them. Luckily neither Beth nor Milo had any more squash or rugby training, and the teachers were winding down the amount of homework. Beth was worried about Milo: he was listless and distracted. He answered her questions in monosyllables and avoided looking at her if he could. There was a coldness she had never felt before between them.

'Do you think this is right? Taking the novel and making a play out of it. Are we right to do this?' she wondered out loud to him. They were sitting in the sixth-form common room, at their usual corner table, where everyone knew to leave them alone if they were working on the play.

'How do you mean?' he sighed.

'Well, I want it to be something special. And now I think, is this really art, when all we're doing is copying the words that someone else wrote? Is that art too, or just plagiarism?'

'I thought this is what you wanted to do?'

'I did. I do. But I want it to be perfect.'

He looked at her and shook his head. 'Not everything has to be perfect, you know. Sometimes, the first time, you just have to—'

'I don't agree. Everything I do, I want it to be the best. Otherwise it's not worth doing. What's wrong with you these days anyway?' she griped. 'Why are you always so moody?'

Milo didn't answer.

'What is it?'

He stood up, towering over her. 'Got a coat?'

She nodded.

'I need to speak to you alone.'

She rolled her eyes but stood up and found her coat, leaving their notes and folders on the table. She followed him out of the room and, instead of turning left towards the stairs up to the main corridor, he turned right, heading towards the end of the corridor where she'd never been before. There were locked storeroom doors to the left and right and at the end, Milo fished out a key from his pocket and unlocked a blue door. He opened it and ushered her through, locking the door again when they were on the other side. Now they were in another corridor, unlit, completely empty and silent. There was a set of narrow stone stairs leading up and outdoors and Milo, ignoring her look of confusion, strode towards them and climbed them two at a time.

The stairs emerged around the back of the tennis courts, behind a small house or hut. He walked past it, not looking back at her. She had to run to keep up as they followed a path away from the school, between woods on one side and a high wall on the other, for about ten minutes. The wall became higher, at least three metres high, and at that point Milo turned a corner and used another key to open a small wooden door in the wall, hidden by overgrown bushes and vines. Again he held open the door for her, without saying a word. She hesitated before she stepped inside. He had to crouch down when he followed her through the door.

It was a walled garden with a neat lawn in the centre, surrounded by a gravel pathway, trees and plants climbing around the outer perimeter by the wall. The frost had covered everything with a fine layer of silvery white, glistening and sparkling in the afternoon sunlight. Beth was speechless. She had never seen anything so beautiful and so calming. She put her hand on Milo's arm.

'Like it?' he asked, looking down at her, smiling, at ease again with her.

'What is it?' she whispered. 'I mean, is it yours?'

'No, it's the walled garden that belongs to the school. Nobody ever goes here though, except me. The new groundsman gave me the key when my dad died. He said it was my mum and dad's favourite place and, unless anyone else found out about it, I could look after it myself and keep the key. Nobody else has ever even asked about it. Nobody else but me has been in here since last year. Until now.'

'Thank you for showing it to me.'

'Come and have a look.'

They walked around the gravel pathway and Milo talked about the plants, the trees, the time he spent here and how much the garden had meant to his parents. They found a moss-covered stone bench in a corner under a weeping willow tree and sat down.

'You're a dark horse. What other secrets do you have, Milo? Or should I call you Dickon?'

'Who would that make you? Mary Lennox, I suppose? I can see the similarities.'

'OK, ha ha. Well, now you've brought me here, you'd better tell me what you wanted to say. What's bothering you these days?'

Milo's face tensed. 'It's about you and Edward. You sent him that poem – don't look like that, he showed it to me – and he's head over heels in love with you. Everyone saw you two creeping off from the rugby game last week, and at the party, he was all over you. Everyone thought you were a couple. Then Edward tells me you're not interested. I haven't seen him looking this down in the mouth for ages, and for Edward, that's really saying something.'

'I thought you weren't interested in school gossip?'

He shrugged. 'It's all everyone's talking about.'

'Really?' She couldn't keep the smile out of her voice.

Milo turned to her. 'That's not a good thing, Elizabeth.'

'Beth. I prefer Beth.' He knew that – why did he insist on using her full name? 'Isn't it?'

He stared at her for a moment, then said quietly, almost to himself, 'I didn't think you would be that cruel.'

'Oh, for Christ's sake. It wasn't like that. This is ridiculous.' She stood up to leave. 'I don't have to explain myself to you.' She sat down again, trying not to lose her temper. 'Even though this is none of your business, or anyone's, and I couldn't care less what anyone thinks, especially you...'

He didn't react.

'...the point is, it was sort of a joke, that poem. I didn't mean for him to go all crazy about it. I've explained it to him, so it's going to be fine. It's all under control.'

She saw his look of mistrust. 'What? What is it, Milo? Spit it out. You're really starting to get on my nerves.' She was so annoyed with him, and knew deep down she couldn't defend her behaviour, which made it even worse, because the only person in the whole school whose opinion was important to her was his.

He stood up from the bench, as if he couldn't bear to be near her. 'That's not how it works. You told him that you love him, you made him fall in love with you and then you just change your mind? Don't forget, he wasn't even interested in you before this; he was perfectly happy before he knew who you were. He's a nice person – he's my friend. The poor guy doesn't stand a chance.'

She laughed shortly. 'How do *you* know how it works? You don't know what you're talking about.' She looked at him, his face neutral, even though she was trying to hurt him. It was driving her mad, the way he was judging her. 'What makes you think you're such an expert all of a sudden?' Her voice rose. 'I didn't ask your opinion and I couldn't give a shit what you think. In fact, the more you lecture me about this, the more I think I did the right thing. You think you're so honourable, but you're such a hypocrite. You're only criticising me because I didn't want to go out with you.' She glared at him, challenging him to deny it.

'No, actually,' he said evenly. 'I haven't thought about you in that way for a long time.'

'I suppose you would say that.'

'Yes, I suppose I would.'

Beth fumed silently. She had been so sure that Milo was still in love with her. She could have put up with his reprimand about Edward if she thought that he was only doing it out of spite – if he couldn't have her, no one could, that sort of thing. Now she could see that he didn't love her any more, that he had kept his promise to be her friend. It was galling, that's what it was.

She narrowed her eyes. 'I'll tell you what, Milo, if I'm such a fucking disappointment to you, then let's say we're not such good friends as we thought we were. Perhaps it would be best...' she stood up from the bench and headed for the small door of the garden, 'if we didn't spend so much time with each other any more. Thanks for your help with the play, but I think I can take it from here.' She stormed out of the garden, leaving him standing unfazed by the bench.

'If you say so.'

Chapter Nine

B eth didn't speak to Milo again for the rest of the term. She was so angry every time she saw him, and it infuriated her how he would meet her stare with a calm smile. Once or twice, he looked as if he were about to burst out laughing at her, which only wound her up more. The script for the play was finished, and the secretary had typed it out and given her three copies. Beth went alone to deliver the script to Mr Gifford. He promised to read it over the holidays, so they could meet in the first week of term to discuss any improvements.

On the last day of term, Anne arrived to pick her up in her ancient yellow VW Golf, took her home to Melchester and told her she had an hour to pack a bag.

'I couldn't bear to spend another dreary Christmas in England. I've splashed out – we're going to Florence tonight. Luxury hotel, art galleries, fancy-pants restaurants, designer shopping. No expense spared.'

All thoughts of Edward and Milo flew out of Beth's head. It was the best holiday of her life. On New Year's Eve, when they arrived back home from the airport, there was a message for Beth on the answer machine from Livvy, inviting her out that night. They would pick her up at six, and she was to wear something 'not too flimsy' and 'dancing shoes'.

'It sounds like you're going to a rave,' said Anne.

'A rave – what on earth is that?'

'What do they teach you at that expensive school of yours? It's a dance party, usually in a field or a warehouse. They set it up without proper licences and everyone finds out where it is at the last moment, so the police can't close it down too quickly. Wear trainers and take a bottle of water with you. And stick close to your friends – if there is a police raid and everyone does a runner, you'll need to be together.'

'How do you know all this? Actually, please don't tell me, I don't want to know.'

Sure enough, when Livvy and BJ picked her up, they'd found out about a rave that was happening at a deserted barn in between the town of Shottsford Forum and The Island. Beth was worried that it was too close to school, but the Roses had checked out the location on a map and said it was miles away so it wouldn't be heard, and also that all the teachers would be away right now.

'Are we picking up Melanie or not?' asked Billy. 'What did she say in the end?'

'Nope, she's not coming,' said Livvy, her eyes twinkling. 'Guess what – she's got a date tonight.'

'Who's the lucky man?'

'Dunno. She wouldn't say. She said she wasn't sure if it was happening, then suddenly it was, but she didn't want to say who with.'

'With whom,' said Beth.

'Stop doing that!' all three of them shouted at her.

Beth attached herself to the Roses at the rave. There must have been about a thousand people there, and it was so loud they couldn't hear each other talk. The music was totally new to Beth, like nothing she'd ever heard before; the crowd was going mad. At about eleven o'clock they went outside for a break, and Beth heard someone call her name. She looked over to a group of boys who were sitting on some straw bales. Livvy and BJ were already walking over there before she recognised them – they were from her old school, and among them was her former antagonist, Steve aka Ferris Bueller. Too late to change direction, she introduced everyone. Billy lit up and passed round a joint, and Bueller offered them some pills. Billy and Jake took one each.

'What are they?' asked Livvy.

'Ecstasy.'

'Umm…' She hesitated, looking at her older brothers. 'Have you taken it before?'

'Couple of times.'

'What does it do?' said Beth.

'Just makes the music more intense, like it makes more sense, and gives you a good buzz.'

Livvy turned to Beth. 'What do you think? Shall we try it?'

'Want to do a half each?'

They swallowed half a pill each, drank a beer and went inside to dance again.

It was nearly midnight when Beth found herself outside again, but she couldn't see the others. She wasn't sure if the E had worked properly. At midnight she was sitting alone, cheerful, exhausted and sweaty, and clinked together her cigarette and bottle of beer to wish herself a Happy New Year. Bueller came out a few minutes later, alone. He wished her a Happy New Decade and she decided to be nice to him. He hadn't seen her friends but they sat together for a while and chatted about the rave.

'So, do you know how it all works?' She waved her cigarette at the barn.

'Dunno exactly – but how did you get here?'

'I got a lift with my friends.'

'OK, well, with me it was like this. I was in the pub last week and this bloke came in and was handing out flyers; here, look – like this.' He pulled a folded piece of paper out of his pocket. 'There's a date, see, and a phone number to call. It's from one of them mobile phones. You call it on the day of the rave and they give you map coordinates or a road name. Then you just turn up.'

'But it's so loud – why do you reckon the police aren't here yet?'

'I dunno. I suppose they're all on duty in the town centres, and this is so far away. Even if some old biddy who lives near here does call the cops, they probably can't be bothered to traipse all the way out here to close it down. They can't spare the manpower anyway, not on New Year's Eve. Every fucker is out in Melchester puking on the streets; that's where the cops are tonight.'

'Is this your first rave?'

'Nah, I went to one in the summer, near Stonehenge, after the hippies had been cleared out. There used to be loads in London, but now everyone goes to the ones in the country. You can get more people together. And the more people there are, the harder it is for the cops to control it.'

'Well, I suppose I'd better find my friends, in case they're looking for me.'

'Or...' he smiled and tilted his head to the side, 'you could let me be your friend tonight...' He leant his face towards hers and Beth, laughing, slid away from him.

'You always were really cheesy, Bueller. Look, can you do me a favour? I'm going inside, but if Livvy and her brothers come out again, could you please tell them to wait here for me? Otherwise we might keep missing each other.'

She struggled through the sweaty, dancing mob, circling round the edges of the barn and zigzagging through the dancers. She made it back to the barn doors without having seen them, and now Bueller was gone too. She didn't have a clue what time it was, but she'd had enough. What the fuck was she supposed to do now without the Roses? They were such airheads; where were they? She had an idea that they might have gone to The Island, either to set up some stupid prank, or maybe they thought that's where she'd be. It was only a couple of miles to the school gates and she was pretty sure she could find the way. With a second wind, she walked away from the pounding beat of the music and followed the track.

After a while, she saw a turning with a lamp post she recognised, and not much later, she saw the school gates in front of her. The archway with the coat of arms and Latin motto had never been more welcoming.

She was about to start walking up the driveway when she spotted a narrow, overgrown pathway to the side of the stone wall. She was so tired that it took a couple of seconds for her to figure out why that path meant something to her. Finally it clicked – it was the path to Milo's cottage. The night he'd fallen off the ladder, this was where it had happened.

Milo. Her exhaustion, the dancing, the beer and the drugs all collided and she had one thought – she wanted Milo. He was what she needed – his calmness, his strength, his safeness. It was all clear to her. She pushed aside some brambles and ran up the path towards the cottage. There were lights on upstairs and downstairs, but all the curtains were closed. She knocked on the door and waited, her breath clouding in the air around her. She quickly pulled her fingers through her hair. She probably looked a complete mess.

When Milo opened the door he was in his boxers and pulling on a crumpled white T-shirt, frayed around the neck. He stopped when he saw her, only opening it halfway.

'Eliza… Beth, is that you? What the hell are you doing here?'
'Happy New Year. Can I come in?'
'How…? What…? No, no, you definitely can't come in,' he

stuttered as she tried to push the door open. 'No, it's... it's not a good time.'

'What are you talking about?' She ducked under his arm, into the warm, cosy kitchen. The embers of a fire were glowing in the grate and she sat down heavily on a chair by the table.

'This is lovely, Milo. You really are very domesticated. What have you been up to tonight?' She looked over to him, still standing at the half-open door. 'Close that, will you, there's a bit of a...' She stopped talking and followed his eyes to where they had glanced upwards to the top of the stairs. She looked back at the table. A candle, two wine glasses, two plates, two sets of cutlery. 'Ah. I see. It really isn't a good time. Who is she? Oh, it doesn't matter, don't tell me. Oh my God, is it Mel?'

The expression on his face told her she'd guessed right.

'Oh shit, how embarrassing to burst in on you like this. I lost Livvy at this party, and I thought maybe I could use your phone...' She tailed off. 'I'm so tired. I know this is a lot to ask, but could I kip on your sofa? I don't know what else to do. Please?'

She could feel her eyes drooping; her shoulders and arms were heavy as she spoke. Milo pointed to a shabby sofa near to the fire, mumbled something about a blanket and left the room. Beth staggered over to the sofa and lowered herself down, drifting down, down into the absolute bliss of it. Through half-closed eyes she saw Milo return and felt a blanket spread over her. She reached her hand out and clasped his. A sleepy smile of gratitude spread over her parted lips. She murmured, more to herself than to him, 'You're such a legend, Milo.'

'I know.'

And she smiled again.

Milo trudged upstairs and creaked open his bedroom door. Melanie sat fully clothed, where he had left her, on the edge of the bed. He looked at her, awkward and embarrassed, not wanting to be the first to speak.

'It's OK, Milo, I know you're too nice to say it. It's really OK.' She held up her hand when he tried to speak. 'It's obvious how you feel about her. I knew before I called you about tonight.' She swallowed and tried to smile. 'Would you please call me a taxi now?'

'It's so late. Why don't you stay here? I'll make up the bed in the other room for me.'

'Thanks, but if it's all the same to you, I'd like to go home now.'

Half an hour later, he watched the taxi pull away, closed the front door and leant with his back against it, his shame mixed with relief. He glanced over at the sofa and was tempted to spend another night sitting watching Beth sleep, but Melanie's parting words rang in his ears: *If you ever feel like trying to get over her with me, let me know. Beggars can't be choosers.*

Beth woke at midday on the first day of 1990. While she'd been asleep, Milo had chopped some logs, washed and cleared up from last night, made her some strong coffee and cooked her a fry-up. Mel was nowhere to be seen. They sat eating, drinking and talking in front of the fire until it started to get dark again. Where had the time gone?

Beth stretched out on the sofa, yawned and said, 'I'm not really sure I can be bothered to move again today. Anne's not home anyway, she's in London. Shall I stay another night here? Or do you have plans with Mel?'

'Ha ha, very hilarious.'

He put some potatoes in the oven and produced some fresh cheese and salad from the fridge. Beth watched him and wondered if they were leftovers from his dinner with Mel last night, which was now fading into a distant memory. He fetched some glasses and a bottle of wine. Beth winced as she took the first sip.

'Oh, sorry, is the wine not a good vintage?' he asked.

'No idea, but it's hurting my hangover.'

'Hair of the dog. It's the only way.'

She downed the rest of the glass and refilled it.

'That's the spirit.'

Beth looked around her, taking in the bookshelves stuffed with old books. The phone rang and Milo answered it, and she heard him say quietly, 'No, not today, mate... tomorrow's good, I'll see you there. OK, eight o'clock. No, umm... I'll tell you tomorrow.'

'Who was that?' *Perhaps another girl?*

'Some friends from the village; they're heading down to the pub, they called to see if I wanted a pint and a game of darts.'

She moved over to the record player and stacks of records in the corner and flipped through them. 'Bob Dylan, Cat Stevens, Otis Redding, The Beatles, Nina Simone, Frank Sinatra... are all these yours? Don't you have any new music? From people who aren't practically dead?'

'They're my mum and dad's.'

Her face fell. 'Oh God, I didn't mean—'

'It's OK, I know what you meant. I don't have any money to buy anything new, but I like all this. It reminds me of them.' He took an album called *She Shot Me Down* from her hand and said, 'Not that one, it's too sad; here, put this one on', and handed her *Revolver*.

She wrinkled her nose. 'The Beatles? Really?' She put it on, stepped over to the bookshelf and pulled out a few paperbacks. 'So many books. Have you read all these? Are they yours, or your parents'?'

'They're mostly Mum's. Dad wasn't much of a reader. I've read some of them. I bought some from the second-hand bookshop in the village. Mr Gifford sometimes gives me old copies of books he thinks I'll like.'

'You've got a lot of people looking out for you.'

'I grew up here. It's funny – all the villagers, Dad's friends, think I'm posh. Everyone at school thinks I'm an oik. I don't really feel like I belong anywhere. But everyone's been really nice since... since... I don't feel too lonely.'

'Shit, what did you do for Christmas? Your first Christmas alone. I totally forgot.'

'Guy invited me over to Jersey. His parents gave me the plane ticket for Christmas. He and Theo have another two younger brothers and about twelve dogs. It was so loud and hectic, I didn't have time to feel sad.'

'See, everyone looks out for you.' She threw herself back down on the sofa and sighed. *Here, There and Everywhere* was playing and she listened to it. 'Actually, this is a lovely song. Maybe The Beatles are OK after all. What time is it? I'm wide awake. How about the pub?'

'It's already eleven; we'll have missed last orders. We could go for a walk?'

He found some warm clothes for her – an old coat of his mum's, a spare pair of gloves, a woolly hat and a scarf that he wound round and round her neck.

'Where are we going? Another secret garden?'

'Sort of,' was all he would say.

She followed him in the darkness and grumbled all the way up the hill, but at the top caught sight of the lights and the shadowy slopes rolling towards the horizon and the black sea.

'We used to come here. Mum and Dad and I, for picnics and camping. When I'm up here, everything else, school stuff; it seems less important somehow.'

Beth said, 'You know what I think when I see a view like this? I imagine that on every hill in the whole world, there are two people like us having a conversation just like we are. Not just right now, but ever since there were hills and people and for the rest of time. Pretty depressing, huh?'

'No, I think it's quite reassuring.'

The following morning, Milo gave her a lift back to Melchester in Mrs Toms' borrowed car. For the first part of the journey they sat in silence, but Beth shuffled up in her seat and cleared her throat.

'I had a really nice day yesterday, Milo; I'm so glad I found your cottage again.'

'Me too.'

'But, you know, we haven't really talked about a couple of things. I suppose we should get them sorted out or we'll have it hanging over us.'

'Go ahead,' he said.

'Well, first of all, about Edward. You told me what you think and I understand that he's your friend and you're worried about him. I'll sort it out, I promise. I like him too, I won't hurt him. You'll have to trust me. Agreed?'

Milo nodded, but didn't say anything.

'OK. Good enough. Also, about Melanie. I don't want to pry, if you don't want to tell me. But—'

'Nothing happened. You sort of interrupted it with your surprise visit.'

'She's nice.'

He shrugged. 'She's OK. I don't think she likes me any more, though.'

Beth sat back in her seat and looked out at the Wessex countryside flashing past. She was friends with Milo again. The argument about Edward was resolved, sort of. He hadn't slept with Mel. Not that he shouldn't. But perhaps he could do better than her?

'You'll do the play again with me, won't you?'

'Of course.'

Beth clapped her hands over her face. 'Oh shit, I forgot to call Livvy yesterday to say that I was safe, not that she deserves it.'

'It's OK, I called her when you were out cold, Sleeping Beauty. She had something called a "bad trip", whatever that is, and BJ took her home. She's fine. What was it you were all doing anyway?'

Beth explained about the barn and the party, but Milo kept interrupting her.

'What's house music?'

'What's ecstasy?

'What's a rave?'

'Honestly, Milo, you are such a country bumpkin. Don't you know about any of this stuff? It's been around in London for ages.'

Milo looked sheepish. 'I've never been to London.'

'What? Seriously? In this day and age?'

'Mmm. You know, that barn used to be part of my grandparents' farm. I wonder how the rave organisers set it all up, got everyone there?'

'They hand out flyers and you're supposed to call a mobile phone—'

'A mobile what?'

She was about to start explaining what a mobile phone was, when she glanced across at Milo, who was trying to keep a straight face.

'Oh, ha ha, very hilarious.'

Chapter Ten

A week later, school began. This was a big term for Beth – she'd have her *Cold Comfort Farm* script back soon from Mr Gifford and the auditions were planned for the last week of January. She was nervous about Edward; the two-week break didn't seem to have changed the way he felt about her. On Tuesday she spoke to him in the dining hall to make arrangements for her first riding lesson, and during the brief conversation he didn't meet her eyes once. *I must be mad*, she thought; *horses are really not my thing.* But at least it would give her a chance to be alone with him and explain her feelings, or lack of them.

That Saturday, the sun shone and the frost cleared early. It was mild and bright. At breakfast Guy and Milo were talking about that afternoon's hockey team trials. Beth was still unconvinced by the attraction of team sports, and hockey in particular looked like a complete waste of time, knocking a bit of plastic around with some sort of a wooden club – plus, wasn't it a game for girls? But they persuaded her to come and watch for a bit, before she met Edward at the stables.

After lunch she changed into a warm jacket and jeans, and walked down with Livvy and Henry to the hockey pitch. She brought her new video camera, the latest Sony from America, which James had sent her for Christmas. When they arrived, the hockey players had already started so Beth turned on the camcorder and began filming. The coach had set up the pitch so that it looked like an obstacle course, with cones and targets and balls and sticks lying everywhere. She filmed for a while, practising different angles and ranges, at one point standing behind the goal, as close as she dared to the netting. Whoever was in goal was a braver soul than she – the other players were smashing the hard ball at him over and over again, and she flinched when it hit his body pads or gloves, or when he kicked it away with a giant padded boot. She zoomed in as a ball thunked onto his helmet, and then laughed in surprise as the goalie took off his helmet and shook his head from side to side. It was Milo. He gave her the thumbs-up, clipped his helmet back on and faced the next shot. She moved away to the safety of the benches near the halfway line.

Edward turned up at exactly three o'clock as they'd arranged, to take her to the stables. Beth caught Milo's eye and waved goodbye to him. Guy, remembering the catastrophe of the Sherton Abbas rugby game, cracked a ball up into the air straight past Milo's helmet to score the first goal of the afternoon.

'Tsk tsk, eyes on the game, please, goalkeeper,' he shouted gleefully as he collected the ball from the back of the net. He tapped Milo on the shoulder. 'She's like your very own Kryptonite.' And he walked away.

'Wanker.'

Edward showed Beth how to groom, feed and water the horses and get to know them. Gilbert was frighteningly black and enormous, but Caspar, Bonnie's horse, was much smaller, a silver-grey colour, quiet and steady. Just right for Beth to learn on, Edward explained. They put on the saddle and bridle and she sat on Caspar as Edward led him out into the paddock, holding his reins.

The light was fading as they finished clearing away the equipment and sat down on a bench near the stable doors.

'Oh, I have some news for you – I was talking to my mother about your play and she knows a friend of Stella Gibbons, who lives in France but is visiting us next weekend. We'd like to invite you to stay, so that you can meet her and discuss the play. She might have some really wonderful ideas about how it could work.'

'Oh, I'd love to meet her, that sounds awesome, thank you so much. Next weekend would be perfect, before the auditions. Is that really OK if I come and stay for the weekend? Will I meet Bonnie, will she be there?'

Edward stiffened. 'No, she's away at the moment. But listen, I have to tell you something else. My father has set up an exchange for me, at a school in West Berlin, for six weeks. It starts at the end of the month. I wasn't sure I wanted to go away. But I want to get my German up to scratch and it'll be really exciting to be in Berlin at the moment. Also, I know you said at the Christmas party that you wouldn't go out with me... but we get along so well, I love spending time with you. I want to ask you – will you please think about it again, in those weeks when I'm away? I'll miss you so much, I'll write to you all the time, and when I get back, I'm going to ask you out again. Please? May I?' His voice was strained with abject desperation, his body tensed, his eyes wide open.

'Perhaps. I don't know. I'll think about it. I do like you, but I can't promise anything.' She felt like he was wearing her down. The more she said no, the more he persisted. She felt so terribly guilty. Maybe it would be the right thing to say yes. But surely that wouldn't be honest? Oh, she didn't know what to do. He was behaving like a madman. Wearily, she stood up, said goodbye to him and walked out into the dusk.

The orange sunset framed her shadow as she walked towards the open doors at the far end of the stables. Edward sat and watched her black silhouette dwindle into nothing.

The following weekend, Beth and Edward travelled on the train from Melchester to Cornwall together. A car with a driver picked them up from Bodmin station and Beth tried to behave like this was normal. While the driver picked up her bag and opened the car door for her, she caught Edward's eye.

'Your family has a chauffeur, Edward?' she said out of the corner of her mouth as they sat in the back seat. 'What are you, royalty or something?'

Edward smiled at her. He was more relaxed and cheerful than at school. 'Samways is my father's driver – you know, he has to be up and down to London and to the airport. He doesn't like to stay in his flat in London all the time. So if he's driven, he can get on with some work while he travels. Even you, little socialist, can't fault the logic in that.'

Less than ten minutes later, the car turned into a tree-lined gravel driveway, through a set of stone gateposts and low iron railings, and approached an old, three-storey granite manor house. Beth gasped at the beauty of it. The sun was setting behind the low stables to the right of the house. The gravel crunched under the wheels of the car as they slowed at the imposing entrance. Beth grabbed Edward's hand. He froze, a look of shock quickly giving way to a shy smile of joy as he gave her hand a small squeeze.

'Are you all right, Beth? It's not too much? Do you like it?'

'It's way too much and I love it,' she whispered.

Edward's mother was waiting to greet them as they walked through a stone archway that led into a shady courtyard. She looked nothing like Edward – he must take after his father, who was due back later that evening. She gave Beth a hug, which was when she realised she was still clutching Edward's hand.

He noticed her embarrassment and let her hand go reluctantly. Edward's mother led them both through the door and past a vast staircase in the hallway, into a beautiful living room with windows looking out onto a dazzling frost-covered view, with two enormous oak trees framing the sloping park. There were no other houses to be seen. Trees and ice, all the way to the horizon.

'Is that Bodmin Moor? The light here...' Beth breathed. 'It's so...'

'Isn't it perfect?' agreed Edward's mother. 'This is our favourite room of the house, isn't it, Eddie?'

Beth was offered tea – with a proper cup and saucer – and Edward's mother filled them in about the evening. The friend of Stella Gibbons was due any moment; she'd be staying at the house for a few days. At dinner, a few other guests were expected; in all they would be about twenty people. They needed to dress up.

'Did Eddie mention to bring a party dress? Good. Eddie, take Beth up to the blue spare room, please.'

In the blue spare room – they had more than one spare room! – Beth had a bath in the en suite, changed into her new dress, dried her hair, leaving it down so it fell in dark waves over her shoulders, put on make-up and waited for Edward. Eventually she heard a soft knock on the door and jumped up to open it.

'Wow,' he stammered, 'I... you look...'

'You don't look so bad yourself.' Beth smiled. He was wearing a dinner jacket with a white waistcoat and a white tie. He looked so natural and handsome in it, Beth was again astonished at the change in him. It was like he was one person at The Island and another completely different person here. She hooked her arm through his and they made their way downstairs. They could hear the front door opening and closing, voices chattering, the distant sound of music, and as they came down the stairs, they saw the flowers and candles that had transformed the hallway.

Beth was introduced to Mr Markham, who was as handsome as his son – tall and dignified, not a hair out of place. Edward spent the entire evening at her side, introducing her to everyone, listening carefully when she spoke and watching her when he thought she wouldn't notice. She had a lovely time. She drank champagne and ate everything she was given, even though she didn't have a clue what it was. It all tasted wonderful.

She sat between Stella Gibbons' friend and Edward at dinner, and asked a ton of questions about the author and the book. The friend was interested in Beth's play and said she would come and watch the performance. Beth wished that Edward had also invited Milo – he would have loved it here too, with Edward's family, eating all this posh food.

When all the guests had gone, Edward took Beth to her door and kissed her cheek, murmuring, 'Goodnight.' She thought for a moment that he was about to try and kiss her properly, but he blinked twice and walked off down the corridor to his room.

Chapter Eleven

On Sunday afternoon, Edward dropped Beth off at Bodmin train station, so she could return to school. He was flying to Berlin early on Tuesday morning but wanted to spend Sunday night at home, to see his sister who was returning from her friend's house.

Beth knew she'd miss Edward. He was very attentive and his family were so kind. But she was also a little relieved to have some breathing space. He was sometimes too attentive; it made her feel like she had a bodyguard, rather than a boyfriend. Was he her boyfriend? They hadn't even kissed, and Beth didn't think she wanted to. He was such a clever, interesting person, and very, very handsome. But she didn't know if she was attracted to him; something was missing, some spark.

It was already dark when she stepped onto the connecting train at Exonbury. The train was packed. She was lucky to find a window seat next to a middle-aged lady. She settled down to read her book while the rain drummed on the window next to her head. She might have to ask the lady to wake her up at Melchester; she already felt sleepy, the carriage was so warm.

A voice broke into her thoughts. 'I'm awfully sorry, but I think you're sitting in my seat.'

She looked up from her book, annoyed at the interruption.

'You see, I reserved a seat – look, here's my ticket; seat 22A – I'm afraid I'm going to have to ask you to move.'

Beth hadn't thought to book a ticket, and she was angry with herself and this boy, who looked vaguely familiar. He was about the same height as her, with longish, messy blond hair falling into his eyes, which were an icy green colour, surrounded by long, thick eyelashes. He was grinning at her mischievously.

'Don't I know you from school? Yes, I'm sure you go to my school.'

Beth stood up without answering and rammed her book into the pocket of her coat, reaching up into the luggage rack for her bag as the middle-aged lady moved her legs to one side. Beth lost her balance slightly and the bag dropped off the rack. An arm shot up and caught it easily, pushing it back up onto the rack.

'Tell you what, don't worry about moving, I can find another seat. You stay there, it's all the same to me.' He turned around and sauntered off to the front of the carriage. There were no seats left for him, Beth was sure of that, but she appreciated his manners. She sat down again.

Twenty minutes later, the lady sitting next to her started gathering herself together and as she stood up, she nudged Beth.

'I'm getting off at this stop. Would you like me to tell your friend he can come and sit next to you, on my way out?'

'He's not my friend, I don't know him.'

'He's very good-looking, isn't he; sexy, I mean? Have fun. Bye.'

Beth would rather not have sat next to anyone, sexy or not, but she supposed it was only fair as he'd given her his seat. He soon slid into the seat next to her and without a word, fixed his eyes on hers. She held his gaze for as long as she could, then looked at the back of the seat in front of her. She flicked her eyes back to him and he was still staring at her. Jesus. What was he doing? He looked at her like he was seeing her naked.

Finally he broke the silence. 'So, was I right? Are we at school together? I'm Zack.'

'Zack?' she managed to croak.

He looked like he was trying not to laugh. 'And you are…?'

'Beth Atkinson.'

'Ahhh, yes, I thought that's who you were. You're the one the whole rugby team's so keen on, I believe. It really is a pleasure to meet you at last,' he drawled, never taking his eyes off hers.

'Oh, you're in Milo's rugby team, are you?'

'Milo's rugby team? That's a good one, I must remember that.' At last he broke his gaze and sat back in his seat, closing his eyes. 'You should hear some of the things they say about you, it would make you blush. Mind you, you don't look much like the blushing type, am I right?'

'Not really.' She tried to keep her voice level. 'Look, do you… would you like your window seat? I'm reading, so it doesn't make any difference to me…'

He shook his head and so she opened her book again and pretended she was concentrating on the words. He took the hint and settled back in his seat, closing his eyes and smiling. When she realised she had read the same line three times, Beth dared to sneak a look sideways and found herself caught out – he was staring at her again.

'My God, you are quite a beauty, and I should know, I've seen a few girls in my time, but none of them in your league. You're actually giving me a hard-on right now—'

'Don't be so revolting, that's the most disgusting thing I have ever heard,' she hissed. She knew she should try to keep her cool, even though her heart was racing. Who did he think he was? Nobody had ever dared to speak to her like this before. And yet, though her head was outraged, her stomach was turning over and over because – the lady had been right – this rude, arrogant, dirty boy was the sexiest person Beth had ever met. A sixteen-year-old Adonis. They were so close, she could have touched him. He magnetised her and repelled her at the same time. She felt a hot panic, a loss of control, and fought to turn away. With trembling hands and burning with shame, she hid behind her book. She wanted to get up from her seat, get away from him, but her legs wouldn't allow her to move. What was happening to her?

Beth wondered when the journey would ever end, and at the same time hoped it never would. She was desperate to get herself under control. What was she going to do at Melchester, when Zack would get off the train too; what if they had to take a taxi together back to school? Thirty miles in the back of a dark taxi with him. Could he keep his hands to himself? Did she want him to? She imagined him touching her, on her arm or her knee, somewhere totally innocuous, but the thought of that made her stomach flip over again. It would just about be the end of her.

At last, the train pulled into Melchester station and Beth steeled herself to look at him. He was standing up, running his hand through his hair, checking his reflection in the window.

'Would you mind passing me my bag?' she said.

'What's the magic word, young lady?'

'Oh, for fuck's sake, I'll get it myself.'

'My, what language. Not so much of a lady, then, perhaps?' He reached up effortlessly, pulled down her bag and handed it to her. He didn't even lower his voice when he said to her, 'I wish this journey had been longer. More time to get to know each other better. I've got a couple of people to meet in town before I go back to Alcatraz. See you at school.' He turned away from her and moved nimbly through the carriage, which was packed with people struggling with luggage.

Not if I see you first, thought Beth.

Half an hour later, Beth was back at school, lying face up on her bed, staring at the ceiling. The stripes of bright colours on the kikois that Sav had brought back from Kenya for Livvy swirled in front of her eyes as she gazed and gazed at them. Livvy came in after dinner and flopped down next to her on the single bed.

'How was your weekend? How was Edward? Did you snog him yet?'

'Good, nice, and no.'

'You OK? You seem to be rather at sixes and sevens, my lovely friend.'

'Mmm... what? I... umm... met this guy from The Island on the train, do you know him – I think his name was Zack?'

Livvy raised her eyebrows and tucked her hands under her head. 'Ah, what to say about Monsieur Zachary Smythe? Where shall I start? Let me see: his mother is French, interior decorator to the stars, filthy rich of course. Has a place in London, Notting Hill I think. This is the best bit – she had this steamy and long-running affair with minor royalty, the duke of somewhere or other. And she was married the whole time to a doctor, and it carried on, the affair I mean, until he divorced her, leaving Madame Smythe and the duke to carry on more or less in public. They're not married, though. Now and again you see something written about them in the papers, and last year or the year before, Zack, his mother and the duke were photographed in the royal box at Wimbledon, and it was pretty clear that he's Zack's father; they are the spit of each other. The truth were loud.'

'What's that, Livs? About the truth?'

'The truth were loud. What? Why are you laughing? I don't get it.'

Beth clutched her stomach and wiped the tears away from her eyes. 'That is a classic. You mean of course *The truth will out.* Not were loud – will out.'

Livvy looked annoyed. 'Well, that's not how I say it.'

'But it's wrong, how you say it.'

'Says who?'

'Launcelot Gobbo, for one.'

Livvy looked unconvinced. 'I don't know him.'

'It doesn't even make any sense. If anything it would be "The truth was loud."'

'I thought it was, you know, cockney or something.'

Beth started laughing again.

Livvy tutted. 'Do you want to hear about Zack or not?'

'Yes, yes, of course. Carry on, please. Ignore me.'

'Right. Well, of course, Zack isn't the least bit worried about all this, in fact he's rather proud of his "lineage", as he calls it. Apart from all that, he's a good laugh; really sarcastic, you know, very cool and charming when he wants to be. And very easy on the eye, as I'm sure you've noticed.'

'How do you know so much about everyone?' asked Beth, amazed.

'I've been at this school for more than five years now; these are the people I live with. I want to know about them, and I think it's important to know about their families, their parents' jobs, who they are, where they come from. You never know, might come in handy one of these days.

'Anyway, back to Zack. Now the not-so-good bits. He hangs out a lot with the girls in the fourth and fifth years; he likes 'em young, and he's a bit of a tart.'

'How do you mean, a tart?' Beth tried to keep her voice impassive.

'He's been out with a lot of girls, the younger ones I mean; he doesn't do long-term. He's never been out with anyone from our year. So what did he say to you? What did you think of him?'

'I thought he was arrogant, vain and rude.'

'So, you like him then?'

Beth woke up early the next morning, taking a long shower before the morning rush. She chose her clothes with care, let her hair dry naturally and put on a bit of make-up – not enough for the teachers to notice; she knew exactly how far to push it. Then she sat at her desk and did an hour's work to finish an essay on *The Tempest* before breakfast.

'Morning, beautiful,' Livvy mumbled at 7.30, rubbing her eyes and sitting up. 'What are you doing up so bright and early? Blimey, you do look radiant today. What's the occasion?'

'Nothing. I'm off to breakfast. See you in assembly.'

At breakfast, she steered clear of Mel and Justin Ravensdale, who were sitting opposite each other, on their own, at a table in the middle of the dining hall. *That's a new development*, Beth thought, and wondered idly if Milo would mind. Mel hadn't spoken to her since the New Year. As she walked past, Justin whispered something in Mel's ear.

Beth sat instead with a girl called Susanna from another house, who she knew from the swimming team and who was in her history class. Susanna's boyfriend Finn appeared and told Beth that everyone had seen her and Markham at the paddock last Saturday and leaving for the weekend together. Everyone at hockey training had been saying they were shagging, but Milo had got all hot under the collar, not for the first time either, and told them all it wasn't true.

While Finn and Susanna talked, Beth kept looking over their shoulders, wondering when Zack would come to breakfast. She sat there for over an hour, other people coming and going, the table filling and emptying. Still no Zack. She sighed, exasperated, gave up and went to fetch her books for her first lesson.

All day she looked for him. She didn't know which A Levels he was taking; he wasn't in any of her classes. At lunch it was the same story: she sat there for ages and looked around, but he didn't show up. It was like he wasn't in school. Annoyed, she made her way to the pool for swimming practice after lunch.

She changed into her swimming costume, showered quickly, grabbed her goggles, cap and towel and pushed open the door out of the changing rooms into the pool area. And there he was. Sitting on one of the benches, alone, in a pair of red swimming shorts. She looked down at her feet and ignored him as she tried to walk past.

'I dreamt about you last night,' he said, loud enough for her, but nobody else, to hear.

She stopped in front of him and held her towel in front of her body. 'I didn't know you did swimming.'

'It was a very enjoyable dream. I was rather sorry to wake up.'

'Did you switch sports?'

'I've been trying to find you all day to tell you about it.'

'Well, here I am.'

'Yes, here you are.'

Beth's heart was thudding painfully in her chest. She had to try and breathe. *Look normal.* She put her hand on her hip. *Breathe.* 'And?'

'You want me to tell you now? Here? In front of all these people?' He smirked, stood up and stepped towards her. Close up, she could see his smooth, hairless skin and the wiry muscles of his chest and arms. He moved slowly, his head cocked to one side, and put his mouth next to her ear. 'So you *do* blush. Let's talk about it later.'

Shaking, her legs almost giving way underneath her, she remained rooted to the spot while he sauntered off towards the rest of the group, who were warming up near the diving boards. She gathered herself together and joined them, keeping her distance from Zack, who looked bored by everyone and everything. She made it through training, just about, and hurried to the changing rooms, turned the shower up as hot as it went, and stayed in it for as long as she could bear, until she was sure everyone else would have left the sports hall.

Having been unable to catch a glimpse of him all morning, now she saw him everywhere she went. He always stared at her with that arrogant, penetrating gaze, and every time she had to look away before he did, unable to bear the way it made her feel. She felt like she had a flashing neon sign above her head reading, *I WANT YOU.*

She had a double free period at the end of the day, so went to one of the libraries off the main corridor and tried to concentrate on reading about the Spanish Civil War for her history class tomorrow. The page swam in front of her. She felt a tap on her shoulder, and Theo Revel, Guy's thirteen-year-old brother, gave her a folded note, smiled shyly at her and sat down at a table on the other side of the room. Confused, Beth unfolded the note. What did Theo want? Was it a note he'd delivered from Guy or Milo?

Later is now. I'm waiting outside. Z

Shit, thought Beth, *I can't go, I'm going to make a total fool of myself. I'll ignore him, stay here, where it's safe.* She was trembling again; why did even the thought of him affect her like that? *Relax, breathe, calm down.* She remained in the library until the bell rang for dinner, staying seated until the room had emptied, giving Theo a wave as he walked by.

She sat for a while longer, nervously drumming her fingers on the desk, staring out of the window at the darkness. Five, ten minutes went by; she didn't know how long. When she was sure he wouldn't be waiting outside any more, she gathered all her unread books together and put them in her bag. She turned towards the door and nearly screamed to see Zack sitting on a desk at the back of the library, feet up on a chair, staring straight at her.

'Are you by any chance trying to avoid me, Atkinson?' He was smiling as usual, a smile that said, *I know the effect I have on you.*

'Christ alive, you scared the crap out of me. How long have you been there?'

'Long enough. Come here.'

114

'Look, whatever creepy shit you want to describe to me will have to wait. I'm not interested. I've heard about you.'

'Been checking up on me? How sweet.'

Beth moved up the central aisle between the desks towards the door, but as she drew level with him, he said, 'I've been checking up on you too, and it would seem I've got my work cut out for me. Half the school's got a crush on you, including our esteemed head boy and our mutual friend Farmer West.'

'Didn't your mother tell you not to listen to gossip?'

Zack shrugged. 'Only passing on what I heard.'

Beth pretended to be bored. 'All right then, what've you heard?'

'That you and West spent the night together, in the summer holidays after the Melchester races.'

Bloody Livvy.

'And that you went skiing with Markham and his family at New Year.'

'That's not true; Edward asked me but I didn't go. And Milo and I are just friends.'

'Clearly, he doesn't quite see it that way. Or Markham. Mind you, I don't blame you for blowing them out. They've got to be two of the most boring people I've ever met. You're too good for them.'

'Oh, but not too good for you, I suppose?'

'Touché, Atkinson.' He sprang down from the desk and stood between her and the doors.

She took a step back and bumped her hip into a desk on the other side of the aisle. *Shit. Ow. If he comes any closer now, I don't know what I'll do. Jesus, what do I do?* If she could just concentrate on his mouth, on that one part of him, maybe... maybe... *Oh fuck, this isn't working.*

He stood still and gazed at her with his pale green eyes, as if he knew how uncomfortable he was making her. 'I feel like I know you,' he said in a low voice.

'Well, you don't.'

'I know one thing. You're the kind of girl that makes everyone unhappy.'

'Wh… what? Why?'

'You're so beautiful, you make all these boys fall in love with you. Then you break their hearts. After that, they're not interested in any other girls, so you break the hearts of the girls too. Everyone's unhappy, all because of you.'

Beth thought of Milo and Melanie at New Year. She frowned. 'Bullshit, stop talking crap.'

Zack laughed. 'OK, I will. But it's true that you're beautiful and it's true that I dreamt about you last night and I'm hoping to do so again tonight. To be continued, Atkinson.' He stepped away from her, blew her a kiss and turned and left the library.

It was the same story every day that week. She saw him at swimming practice, and it mortified her that they were so close to each other, with not many clothes on. She saw him at lunch, staring at her, making her look away quickly, down at her shoes, anywhere but at him. She saw him in the corridors, in the tuck shop, in the library. And every time, even though there were loads of people around them, the way he looked at her or spoke to her made her feel like they were all alone.

On Thursday, she sat with Milo at breakfast as they ran through the plan for the *Cold Comfort Farm* auditions that evening. They arranged to meet at the theatre after their final lessons of the day. When Milo left the dining hall, which was by now almost deserted, Beth noticed he'd left his tatty jumper on the bench next to her. She heard his footsteps return to collect it and picked it up, holding it out to him without looking up from her folder.

'Thanks, but it's not my size,' drawled a low voice.

Beth jumped. 'What do you want, Zack?'

'Bit snippy, aren't you? I'd like to audition for your play.'

Beth frowned. 'Which part?'

'Seth Starkadder, of course.'

'You're not right for that part.'

'Why not, may I ask?'

Beth stood up, closed her folder with the photocopied audition scripts inside it and put it into her bag along with her tattered copy of *Cold Comfort Farm*. She ran her shaking hand through her hair. *Get a grip*, she thought.

'OK, come if you want. I'll put your name on the list.'

'Maybe I'll surprise you. Where and when?'

'Theatre. Five till seven.'

'I'll see you at seven.'

She shook her head. 'No, we're finishing at seven.'

'We?'

'Milo, Livvy and Henry'll be there too.'

Zack paused and looked at her. 'Actually, I'd prefer to audition for you. Alone.'

Beth felt dizzy at the thought of being alone with him. Why was she being so pathetic? 'You're not the only one who wants that part. We've got fifty people auditioning. So I'll see you between five and seven, or not at all. Up to you.'

She walked away from him, her head pounding and her heart racing, thinking about it over and over. *Alone. With. Him.*

Beth couldn't concentrate that afternoon in her lessons. She went down to the theatre much earlier than she'd arranged to meet the others, and sat in the middle of the seat rows, staring at the dimly lit stage.

Milo, Livvy and Henry arrived shortly before five o'clock, when the first few people trickled in. Livvy accosted them in the foyer, arranged them into girl-boy pairs and gave them all a script and a time slot. They settled down to watch the stage.

They found their Flora Poste fairly quickly, a girl called Alice in the fifth form, pretty, petite, with sharp features and neat, straight hair. Henry auditioned for Charles Fairford, a small but important part, and he was great. Guy didn't read from the audition pages but did a hilarious Aunt Ada Doom monologue, which Beth wasn't sure about, but the others voted her down. They had all the Pioneers-O and the Starkadders, except for Seth. None of them were satisfied that anyone they'd seen had the right 'raw, animal sexiness,' as Livvy put it, giggling.

'Milo, why don't you do it?' asked Henry.

'Me? No, no way. I can't act. At all.'

'Oh, go on, give it a try,' pleaded Livvy.

Milo looked at Beth. She shrugged her shoulders and smiled.

'No, I can't. All those people looking at me, I'd shit myself.'

'Chicken.'

Disappointed, Livvy and Henry cleared up their notes and lists.

Beth kept glancing up towards the door at the back, and the clock at the side of the auditorium. 'I'll see you at dinner,' she said, shuffling through the scattered pages on her seat and not meeting their eyes. 'I want to write down some stuff before I forget it.'

The other three trudged up the steps and left her there, flicking through a pile of paper. As soon as the door slammed shut, she breathed out and sat down. She stood up again, fiddling with her fingers. Exasperated, she stuffed all the paper into her bag and walked down the aisle towards the stage to collect the scripts that had been left there. In the distance she heard a boom of thunder, so loud that it echoed in her ears and made her throat thud. Hailstones were pounding on the roof. There had been a storm warning on Ceefax that lunchtime.

She sat on the edge of the stage with her legs dangling down, looking out towards the rows and rows of seats. She thought of Milo, and how he couldn't face performing in front of all those people. She was the same. She wanted to be behind the camera, not in front of it.

Her thoughts were interrupted by a creak at the back of the stage. She whipped her head round and saw Zack standing by the wings, with that same arrogant, mocking stare. She was agitated and at the same time relieved that she was alone with him and that the others had gone.

'You're too late. Auditions are over.'

'I wanted to show you what I can do alone. I couldn't imagine you'd want the others to see it too.'

Beth hesitated. She had heard that he could act, and had been annoyed to say the least that he hadn't turned up to the auditions. And now here he was, clearly having waited until everyone else had gone. He was so irritatingly sure of himself. She couldn't give in, she mustn't.

'No, you're too late, the others have gone. I don't have time.'

'It won't take five minutes.'

He was near her now, and she shook her head, but not in a very convincing way. Lightning flashed beyond the narrow windowpanes in the doors to the foyer and she felt a shiver run through her. She tried to hide it.

'Close your eyes.' It was almost a whisper. She obeyed. For a moment she thought he'd left, but she heard him move towards her and his clear, slow voice drifted to where she sat.

'*She walks in beauty, like the night*
Of cloudless climes and starry skies;
And all that's best of dark and bright
Meet in her aspect and her eyes...'

Beth began to open her eyes and felt his fingertips softly close them. She couldn't... she mustn't... what was she supposed to do? Dizzy, weak, she gave in.

'*Thus mellow'd to that tender light*
Which heaven to gaudy day denies.
One shade the more, one ray the less,
Had half impaired the nameless grace
Which waves in every raven tress...'

His hand ran through her hair gently, and she shivered again as he stroked it off her neck. She tried to move, but it was as if she was pinned down to the edge of the stage.

'*Or softly lightens o'er her face...*'

His lips were almost touching her neck, and without noticing how, she knew she was pressing her face towards the sound of his voice, wanting his touch.

'*Where thoughts serenely sweet express*
How pure, how dear their dwelling-place.
And on that cheek, and o'er that brow,
So soft, so calm, yet eloquent...'

She could feel his breath over her face and his lips touched her forehead as he spoke the words.

'*The smiles that win, the tints that glow,*
But tell of days in goodness spent,
A mind at peace with all below,
A heart whose love is innocent!'

She dragged her eyes open, his face was so close, his eyes bright and mocking; she reached up to him and held the back of his neck, pulled him to her and they kissed.

Chapter Twelve

Milo had been wondering, ever since Beth had returned from her trip to Cornwall, about the change in her. She had a strange new glint in her eye. Could something have happened between her and Edward? She'd said at New Year that she wasn't interested in him, which had alleviated Milo's jealousy and made it easier for him to stick to his New Year's resolution to waste less time thinking about her. But by now Milo knew Beth well enough to know that he could never be sure what she was going to do next. He had the impression that she didn't even know herself. It wasn't that Milo thought she had lied to him about her feelings for Edward, only that she might have changed her mind. She did that a lot. He wanted to talk to her about it, but was wary of starting another argument. She only talked about meeting Stella Gibbons' friend and the new ideas she had about the play. One minute she was babbling, spilling out ideas so quickly he couldn't keep up, the next she was silent, her eyes darting over his shoulder, or with a glazed-over look that made him feel uneasy.

When he left the theatre on Thursday night, fat raindrops became heavier and harder and the storm began. He grabbed an umbrella that was lying near the dining-hall door and sprinted back through the hail towards the theatre to take it to Beth. He entered the foyer as a rumble of thunder burst. Leaving the umbrella on the floor, he reached out to open the door to the auditorium, which had a thin strip of glass in it. What he saw made him freeze. Beth was sitting on the stage, her legs dangling down, her arms by her sides, her head tilted back, and she was being kissed by a boy on her neck.

Milo felt cold all over and his heartbeat slowed. He gripped the door handle until his knuckles were white, wanting to leave, his legs like lead. He turned his head away, but looked back again as Beth raised her arms and held the boy to her as she kissed him back. It was a strange feeling he had, of being revolted and yet fascinated by the sight. He couldn't stop looking. He had the same sick feeling of joy that he'd felt that night when he saw her swimming naked in the pool.

Milo finally managed to tear himself away and, forgetting the umbrella, trudged through driving hailstones to dinner. Without a word, he sat down opposite Henry and Livvy and mechanically chewed at his food, his mouth so dry he had trouble swallowing. A few minutes later, Beth rushed in, sat down next to him and he couldn't even look at her.

'There was one more person to audition; he's brilliant, for Seth, I mean.' Her voice was husky and excited.

'Who? Who's going to be Seth?' asked Livvy.

And Milo, in the second before she said it, realised that he recognised the boy she'd been kissing and gripped the edge of the bench with horror.

'Zack Smythe. He's perfect,' sighed Beth.

Later that night, around midnight, Milo gave up on sleep, tried to read, couldn't concentrate and lay in his bed, feeling like he'd been knocked out in a fight. He went to the loo and on his way back, saw a light under Guy's door. He knocked softly and went in. Guy was sitting up in bed with his Walkman headphones on, reading a copy of *Sports Illustrated* with Michael Jordan on the front cover.

'Hey, big man.' Guy took off his headphones and closed the magazine.

'I can't sleep.'

'Something on your mind?'

Milo sat down on a beanbag next to Guy's desk and thought. Guy waited patiently.

'I saw... I saw Beth getting off with Zack this evening.'

'Oh. Bummer.' Guy knew how he felt about Zack. And how he felt about Beth. 'What're you going to do?'

'Nothing. What can I do? I mean, I want to do something. But I don't know what.'

'Yes. Well, that's clear then.' Guy grinned.

'It's complicated. I don't want Beth to think I still like her—'

'Even though you do?'

'No. I mean, yes. But not really. But I want to tell her what a tosser he is. Just so she knows.'

'A need-to-know situation?'

'Don't take the piss. I'm serious. You know how he is. He'll break her heart into tiny pieces.'

Guy considered this. 'Beth's a big girl. Maybe she'll break his heart. That'd be worth seeing. This isn't part of the charming Virgin Project is it? Is she...?'

'How would I know?'

Guy raised an eyebrow at him questioningly.

'Livvy says she is.' Milo felt sick.

'Look, I know you think the sun shines out of her arse. And she is very hot. And she smells so good—'

'Is there a point to this?'

'Yes. Don't interrupt. My point is, she is a truly wonderful girl and you've put in a lot of spadework with her. But you're so rubbish at showing your feelings that she probably doesn't have a clue you're still after her. Then in swoops some other dickhead and sweeps her off her feet. This was bound to happen.'

'But I did ask her out.'

'Yeah, but when was that? Years ago. The trouble with you is, you're too chickenshit. You won't convince her if you keep backing off every time she knocks you back.'

'Well, thanks for that excellent advice, Guy, but that's actually not my problem at the moment. There is this small matter of trying to make her see what an evil bastard Zack is. What am I supposed to do?'

'Just go and talk to her and tell her about his virgin-chasing. That'll do it, I reckon. And it's not even lying; he really has given us all the material we could ever need, in those interesting chats we used to have after rugby training. We'll see if he can charm his way out of that one – or into that one, in this case. Sorry.' Guy gave Milo an encouraging smile. 'Come on, this might be your last chance. It's not difficult – here, I can make a list for you if you like.'

'No, that's OK, I can manage. Thanks,' Milo sighed as he got up from the beanbag and padded back to the door. He knew Guy was right, but he wasn't looking forward to this conversation.

As he closed the door he heard Guy say, 'Ahh. Young love.'

In the morning, Milo tried to figure out how to get Beth alone and what exactly he was going to say to her. He couldn't tell her about Zack and Bonnie, but he could tell her all the other stuff that would horrify her. He had to talk to her soon, before Zack got his hooks into her, before – Milo's blood went cold at the thought – he slept with her.

He was supposed to have dinner with the Tomses that night, but he asked if he could skip it as he wanted to go to the cottage and check everything was all right after the storm. It wasn't easy to convince Mrs Toms that he was OK; she was, as ever, on the lookout for Signs of Grief and he was pale and exhausted from a sleepless night. Milo felt a flash of shame that, instead of grieving for his mum and dad as she thought he was, his only thoughts were for Beth. He put on his tracksuit after dinner and ran through the woods, jumping over several fallen tree trunks, splashing through the mud, until he reached the cottage, where everything was fine. He waited for about an hour until he knew everyone would be in their houses, put on a pair of boots and a warm coat, gloves and a hat, grabbed a torch and headed back through the woods.

He knew that Beth liked to go night-wandering, leaving her house through a window after lock-up time to go for a smoke in the woods. He'd shown her the best places and knew which ones were her favourites. She also used to sneak away from The Island on Saturday afternoons, take the bus or a taxi to Melchester and go to the cinema. These excursions kept her sane, she said. Being 'locked up' gave her the shivers. Milo was worried about her running into a teacher and had introduced her to the eleventh commandment of The Island: *Thou shalt not get caught.* She didn't intendeth to.

Usually he wouldn't have needed the torch to find his way about, but tonight was a new moon and the woods were changed after the storm. Fallen branches cracked under his feet and once he tripped over a tree that had come down. Through the thick, dripping trees, towards the river, he saw a red glow in the dark boathouse window. He nudged open the door.

'Beth. It's me.'

'Milo? You scared me. What are you doing here?'

'Looking for you.'

'Huh. Come and sit. You OK?' She turned the torch around and shone it in his face. 'Why are you always so grubby?'

He sat down near to, but not touching her. There was a long silence. He'd been trying to decide what to say all day, but now he was here, the words had disappeared from his brain. He wished he'd taken Guy up on his offer of that list.

'Did you have something you wanted to say to me? It's just, I'm sort of meeting someone tonight.'

'Oh. Who?'

She was flicking the torch on and off, on and off. 'Actually, it's Zack. He'll be here any minute.' He thought he heard her voice tremble as she said it, which did not bode well at all.

'Well, I'll make it quick. It's about Zack. I don't think he's good enough for you.' Milo rushed the words out before he could change his mind.

Silence.

'Go ahead,' said Beth eventually.

'He's not nice to girls; I don't think he'll treat you well.'

'Unlike you or Edward, I suppose?'

He sighed. 'I'm not talking about me or Edward, or if I am, then only in the sense that neither of us would wish you any harm. And Zack is going to hurt you, sooner or later. He always does.'

'I can take care of myself.'

'I know you can, I'm not trying to interfere, but you don't know him like I do. He's basically a liar. He uses people and he won't be faithful to you.' Milo wasn't sure how far to go. Could he tell her about the revolting things Zack had said? What if they'd already done some of them together?

'It's OK, I know about his reputation with the ladies. I just like him.'

'What's wrong with Edward, anyway? I thought you liked him? Don't you think he'd be better for you? He's such a nice bloke.'

'God no, not Edward. He's really not my type,' she sighed, and lay back on the blanket.

'You have a type?'

'I do now.'

126

'Oh shit, Beth, please don't do this. Not with Zack. He's going to use you and then throw you away, just like all the others.' Milo was panicking. He was whispering, so they didn't get caught by any of the teachers, but his voice was harsh and desperate.

She laughed. 'Don't be so melodramatic. You know, you don't have to try and save me every time you think I'm in danger. Sometimes I think you're trying to protect me from the big bad world, but you don't get it, do you? I want to find out everything for myself. You're not my dad, Milo. You should just back off and let me make my own mistakes. It's really quite boring of you. I mean, what's the big deal about Zack? Why does everyone think it's so wrong to sleep with anyone who's slept with someone else?'

'It's not just that, it's—'

'You're such a sheltered child. You've been stuck here on The Island your whole life. You've never even been to London. You've never been abroad.'

'I have – to Jersey.'

'Jersey doesn't count. You think you know what's right and wrong, but it's not that simple. We're almost adults now; there are no goodies and baddies.'

'I never said there were,' he mumbled.

'Listen. Bad people can sometimes do good things. And good people can sometimes do bad things. There's really no harm in it. The world keeps turning. You need to get over it. It's funny, Milo, but I somehow get the feeling that you're living your life vicariously through me.' She paused, and he knew from the look on her face that she was wondering if he knew what 'vicarious' meant.

'That's not what I'm doing, I'm telling you – I know this guy and he's no good for you. He'll take advantage of you. I don't like him.'

'Well, I most certainly do. What makes you assume it's him that's going to be doing the advantage-taking? Now please, get lost, because I'm waiting for Zack and I'm not sure your delicate eyes will want to see what's going to happen.'

'Please, Beth.'

'Off you go. Look sharp.'

In the dark, Milo was fighting off tears. He had totally failed. But he couldn't betray Bonnie and Edward, so there was nothing left but to go and hope that somehow Zack couldn't make it. He stumbled away from her, a hard, painful lump in his throat, forgetting his torch, thankful for the darkness, and crashed through the woods towards his cottage.

Beth lit a cigarette and waited for Zack. She didn't have long to wait.

'Hello, sweetheart, fancy meeting you here. Who was that?'

'Nobody.'

He sat down behind her and wrapped his arms and legs around her, took a drag from her cigarette and, gently taking her chin and twisting her head round to him, kissed her for the second time.

Chapter Thirteen

Despite her bravado with Milo, Beth *was* worried about Zack's reputation, or rather his greater experience, with the ladies. She didn't care that he'd slept with loads of other girls. In fact, it made him more exciting. What niggled her was that the next inevitable step for them was sex and she didn't know if she'd get it right, or if he'd lose interest in her once they'd done the deed.

They always met outdoors at night and as his lips, cold on the outside, kissed hers, she felt herself warming up and then he'd blow on his hands and rub them together before he slid them up underneath her coat and layers of jumpers. When he touched her skin she melted, her stomach turned to hot liquid, her head boiled. She didn't know how she was going to be able to hold him off much longer, or even if she wanted to.

On the morning of Valentine's Day, Beth gathered up her larger-than-usual pile of post and stuffed it all in her bag on the way out of her house for breakfast. On the grass slope above a low wall to the side of the road sat Zack and Justin, hunched down together and talking in low voices. When Justin saw her coming down the hill, he stood up, slapped Zack on the back and slouched away.

Zack waited until she was level with him before he took her hand, pulled her to him and whispered in her ear, 'Happy birthday.' She felt a tingle run down her body and back up again.

'I didn't know you knew.'

'The whole school knows when your birthday is,' he replied with a smile on his lips. 'I've got something for you. Close your eyes.'

She was expecting a kiss, but felt something heavy, metallic and cold in her hand.

'Like it?'

She opened her eyes. 'A watch?'

'Not just any watch. I had it inscribed, see, here on the back...'

Beth read the inscription. 'I can't accept... It's too much – a TAG? It's beautiful, but you can't give me this.' She held it out, offering it back to him, but he jumped up and sprang down onto the road, laughing, walking away from her. 'Please, Zack – I don't even wear a watch. Don't tease. It's too expensive. I'll lose it or break it or something.'

She ran after him and put her arm through his, slipping the watch into his coat pocket. He turned towards her. He held the tops of her arms, slid his hands down to take hers, let go of one of them, fished the watch out of his pocket and put it on her wrist.

'Take it, it's yours. Don't break it, don't lose it.'

She searched his eyes and saw something new there, like she was seeing him for the first time with all the confidence and the sarcasm gone from him, and the gift was so special to her because it came from him in that moment, from something that she thought might be love.

At breakfast they sat close to each other, opening her presents and cards.

'Who's Moneypenny?' Zack said as he read James' birthday card over her shoulder. 'Whoever she is, she doesn't like you very much. She's sent you a book, of all things. You're seventeen, not seventy. *A Prayer for Owen Meany*. How utterly depressing.'

Beth noticed the inside cover as he dismissively flicked through it. 'Let me see. Holy shit. He's signed it himself.'

'Who?'

'John Irving.'

'Who's John Irving?'

She tapped the front of the book, but it made no impression on Zack. It was probably better that way – she couldn't explain how James and John Irving would know each other. Get him, though – her shy Uncle James hobnobbing with famous authors.

She started opening the other envelopes. There were love poems, quotes from song lyrics, even a card that said, *Marry me*. They laughed until their stomachs hurt, despite the fact that the dining hall was full and everyone was watching them.

'I don't think you're going to get many cards next year; I'm getting some very sulky looks,' he murmured into her ear.

'I don't want many next year. Only one, in fact.'

'Here's the last one,' said Zack, looking at a small box-shaped parcel. 'Hang on, it's from Berlin. Now...' He pretended to rack his brains. 'Which one of your many admirers is in Berlin?' He tossed the box from hand to hand, pretending to drop it.

Beth snatched it from him. It felt disloyal to Edward, but she couldn't read the card without Zack seeing it too. She felt a pang of guilt as he read out loud in a snide voice, '*Darling Beth, I can't wait to see you on 4th March. Have a nice birthday. All my love, Edward.*' Zack mimed a yawn.

She slowly tugged the cream ribbon off the box, glancing at Zack, who lifted his eyebrows snarkily. She opened it and inside was a watch. Beth frowned and looked uncomfortably at Zack. He was smirking.

'Well, you can never have too many watches.'

They both burst out laughing again.

Milo came to breakfast, saw Beth with Zack and bit his lip. He found Guy and Theo sitting together. Guy, uncharacteristically, had his arm round his little brother. Theo said a small 'Hi' to Milo and left.

'He all right?' asked Milo.

'Nope, not really. He's gutted actually. Atkinson and Smythe are sitting over there taking the piss out of all her Valentine's cards. Theo's got such a crush on her. I can't concentrate on my breakfast; the noise of breaking hearts is fucking putting me off.' He got up angrily and stomped away, as if he blamed Milo. He came back a minute later. 'Oh, by the way, you know that Swatch watch you were going to give her? Don't. She got an obscenely expensive one from Smythe and apparently Ed Markham's sent her a watch too. Don't give them the satisfaction.'

'Thanks for the heads-up.'

'Honestly, Milo, stop me if you've heard this before, but I can't understand why you're so gaga about Atkinson. Lately, she's turned into a right bitch.'

'I thought you said she was hot, and the girl of your dreams?'

'Yeah, well, I have very low standards.'

Milo took Guy's advice about the watch, but he had another surprise for Beth, which he and Anne had been arranging for weeks. He needed to get her away from Zack, but they were stuck together like glue. At lunch break he found them in the sixth-form common room watching TV, her arm around his shoulders and his hand resting on her thigh. *It's like he's marking his territory or something*, thought Milo with a wrench in his stomach, which he tried to ignore.

'Hi, happy birthday,' he said in a quiet voice as he towered over them.

'Hmm… what? Oh, hi, Milo, didn't see you there. Thanks. I'm having a lovely birthday. D'you like my new watch?'

'Yes, it's very nice,' Milo said mechanically, and he saw Zack sit up and study him with a malicious grin on his face. 'Can I talk to you alone, please?'

'What's up, West? Don't tell me you bought her a watch too?'

Milo couldn't help blushing, even though he was sure it was just a wild guess on Zack's part.

Zack looked delighted to have hit the mark. He sat back in his chair, stretched out and laughed. 'It's absolutely my favourite thing to be in the middle of this love triangle, or hexagon, or whatever it is these days.'

Beth dug him in the ribs and mouthed, *Be nice.* When he ignored her, she stood up and smiled awkwardly at Milo. He inclined his head towards the door.

She nodded and then turned to Zack. 'See you later.' She bent and kissed him lightly on the mouth, but he held her neck and pulled her to him, prolonging the kiss. Milo blinked and looked away.

'Don't do anything I wouldn't do, West.'

Outside the common-room door, Milo heard a loud burst of laughter. He turned to Beth. 'You've got a couple of hours now, haven't you?'

'I have to be at swimming by 2.30.'

'OK, well, let's get a move on, then.'

'Where to? The secret garden?'

'Nope. Follow me, please.'

Now that he was away from Zack, he could enjoy the moment he'd been planning. Round the back of the school, through the woods towards his cottage, there was an easy silence between them, their discord about Zack forgotten. The woods were silent too, as if they were helping Milo keep the secret. Once they'd reached the main gate, he took her a little further around the back of his cottage, where there was a wider track that led to a row of low wooden sheds, behind which was a high hedge bordering the cottage's garden on the other side. Milo stopped, dangling two keys in front of her face.

'Happy birthday. Joint present from Anne, James and me. Well, it's really from them; I'm just the middleman.'

Beth raised her eyebrows and her face broke out into a grin. 'What is it?'

'Open the shed with the key and you'll find out.'

'Tell me first.'

'Nope. My lips are sealed. Open the door.'

'Will I be surprised?'

'Open the door, will you?'

''Cause I don't like surprises.'

'Shame, this is a good one. Are you going to open the door or not?' He was tapping his foot, waiting for her to make up her mind.

She took a deep breath and stepped towards the door. She reached out her hand, slotted the larger of the two keys into the padlock on the shed door, closed her eyes and clicked it open. With a slow creak, the door swung open, and there stood an ancient pale green VW Beetle.

She squealed with joy. 'A car. Oh wow. Is it really for me?'

They climbed in and Milo explained that the present was three things: the car was from James; driving lessons from Anne; and the shed, Milo's contribution, was its secret parking space while she was at school. She wanted to take it for a ride straight away, but Milo reminded her that swimming started in fifteen minutes. She locked the padlock and, before they began walking back up to school again, she put her arms around Milo and kissed him on the side of his chin. He blushed, and his heart pounded through his jumper.

'Thanks so much. This is my favourite birthday ever.'

As they walked, Milo asked her to keep the shed a secret. She mustn't get caught taking the car in or out of there, because he'd promised the headmaster that this sort of thing wouldn't happen. Beth agreed. Milo thought to himself, *First Beth's parents, then Bonnie and Zack, now this: I'm quite the secret-keeper these days.*

That weekend, Zack went back to London to stay with his mother, who was having a party at her house. Beth was invited but couldn't make it. She had a swimming gala on Saturday, which Zack was bunking off, and she was singing a solo in the school choir concert on Sunday. She was disappointed she couldn't meet his mother, but Zack said there'd be plenty of time for all that. He said he'd miss her and asked for a photo of her, which she thought was sweet. She gave him one that Livvy had taken with her camera before the Christmas party.

When he'd gone, she rushed through her homework, which she'd been neglecting these past few weeks, and caught up on some sleep, which she'd also not had much of. She wrote a long-overdue letter to Edward.

17th February 1990

Dear Edward,
Thanks for your birthday card and the watch. I don't want to hurt your feelings, but I have to return it to you. It's not that I don't like it, it's really a lovely watch, but I can't accept a gift like that from you.

I've told you all along that I want to be friends with you, and I know you want more but I've made up my mind that I can't be your girlfriend.

I'm not sure whether I should tell you this, but it's going to be more difficult if you hear it from someone else. I'm going out with Zack Smythe – it's one of the reasons I can't accept the watch from you. He gave me one for

135

my birthday too. I hope you can return yours to the shop
without any problems.
   I hope you understand, and that we can be friends.
   Please write and tell me how you are, and how Berlin
is. I'll give Caspar and Gilbert a kiss from you.
   Beth

That should do it, she thought. *He can't argue with that.*

On Sunday night, after the concert, she waited in her room,
hoping Zack would be back on an early train. She hadn't changed
out of the dress she'd been wearing for the concert and, as she
looked in the mirror in her and Livvy's room, she was pleased
with her reflection. She wanted to see him so badly. Since they'd
got together twenty-four days ago, this was the first time they
had spent apart, and this weekend she'd thought about him
every minute.

Later that evening, when Beth had decided he wasn't coming,
she and Livvy sat in Livvy's bed in their pyjamas.

'How's it going with the lovely Zack? I don't see much of you
these days,' asked Livvy.

'Great. Really good.' She paused. 'I got a lecture from Milo
about him. I thought he was going to force me into a chastity belt.'

'Have you...? You know, have you done it with him? Zack, I
mean, not Milo.'

Beth swallowed. 'Livs... promise you won't tell anyone about
this?'

Livvy nodded solemnly and drew her finger and thumb
across her mouth.

'I really want to, but I've never... I've never slept with anyone
before. What's it like?'

'Search me.'

'Really? You've never had sex either? *Really?*' Beth was
astonished. She'd thought everyone but her had done it.

'Nope. I nearly did once, but it didn't quite work out. I was having a delightful snog with Henry and we thought it might be fun, and then it was just too embarrassing, when we got our clothes off. We did a bit more snogging and left it at that.'

'So let me get this straight. You and Henry kissed when you were naked and then... stopped?'

'Yep. Then we went to sleep and it was lovely.'

'Livs, I've got to talk to someone about it or I'll burst. I am absolutely begging for it with Zack; I can't even think about anything else but him. He makes my knees go wobbly. If I were naked with him, I wouldn't be able to stop. I can't resist it for much longer.'

'So why don't you give it a whirl?'

'I don't know what I'm doing. What if I'm rubbish and he doesn't like me afterwards?'

'Well, as I understand it from my oversexed brothers, it really isn't like that at all. You sort of go with the flow – I believe that was the gist of what they said; not entirely sure because they make me want to throw up when they talk about sex. But listen. There's one thing I think I should tell you about Zack. It's what I said before, about his... umm... penchant for younger girls. He sort of has this reputation – how do I put this? – for dumping girls after they've had sex with him. And,' she took a deep breath, 'also, he gave one girl trich.'

'What's that?'

'Trichomoni... trichomosis, or something like that. It's an STD. It's really minging, and it's so unfair because the girl gets it badly, pus and pain and everything, and sometimes the boy doesn't even notice he's got it.'

Beth thought about this for a moment. 'I don't believe it. It's bullshit. He told me he's never had sex without a condom. So that can't be true, can it?'

Livvy shook her head.

'Do you think that's true? About him sleeping with girls and then chucking them?'

Livvy nodded.

'But maybe… I don't mean to sound conceited, but if he's always gone for younger girls, with me it'll be different. Don't you think?'

Livvy shrugged.

'Oh, can't you say something helpful?'

Livvy groaned. 'I don't know what to say. You'll get so cross with me. You're obviously crazy about him, so if I criticise him you'll hate me now, and if I sugar-coat it you'll hate me later, when…' She clammed up.

'So you *do* think this is like with all the other girls. Well, it isn't. He told me about the others. He likes me because I'm older than him and we can talk, we're on the same level. It's different.' She got out of Livvy's bed and climbed into her own.

'Don't get into a ginormous huff with me. You always do this – you ask me what I think and then you completely disagree with me. So what's the point of asking me in the first place? You're so arrogant, you treat me like a servant. Stop acting like everyone is so inferior to you. Especially me. I'm fed up with it…' Livvy ground to a halt with a shocked expression, as if she couldn't believe she'd dared to say all those things to Beth. She lay back in bed and pulled the covers over her head.

There was quiet for a few seconds before Beth's footsteps padded over.

'Hey.'

'Hey what?' came Livvy's muffled voice.

'You're so sweet when you're angry. I promise I won't be arrogant and superior any more.'

'Or scary?'

'Or scary.'

Livvy poked her head out from under the covers and took a deep breath. 'OK. But you should carry on being scary to Zack otherwise he'll have his wicked way with you. I agree with Milo – the longer you keep your legs together, the better.'

Chapter Fourteen

'Ready for your first lesson?' asked Milo, a smile fixed on his face as he unlocked the shed.

'Yes. You look more nervous than I am,' said Beth, patting him on the shoulder. 'Which is kind of insulting.'

He rolled his eyes at her and waited for her to unlock the passenger door before folding himself into the tiny space.

'You make this look like a toy car.'

He showed her how to start the car, reverse, use the clutch and the accelerator, change gears and brake. She practised on the track for an hour until he was sure she was ready, then they set off to Melchester.

'What are you doing this half-term? Jet-setting off to Italy again? Watch the red light,' he said.

'Nah, I've got a ton of homework to do and then I'm going up to London for a couple of days. Shopping and a party.'

'Who's having a party? Slow down, watch that car.'

'A friend of Zack. Or Zack's sister. Or someone.'

'Zack has a sister? Change into second.'

'I thought you said you knew him from way back? How do you know him anyway?'

'Oh, it's a long story. Check your mirror. Indicate.'

A song came on the radio, *Come On Eileen*, and they sang along to it. When it had finished, Milo said, 'So, is that an old song or a new song, would you say? The speed limit's thirty here.'

'Well, out here in the sticks, it's brand new, because you're all so behind the times, but in London it's an oldie.'

'What're the kids listening to in London, then? You can't overtake here.'

'Dunno, I'll tell you next week.' She heard Milo chuckle. 'What's so funny?'

'Not so much funny, really. I was thinking, for you this song is old. For me, it's quite new. Some people at school think that everything old is rubbish – old music, old clothes, old books, old people – but if you think about it, everything gets old sooner or later. As soon as something's happened, it starts to get old.'

'Yeah, but what makes it good is not that it's new, but that it's original. Something that makes you feel like you've never felt before. It's exciting.'

'But that's just perception. Really, there is nothing new. Everything is a rearrangement of the same words, the same notes, the same colours. That's not original, it's just a new version. Same stars, different constellation.'

'How poetic. Also, how depressing. Or are you going to tell me you think that's reassuring too?' She turned her head quickly to Milo.

He was grinning. 'Yep, I reckon. Don't look at me, look at the road.'

When they arrived at Beth's house, Milo came in to say hello to Anne and then left to catch the bus back to The Island. Later that afternoon, the phone rang. Anne answered it.

'Oh, hello… Edward? Let me see…' She held out the phone to

Beth but, seeing her niece shake her head, continued, 'Edward, sorry, she's not in at the moment. Yes, I'll tell her, tomorrow evening...? At home – OK, goodbye.' She put down the phone. 'Edward would like you to call him tomorrow evening at home.'

'Is he back from Berlin?'

'He's flying in tomorrow, and will be in Cornwall by the evening.'

'Oh, shame. I'm getting the first train to London tomorrow.'

Anne gave her a searching look. 'Tomorrow? I thought you were going on Monday?'

'Changed my mind.'

'When?'

'Just now.'

'I see. Well, far be it from me to interfere in your love life. Have fun, but make sure you don't go anywhere near Brixton. There's a whole heap of trouble brewing around the poll tax demonstrations.'

'How do you know about all these raves and riots and stuff?' Beth said, in awe of her aunt.

'It's called the real world, Beth.'

She was going to check in at James' flat in Clapham and meet up with Zack after she'd done some shopping. The party was on Monday night. When she stepped off the train at Waterloo station, the first person she saw was Edward. It was too late to turn around or hide – he'd seen her too. She forced a smile onto her face and walked slowly towards him.

'Hello, Edward, how are you?'

'Beth. Hello.' His smile was nervous; he looked pale and had dark circles under his eyes. 'I was going to call you later. I got your letter. I had to speak to you. Do you have time to talk? My train home doesn't leave for another hour.'

They found a café and sat down in the window, opposite each other. Edward sat silently for a minute, stirring his coffee. Beth lit a cigarette.

She broke the ice. 'How was Berlin?'

'Fascinating. Euphoric. Agitated. How was The Island?'

Beth thought, *Strangely enough, exactly the same.* But she said nothing.

'I'll get to the point. About Zachary Smythe. I think you're making a big mistake. He's—'

'Edward, excuse me. I think you should be careful what you say now. I'm not going to sit here and listen to you insult my boyfriend.'

He winced at the word, and she tried to be gentle.

'I never promised you anything, only that I'd think about it. And I thought about it, and I don't want to go out with you. I chose Zack.'

'I can't let this happen again...'

'Again? What do you mean, again?'

'He's promiscuous. He doesn't respect girls. He's a sexual deviant.'

'A what? Are you joking? Oh, you're not joking. But... a sexual deviant? Edward, you should hear yourself.' She softened her voice. 'Look, I've already had this lecture from Milo. He's worried about me, you're worried about me. I get it. But I feel good about this. I'm happy. And I don't care that Zack's slept with loads of girls. Like I told Milo, I can take care of myself.'

'Is there no way I can change your mind? Come with me to Cornwall. Spend half-term with me. We can ride, get away from it all.'

'I don't want to get away from it all. I want to get into it all. I want to spend half-term in London with Zack. I don't care what you say. It's my choice.'

She stubbed out her cigarette and stood up to go. Edward's hand flashed onto hers. She tried to pull away, but he gripped her hard.

'Have you slept with him?'

'What? I'm not going to answer that.'

'Then you have.' His shoulders drooped. The shadows under his eyes gave him a haunted look. Still gripping her hand, he muttered something under his breath and stood up, pulling her to him. When she raised her eyes to his, she saw with a jolt that they were cruel and bitter.

'I won't let it happen. I'll do anything to stop it. You stay away from him or I'll get him expelled.' His voice was cold and frightening.

'For what? Edward, expelled for what? I don't understand why you're so bothered about this.'

She managed to pull away from him, and he muttered again under his breath.

'What – what's wrong?' She was frightened, but in his eyes she saw something desperate and wretched and couldn't be angry with him.

'He'd better keep his hands off you. Tell him that from me. If he doesn't, and I catch him, tell him – and use these words – this is the end.'

He left the café, and Beth lit up another cigarette, ordered another coffee and sat staring into space. By the time she'd finished them, her hands had stopped shaking and her thoughts had turned to her favourite subject: Zack.

That night, Beth went alone to the cinema on the King's Road and watched *Dead Poets Society*, which she'd been meaning to see since Christmas. She stayed overnight at James' flat, had a bath and went to bed early. She had a strange dream. She was in a maze, and it was a frightening place, full of shadows and unknown dangers. She was struggling to breathe; the air was stifling. She understood that the maze wasn't safe for her. She didn't know where to turn. Three figures loomed in front of her: Milo, Edward and Zack. They beckoned to her silently, and she knew that one of them would help her escape the terrors of the maze. She looked from one to the next, at their outstretched hands, and slowly walked towards Zack. The dream ended and she woke up, her breath coming in great gasps as she tried to calm down.

So much for beauty sleep, she thought ruefully.

The next day she shopped and afterwards went back to James' for another bath. She wanted to look her best when she saw Zack that evening. They were having dinner with his mother. As she made her way over to Notting Hill in a taxi, she wondered about the dream and about what Edward and Milo had said to her. Why were both of them so worked up about Zack? Perhaps they'd heard some of the same rumours that Livvy had heard. But Beth was mad about Zack and knew he was telling the truth. He was right for her.

The dinner with Zack's mother was fairly nerve-racking. Madame Smythe was charming, but the way she looked at Beth, as if searching for something, made her feel like she was being investigated.

'You are a very beautiful girl, Beth. We must try to get you signed up with an agency when you've finished school,' she declared matter-of-factly.

'An agency?' Beth said.

'Modelling. Or acting. You would be fabulous, a big success.'

'Oh, no, no, I don't want to be a model. I would hate it. I hate the thought of all those strangers staring at me.'

'Really? Shame. I would have thought you'd be a natural.' Again, that searching stare.

Beth felt a flicker of fear about the direction this conversation was taking. James and Anne had warned her that there might be people of their generation who would remember her parents. Anyone with a decent memory would see the resemblance between her and her mother.

'Actually, I want to direct. Films,' she said.

Madame Smythe clapped her hands together. 'What a wonderful thing. And you know, Zachary wants to act. I am sure you will be a wonderful couple, so famous, so beautiful.'

Zack lit a cigarette and offered one to Beth. She glanced at Zack's mother, who was also lighting up, and took it.

'Well, *Maman*, that's enough planning our shining future together. Didn't you say you were going somewhere this evening?'

Madame Smythe rose, kissed his cheek and left the room.

'Sorry about that, she gets a bit carried away,' he drawled.

'She's… umm… nice.'

'Nice? She's old. She's sad.'

'Well, it's something that she cares about you, your future.'

'Huh. It's always the same thing with these oldsters. All they do is drone on about the past and the future. Who gives a shit? Today – that's all there is.'

'Carpe diem?'

'You're not going to get anywhere with me by quoting Latin. Talking of getting anywhere with me, would you like to see my bedroom?' He smiled, stubbed out his cigarette and grabbed her hand as she stood up.

He led her downstairs into the cellar. Beth loved his room: it was huge, with photos and posters all over the walls, a TV in one corner, and on the floor a stereo with tapes and CDs strewn around it. She looked around for somewhere to sit, but there was only the double bed. Zack switched on a couple of lamps, put on a Lenny Kravitz CD and, holding her forearm, walked Beth towards the bed. Her heart was pounding; he must surely be able to hear it. She sat on his lap and he kissed her, his hand sliding down the side of her hip to the bottom of her skirt. She pulled her face away from his and pressed her legs together. His eyes met hers, asking the question.

'I… I wasn't going to stay tonight. I didn't bring anything… I don't have a toothbrush,' she said lamely.

'We could share?'

Beth chewed her bottom lip. 'Won't your mother mind?'

Zack's hand left her leg and he wriggled out from underneath her. 'Is there a problem? I've been waiting for you to make up your mind about this. It's always too cold, we're going to get caught, it's not private enough...' He raised his eyebrows.

'I do want to, it's just...'

'Just what?'

Beth swallowed. 'Nothing. Yes. I want to.' She felt brave and grown-up.

Mollified, Zack leant over to her, kissed her again and pushed her gently back onto the bed, sliding his hand slowly up her skirt. She couldn't help it – she groaned with pleasure.

'I really do love this skirt,' he mumbled into her neck.

His hand circled around to the backs of her thighs and pulled down her knickers. She helped him with her skirt and his jeans, and they both took off their T-shirts. Beth unhooked her bra and he moved closer to her again. He kissed and stroked her all over. She'd never felt so warm and so alive. He moved closer again and she thought her skin would burn. He put his hand between her legs. She gasped and clapped her hand over her mouth.

'It's OK, you can do what you want here.'

She smiled at him, eyes wide open. 'Do you... have a...?'

'Uh-huh.' He rolled away from her and opened a drawer in the bedside table. His back tensed. 'Oh, fuck.'

'What?'

'Sodding Justin. I said he and Melanie could come here yesterday and look.' He held out an empty pack of condoms.

They looked at each other, and he said, 'I'll be careful, I'll pull out in time.' Beth shook her head miserably. Zack groaned in frustration and rolled onto his back. There was a stony silence.

'Isn't there... anything else we can do, for tonight?' she asked in a hopeful voice.

Zack rolled to her. The smile was back. So was the hand. Now they were kissing harder and she couldn't think straight, and she was so hot and felt his finger inside her rubbing and she was lifting her hips, arching her back and there were hundreds of tiny explosions all over her body, electrifying her. Eyelids half closed, she kissed him again as he took her hand and put it on him.

'Hold it here. Move it up and down. Yes, slowly, that's it.'

Afterwards, they fell asleep in each other's arms. Beth forgot to brush her teeth.

She woke up in the morning and felt the soft underneath part of his upper arm around her neck.

'Zack?'

'Mmm?'

'You know all that stuff we did last night?'

'Mmm?' He opened one eye.

'Can we please do it again now?'

Later that evening, after Beth had been back to James' to shower and change, and Zack had gone condom shopping, they met at Holland Park tube station and walked for a few minutes to a crescent road of white four-storey houses with white pillars outside each front door. Zack rang the bell of number five and a tall, blonde girl peeked round the door.

'We brought champagne. And drugs,' said Zack.

'Then you may enter,' replied the girl, grinning. 'Hi, who are you?' she said to Beth.

Beth glanced at Zack, who shrugged. 'I'm Beth, Zack's girlfriend,' she mumbled, annoyed that Zack hadn't told the girl about her.

'Are you indeed? I'm Annabel.' She grabbed Zack's hand and gave him a quick kiss on his mouth. She pushed him inside and turned to Beth. She looked her up and down and Beth squirmed with embarrassment. She raised her eyes from the pavement and was amazed to see the girl laughing.

'What? What's so fucking funny?'

'Temper, temper, young lady. Look, come.' Annabel

beckoned Beth through the door and made her stand beside her opposite a full-length mirror that dominated the hallway. Beth gazed at their reflections: both the same height, the same build, the same long, slim legs clad in miniskirts, the same shape all the way up and down. Only, Annabel's hair was bright blonde and her skin was deeply tanned and Beth's dark hair contrasted with her pale skin and the faint blush on her cheeks.

Beth finally got the joke and turned to Annabel. 'We're like negatives of each other.'

Annabel put her arm through Beth's and they left the hallway and entered the high-ceilinged living room, full of people and noise.

'Finally,' said Annabel.

'Finally, what?'

'Finally, someone I can swap clothes with.'

A few hours later, Beth sat on a sofa wedged between two people she didn't know, who were talking over her as if she weren't there. She stifled a yawn, looked around for Zack but couldn't see him anywhere, and took in the room. Guests were draped on the floor, on windowsills, on a coffee table, on a piano, in an empty fireplace, on an expensive-looking antique sideboard. Someone was even sitting in what looked like a magazine rack. The doorbell rang and finally she saw Zack when he went to answer it. He came back in with Justin, talking intently in his ear, with one arm slung around his shoulder. Justin nodded a couple of times and peeled away from Zack when he saw Beth looking at him.

'Lucky I can lip-read,' she said when Zack finally made it over to her.

'What do you mean?' he said sharply, momentarily losing his usual composure.

'You and Justin. Up to no good.' She smiled, and made room on the sofa for him. He looked at her closely and flopped down beside her.

'Yeah, we're planning to take over the world in approximately...' he checked his watch, 'three hours, fifty minutes and twelve seconds. We needed to get a few final plans straight. Want a drink?' He jumped up again from the sofa and headed off in the direction of the kitchen.

Beth sighed and sipped her full glass. This party wasn't exactly what she'd been expecting. Zack hadn't introduced her to anyone, not even the hostess really, and everyone here was much older and more sophisticated than her. Even Justin was avoiding her, with that shifty look of his. She didn't know what to talk about; everyone else knew each other and they were talking about a whole other bunch of people she didn't know. She felt miserable and out of her depth. Also, she had a humungous zit on her forehead.

She saw Zack disappear for the millionth time towards the kitchen and went to find him, if only for something to do. As she pushed open the door, she froze. Annabel was sitting on his knee at the table, his hand on her thigh, doing a line of coke. They both smiled at her, completely unperturbed. Annabel handed the twenty-pound note she'd used to Zack, slid towards the fridge and pulled out a new bottle of champagne. She asked Beth to open it for her while she fetched some glasses.

Beth peeled back the foil and twisted the cork. The bottle exploded all over her hair and clothes. She screamed, standing in the middle of the kitchen, everyone around her laughing. Zack was smiling at her in a knowing way. Knowing her temper would get the better of her and she'd start shouting at someone. Beth took a deep breath and tried to smile. She knew it was more like a grimace but it was the best she could do. She thought she saw Annabel wink at Zack, but ignored it. Her voice came out higher than usual.

'Annabel, could I borrow some clothes please?'

'Of course, darling. No probs. Up the stairs, third room on the left. Take anything you like.'

Beth wandered through the quiet upper floor of the house and finally found the right room. She checked the wardrobe and found some clothes she thought might fit her. There was a four-poster double bed against the back wall. *Why do all these rich kids have double beds?* she thought. *Do their parents actually want them to have sex all the time?* As she approached the bed, she saw a piece of paper placed on one of the pillows which read, *Don't even think about it, Zack.* Oh, great.

She went into the en-suite bathroom to change. She washed her face and rinsed her hair, putting it up in a ponytail, wiped off the mascara that had run down under her eyes with one of the pristine white towels hanging on a rail, and stepped out of the bathroom.

'Looking good, Atkinson.'

Beth stopped in her tracks. Zack patted the bed next to him with a small smile on his lips.

'Come here. I'd like to have a closer look at that skirt you're wearing.'

'I don't want to.' But she really, really did and he knew it.

Zack shrugged. He got up from the bed and started walking towards the door.

'What's the idea with you and Annabel? I haven't seen you all evening and… what was that, in the kitchen? And why is the witch giving me shaken-up bottles of champagne?'

'It was just a joke. Don't get your knickers in a twist. It's 'cause you're the new girl. It's like an initiation. They do it to everyone. You passed, by the way.'

'Well, that's good to know. Phew. I'll be able to carry on with my life now. But you still haven't answered the question – what's going on between you and Annabel?'

He shrugged again.

'What's that supposed to mean? You've slept with her?'

'Once or twice.'

'When?'

He sighed. 'I don't know. Memory's hazy.'

'Why?'

'Because she's hot.'

'No, I mean why's your memory hazy? Is it since we've been going out?'

'Probably – I can't remember, OK? It's really unimportant anyway.'

'Unimportant? Un-fucking-important? What are you on? How fucking dare you?'

'Jesus, Beth, calm down. What do you want me to say? I never promised you I wouldn't sleep with other girls. It's only Annabel, you know. She's an old friend of mine.'

Beth couldn't believe that Zack was being so brazen about it. Her heart was beating so fast. She was speechless. She sat down on the floor and hid her face on her knees. She felt like crying but didn't want to give him the pleasure of seeing it. She hoped he would just go.

'Beth.' He was sitting cross-legged opposite her.

'Go fuck yourself.'

'Don't be such a drama queen. Look, I really like you. But it's not like we're married or anything. I like girls, OK? And I wasn't lying when I said you're the most beautiful girl I've ever seen. But school is… different from here. We can go out, you and me, at school, but when I'm here and you're not – well, it's OK for me to see other girls and you can see other boys.'

'But I don't want to see other boys. I thought we had something special. Just you and me.' She tried to stop her voice from whining.

'Can't you see how boring that is? "Just you and me." Come off it. We're young, rich and good-looking. We can do anything we like.'

Beth felt miserable. None of this made any sense to her. 'But… we were going to… tonight. Have sex.' Tears sprang into her eyes. She brushed them away with the back of her hand.

'The night is young. I'm looking forward to it. Nothing's changed.'

'Everything's changed. How can I sleep with you now? You're not even denying anything. Was Annabel at your house the night before last, when you said Justin used up your condoms? Is that what you were talking about earlier?'

Zack's lip curled up, a bored expression on his face. 'I thought you were different from all the other girls – cooler, more up for a dare. My mistake. But the offer's always open.'

With his thumb, he wiped away one of her tears. The electricity coursed through her body and she flinched away from him.

'It's only sex, babe. It's supposed to be fun. You shouldn't take it so seriously. Think about it, yeah? Later.' He stood up and disappeared out of the room.

Beth dried her tears and washed her face again. She looked at her reflection in the mirror in Annabel's bathroom. She looked young without make-up. She stepped over her champagne-soaked clothes on the bedroom floor, found her coat and left the house, confused and despondent. He'd made her feel like a naive schoolgirl, which she supposed was what she was. But she'd been so ready to sleep with him and now she had to go back to school next week and everyone would know within hours what had happened. *The truth were loud again*, she thought, and felt a pang, wishing Livvy was here with her.

She walked around Holland Park for a while, stopping in a Wimpy to eat a giant hamburger and an ice-cream sundae, which made her feel sick. London was such a cool place, and everyone at the party had been so witty and good-looking. Zack had at least been honest with her in his own way, and she had known from the start that this thing they had wasn't going to be happy ever after.

She wandered around the streets, watching people going in and out of bars, in couples, in groups or alone. They all ignored her.

She was nothing in this city. She felt dirty and knew she needed to wash her hair. What was she going to do about Zack? She didn't love him, and she knew he didn't love her. Fine. But she did want to sleep with him because he made her feel like she'd never felt before. Just thinking about him – his body, his skin, the way he held her, hard to him, when he kissed her – made her blood rush. If she said yes to him, she would be able to keep him for herself, at least for a while longer. It was enough. He had practically dared her to go ahead. And she could never resist a dare.

She looked at her watch. Past midnight. She thought she knew the way back to the party, but took a wrong turn and didn't recognise where she was. She found herself back at Holland Park tube station and there was a map in the entrance. Checking the directions, she set off with a new sense of purpose. She was going to Zack's house to have sex with him. To have sex for the first time with a horrible, beautiful boy and she was going to enjoy every minute of it.

But when she got there, there was no light on in his cellar. She didn't want to ring the bell in case his mother answered. So she sat on the doorstep and waited. She was freezing cold, shivering in her coat that wasn't warm enough for the end of February. She nearly changed her mind a few times and once got up to leave, just as a taxi pulled up at the house. For a brief, awful moment she thought he wasn't alone. But he stepped out onto the pavement with a broad grin on his face.

She stood still on the steps, trying to stay calm. He walked up them with slow, easy movements and drew level with her, his eyes glinting in the lamplight.

'Changed your mind?'

'Yes. But you'd better get me inside double quick before I change it again. Also, I desperately need a wee.'

Laughing, he took her hand and unlocked the door. He opened it for her and waved her inside. 'Come on in, we've got a long night ahead of us.'

Beth wrenched herself out of Zack's bed on Tuesday to return to Melchester. Anne had booked her a fast-track course of driving lessons for the rest of the week, with a test on Saturday which she desperately wanted to pass, so that she could use her new car. She did. On Sunday she drove the car back to the shed at Milo's house and hitched a lift up the driveway with the next taxi she saw, which happened to contain Alice, her leading lady from *Cold Comfort Farm*. It reminded Beth that there were less than five weeks until the opening night.

Beth was reading on her bed that evening when Livvy walked in, struggling with her suitcase. She collapsed on the bed next to Beth.

'Hello, roommate. So, how did it go?'

'I passed.'

'No, not your driving test, you div. I meant with Zack. How did it go? How was all the sex?'

Beth put down her book. 'How do you know that there even was sex?'

'Because you look different. You know, like you've lost something.'

'Ha ha.'

'So come on then, spill the beans. I want to know every single detail. All the ins and outs.'

'Livvy, don't be lascivious.'

'I'm not lascivious. What's lascivious? Tell me later. How many times did you do it? Where did you do it? What positions? Did you have an orgasm? How big is his—'

'Stop, stop, OK. I can't tell you all that.' She paused. 'You'll have to work it out for yourself; I don't even know the words for some of the stuff we did. But I'll tell you this: it shouldn't even be legal, how good it felt.'

'Oh. Wow.' Livvy beamed.

The following morning, they woke up to Livvy's alarm clock,

blearily showering and dressing, not used to the early mornings. Beth pulled back the curtains and it took a moment before the scene in front of her came into focus. Their window looked out onto a grass bank about two metres high that separated the boys' and girls' houses. On it, spring bulbs had burst into flower over half-term. There were daffodils, tulips, and other flowers she didn't recognise, but she could clearly see that the bulbs had been planted to spell out the words *LOVE THE SPRING*. Beth gasped at the beauty of it.

'What's that?' asked Livvy and came up behind her, standing on her bed and putting her chin on Beth's shoulder. 'Oh, cool. What does it say – *love the spring*? What does that mean?'

'Wasn't it there before? I mean, last spring?'

'Nope. That's new. Oh! Do you think someone planted it there for you?'

'Or you.'

'Mmm, less likely. I don't get it, though; it doesn't make any sense – *love the spring*?'

'It's from *Much Ado About Nothing*.'

Blank look from Livvy.

'You know, Shakespeare? *Lovers love the spring*. OK, well, maybe it was for me then.'

They giggled and looked at it again.

Livvy sighed. 'That is seriously romantic.'

At assembly, the headmaster mentioned the flowers in his speech. He was pleased to see that the age of romance was not dead and applauded the long-term planning of the culprit, but the planting of bulbs was still damage to school property and punishable by a month's Saturday night detention. A smile played on his lips as he spoke.

'What does he mean, long-term planning?' said Beth, who knew next to nothing about flowers, to Livvy and BJ as they walked to class.

Livvy replied, 'It's because whoever planted the bulbs must

have done it last autumn. The bulbs lie in the ground all winter and appear in the spring. So wait a minute... if it is anyone who meant it for you, then it wouldn't have been Zack, or even Edward – they didn't know you then. It must have been—'

'West,' butted in Billy.

Jake whistled. 'Damn. That boy's got style, I wish I'd thought of that.'

'It probably wasn't him, and we don't even know who it was meant for,' said Beth.

'OK, Atkinson, you tell yourself that. But you might want to stop blushing before you see your boyfriend or he'll start to get jealous.'

Chapter Fifteen

E dward found the atmosphere at The Island had totally changed since he'd left in January. He couldn't put his finger on it. He felt different himself, having experienced and seen so much in Berlin. But it wasn't that. Things had shifted and he felt at odds with the school, the pupils and the teachers. He was adrift and no one seemed to have noticed.

Was it all about Beth? She wouldn't talk to him, not in public or in private. She wouldn't ride with him, she wouldn't play chess with him, he wrote her notes but she didn't reply. He tried to catch her eye, but she always glanced away. Or was it Zack's fault? When Edward saw him with Beth he couldn't stay in the same room. He didn't know what to say or do when they were there together, arms draped around each other, touching each other.

Or was it The Island itself? Had he outgrown it, or it, him? All that remained between now and the end of his time at school were his rapidly approaching exams, for which he needed to study, but he spent most of the time staring at the walls in his room. He couldn't concentrate and felt that time was slipping away from him. He slept badly and sometimes woke sweating in the night, unable to get back to sleep, afraid of noises and shapes in the darkness. The dark circles under his eyes grew deeper and activities like shaving, ironing his shirts and combing his hair, let alone showering, fell by the wayside.

He felt like he'd lost a game, but he was unsure what the game was supposed to have been or how he should have played it. Maybe Milo would know. He only felt at ease with Milo. The two friends played chess together a few times a week, but never spoke about Zack and Beth. Edward didn't know what the right words would be and supposed that for Milo too, it was a struggle even to think about it.

Edward longed to catch Zack doing something really stupid so that he could punish him. He wanted him chucked out of school. But that was the dilemma – the activities most likely to lead to his expulsion were sex and drugs. And he knew that if Zack was doing those things, it would probably be with Beth. Even though Edward knew that his chance with her was over, he still felt protective towards her and wondered, with an increasing obsession, how he could manage to get rid of Zack without it harming Beth's position at the school.

The closest he got to it wasn't nearly close enough, but he still felt a little happier than usual when he caught Zack smoking behind the sports hall one day, alone. Edward smiled as he gave him a Saturday night detention, looking into his eyes with a great deal of pleasure as Zack angrily stubbed out the cigarette on the wall.

'You're such a dick, Markham. You don't have to give me this,' he said, waving the detention slip at him.

'You want another one?'

'You want to tell me what the fuck your problem is?'

'My problem… let me see. How about this: you knocked up my sister, and now you've moved on to my friend, and you are revolting and don't deserve to be at this school.'

'So, why don't you tell "your friend" about Bonnie then? What's stopping you? I've been wondering about that for a while.'

'None of your business.' Edward turned to leave, wishing now that this encounter had never happened.

'I've been thinking.' Zack followed him. 'About Bonnie. She's on my mind a lot. Last time I spoke to her, she told me that she'd always love me. All that soppy shit, you know how girls are.'

Edward wheeled round towards him, jaw clenched, but said nothing.

Zack continued in his sarcastic drawl, 'So then, all of a sudden, she's apparently not interested. And now I can't get close to Fortress Markham, thanks to you, and so I try to put her out of my mind with a fresh start. So could you tell me, please, whether it's all over for me and Bonnie, or whether you made all that up? And if it is over, what's your problem with me and Beth? Because you know, a man has needs and she's just the girl to help me get over your sister, if you know what I mean.' Zack smirked viciously as he stood blocking Edward's path.

Edward felt the blood rising to his face and rushed at him, not knowing what he was doing, lashing out. Zack skipped lightly out of the way and laughed.

'You're pathetic. You know, I do believe you've helped me make up my mind. Bonnie's family is not quite up to scratch in my opinion. Beth has a much more interesting family, more my sort of thing, you know.'

Edward didn't know what Zack was talking about. He stared at him, confused and in pain. Zack shrugged and walked away. When he was out of hearing, Edward slid down the wall onto the concrete ground, and wept into his hands.

Chapter Sixteen

'Right, listen up, everybody. Milo's handing out a practice schedule. We've got four weeks until the dress rehearsal, and you need to be word-perfect for that, no excuses. In addition, Alice, you'll have extra sessions with Milo to run through your lines. Zack, you and I can practise together.'

As Milo handed out the schedule, he noticed that everyone was paying attention to Beth except Zack, who was sitting next to her, his hand moving slowly up and down her thigh. Much too far up, not far enough down. He caught Guy's eye. Guy smiled sympathetically, put his fingers in his mouth and pretended to be sick.

At the end of the meeting, everyone disappeared except for Milo, Guy, Zack and Beth. They were talking about some band Milo had never heard of when a third-year girl shouted through the doorway that Beth had a call at the payphones. After she'd left, Milo and Guy also moved towards the door, but Zack called over to them.

'Hey, West, hey... West's sidekick... just between us, I

wanted to ask you chaps, what do you really think of the play?'

They both stared at him in dumbfounded silence.

He tipped back in his chair, linking his hands behind his neck. 'I think parts of it are really lame. I'll try and pin Beth down on some of the scenes; I think I could definitely make some improvements.'

Milo opened his mouth and closed it again. He was pretty sure he knew how Beth would react to that conversation, and would have loved to be a fly on the wall. 'Yes, great idea, Zack, you do that,' he said.

Zack ignored the sarcasm. 'Hang on a minute, there's something else. You know Markham? He's losing it a bit these days, don't you think? I was wondering, you're his friend, aren't you, West? Do you think he's all there? I can't make up my mind whether I should talk to his housemaster, you know, so that he can keep an eye on him, make sure he doesn't do something stupid.'

Milo clenched his teeth and took a few deep breaths. It was vital that Zack didn't see how important this was. He left it to Guy to answer and they left the room.

Walking up to their house, Guy advised Milo to try and keep his cool with Zack.

'Look, mate, I'm sorry it's turned out this way. But he's just going to keep winding you up if he sees it's working. We all know how this is going to end anyway.'

'How?'

'Badly. And then you'll be there, her trusted friend, her knight in shining armour, and you'll live happily ever after.'

'Humph.'

'You know I'm talking sense.' He reached up and ruffled Milo's hair, punching him and giving him a dead arm. In return, Milo grabbed his wrist and gave him a Chinese burn.

At this moment they saw Edward, who was looking pale and tired, his shoulders a little less upright than usual, his hair not so perfectly combed back and his shirt unironed. From what Edward had told him, Milo knew that he was struggling even more than he was with the idea of Beth and Zack. Edward had thought that he could save Beth from the same fate as Bonnie. But Milo knew that Beth was different. She was tougher. At least, so Milo hoped.

Milo and Guy exchanged a grim look. They both knew what the other was thinking – Zack was not too far off the mark. Edward was losing it.

A week later, Milo was in the packed sixth-form common room, sitting on one of the bar stools, talking to Guy, when *Neighbours* finished and the news came on. Usually someone switched it over, but today there was a story about a British journalist who had been executed in Baghdad for spying, and there was an interview with Mr Markham, who had tried without success to intervene. Milo looked around, but Edward wasn't there. Where did he spend his free time these days?

The next item was introduced – a book written by British author James Hurst about his sister and brother-in-law, a famous model and fashion designer whose sudden deaths in 1974 had shocked the world. Milo's eyes locked on to Beth, who was sitting with Livvy on the sofa nearest to the TV. She glanced over her shoulder, her face ashen, her eyes panicking, and found Milo. He tried to smile at her, *stay calm, stay calm*, as everyone's voices drowned out what James was saying, talking about the book – 'Have you read it? Can I borrow it when you're finished?' Pictures of Beth's parents flashed up on the TV.

The next news item was a related feature about a new kind of model called a 'supermodel', of which there were only a handful in the world, models that charged the highest fees and were the most sought after and successful. Milo stood up, ignoring Guy, who was in the middle of sharing his extremely personal feelings about Linda Evangelista, and went over to Beth. He crouched down behind the sofa and laid his hand on her shoulder.

'OK?' he whispered in her ear.

She nodded.

'Wanna get out of here?'

She nodded again.

'It's OK, you know,' Milo explained when they were outside, alone. 'Nobody knows who you are. They can't connect James to you and so they won't make the connection between your parents and you.'

'But those photos… someone will notice one of these days. Do you know, I can't even change my hair to disguise myself. She had ten years of photographs taken with her hair short, long, blonde, dark, every style known to man. Anne told me that she was on the cover of seventeen separate *Vogue* issues. I can't do anything.'

'It's going to be all right and then when it's not, we'll have to deal with it. Until then there's nothing we can do. Just ignore it, act normally. It's the only thing to do.'

'I'm dreading it, Milo.' She sat down on a bench, pulled her legs towards her and put her arms around them. 'I wish James had never written that book. I wish we'd left it all alone. I don't care about having all this money. I'd give it away tomorrow if it meant that I could avoid this happening. I don't want anyone to stare at me and talk about me, and I don't want to be famous. Not for that, anyway.'

'It's going to be OK. Try to relax.'

But Milo could see that it was on Beth's mind more and more. He privately thought that she was lucky to have got away with it for so long, but she had convinced herself that she was going to make it through school anonymously and anything else was a disaster.

They walked down to the river together, leaving the school and its noise behind them. The sunny day reminded Milo of the first time he had seen Beth, a year and a half ago. She told him about the fear she had of being someone else's property – the daughter of someone, the wife of someone. It would drive her crazy, she said, if she couldn't create something interesting or original of her own in her own way.

'It's like my mother – what did she ever do that was her own? She couldn't do anything or say anything without it being commented upon. *What's she wearing? What's she done with her hair? What's she eating? Who's she with?* Nothing was private, so in the end, it's no wonder she was a nutcase – how could she have known what was real and what not? I don't want my life to be like hers. It would kill me.'

They sat down by the river. It was a picture-perfect scene – from the blue sky, sunshine filtered through the trees that framed the river. The shouts and laughter of the rowers barely registered with Beth. She remembered how, that first day at The Island, eighteen months ago, she'd been so thrilled to see the rowers on the river, and now it seemed totally normal to her.

As they walked back to school together, Beth asked if Milo had seen the '*love the spring*' flowers outside her house.

'I heard about them, but I haven't been up to look yet. Are they pretty?'

She glanced sideways at him. He wasn't blushing; he looked totally normal. These days it was getting more difficult for her to read him.

'They're really pretty. Why don't you come up now? They won't last much longer, will they? The flowers, I mean?'

'Mmm. Should be all right for another couple of weeks. Then the flowers will die back, but they'll be there again next spring.'

'Aha. You seem to know a lot about these flowers.'

'It wasn't me.'

'I didn't say it was. You just said it was, though.'

'No, I said it *wasn't* me.'

'It's OK. My lips are sealed. I think it was a lovely idea. So does everyone. You should be proud of it.'

'I would be, except it wasn't me.'

'Suit yourself.'

They reached Norcombe House and stood looking at the flowers. Beth was suppressing a smile. She looked at him again, but he was just standing there with his hands in his pockets. She gave up. Before she left him, she hesitated, looking slightly bashful.

'I have to ask you a favour. It's about the play. I can't carry on learning lines with Zack; we... umm... we get a bit distracted. Will you take over and get him to learn his lines? Please? I'll do the sessions with Alice.'

'Alice is fine, she knows her lines. She's word-perfect.'

Beth glanced at him. Again, his face wasn't giving anything away. She was still suspicious, though. She'd seen the way Alice gazed at Milo, like he was a living god. What on earth did those two get up to when they were alone? Still, if Milo was right and Alice was word-perfect, they obviously must have learnt some lines between snogs.

March turned into April and Milo was really, really worried about Zack's attitude to the play. He was always late to their one-on-one rehearsals and sat there trying to change the subject, which infuriated Milo.

'What are you playing at?' he growled at Zack once, when he had fouled up every line of the scene where the American agent comes to the farm and takes Seth away to Hollywood. 'I thought you wanted to be an actor. Why won't you learn your lines and do this decently? You never know when someone might be in the audience who could spot you.'

'Here? At this school? You must be kidding. Who would come here to see some stupid school play? This part sucks. Seth doesn't even have any decent lines, he just glowers and struts around. I only auditioned for the part to pull Beth.' He crossed his arms over his chest and smirked at Milo.

'Well, now you've "pulled" Beth, learn the lines and don't

ruin her play. You said it: you don't have that many lines – but you are in a lot of scenes and you'll ruin it if you don't know what you're doing. She's going to be so pissed off if you carry on like this.'

'I don't need any advice about my girlfriend from you, thanks, West. I can handle it myself.' He peered at Milo. 'Isn't it time you got over her? Even if she weren't going out with me, I doubt you'd be next in line. She's way above your level and you know it.'

Milo was silent.

'You've got such a chip on your shoulder, always have. It's so sad. You know, you need to get out of this shithole once in a while. You think this play's important? Grow up, would you? You think you're in love with Beth? There are a million girls like her out there, in London, in the big wide world. I'll tell you what, come up to mine sometime and I'll introduce you to this chick I know, Annabel, she'll blow your mind.'

Milo muttered, 'Shut up.'

'What was that, West, I didn't catch that?'

'I said, shut up. Stop being such an arsehole. Learn your lines. Be nice to Beth. Or I'll take you up on that fight you offered me on your first day at school, you little twat.' His face was up against Zack's now; he was shaking with anger. 'I'll forget that I ever made a promise to your father that I'd look out for you. I'll forget that we used to be like brothers and I'll beat the living shit out of you.'

Zack's eyes flashed with fear for the tiniest of moments before he recovered his usual smirk. He scraped his chair, stood up, said, 'I think that went well. Don't you?' and left the room.

Something Milo said must have sunk in, because in the dress rehearsal Zack was almost spot on with his lines and was more or less in the right place at the right time. *He really can act when he wants to*, thought Milo, watching from the wings as Beth sat out at the front and videoed it. You had to hand it to Zack, he was brilliant as Seth.

On the afternoon of the performance, Milo and Guy had just finished hockey practice. They saw a sports car roar up the driveway and, a few minutes later, it sped back past them.

Guy turned to Milo. 'Was that…? No, it couldn't have been. Was it…?'

'Was it who?'

'I just thought I saw Zack in the passenger seat of that Ferrari.'

Milo glanced back, but the car had disappeared around the corner. 'Nah. It couldn't have been. Why would he be leaving school now? We're meeting in an hour for costumes and make-up. We're onstage at seven.'

Guy said with a shrug, 'Must have been some other idiotic long-haired posh public schoolboy in the car. They all look the same to me.'

They didn't dare mention it to Beth, but as six o'clock turned into half past six, they began to worry that Guy's eyes hadn't been deceiving him. Beth enlisted a bunch of third-years and sent them off in different directions to find Zack. To his house, to the library, to the sports hall, the swimming pool. To the woods.

She was storming around looking like thunder. 'Quarter to seven,' she said, 'then we get the understudy ready.' *Who is the understudy*? thought Milo, checking their notes from the auditions. At that moment, one of the boys who'd been sent off to find Zack returned, looking scared.

'I've been to his house and I met his housemaster and he says that Zack's gone home to London, something about his mother being ill.'

'Whaaaaat?' screamed Beth, and the boy scarpered. 'Milo, who's the understudy?'

Oh shit, thought Milo. *As in, hitting the fan.* He gulped. 'Big problem. The understudy is Hugh Hill.'

'And? Where is he? What's the problem?'

'He's... he—'

'He's got glandular fever,' interrupted Guy, trying to save his friend from delivering the bad news.

'Well, then, go and tell him to stop having glandular fever. We need him.'

'They won't let him out of the san. He can barely stand.'

'Whaaaaaaat? What the fuck? So we have no Seth? I cannot believe this. This is not happening.' She thudded down onto a seat and put her head in her hands. 'Think, think, think, what can we do?' she murmured to herself.

Before she had lifted her head, Milo already knew what she was going to say. He backed away. Other members of the cast, who had been hovering in the wings, disappeared; even Guy crept away with an apologetic look on his face. *Bastard.* Milo turned around, and somehow she was right next to him.

'I can't. I can't do it. I already told you, I'd be rubbish. I can't act.'

'Milo, you know how important this is to me; I wouldn't ask you if it wasn't. I need your help. You have to come through for me. You always do. You can do this standing on your head. Only we don't have much time now, so you have to step up.' She looked at him, her face pale but determined.

'You always get what you want, don't you?' he mumbled.

She flashed him a smile. 'Does that mean you'll do it? Yes, of course you will. Thank you, thank you, thank you. You are absolutely the best ever friend ever.' She spun him around by the shoulders and marched him backstage, all business again.

They had five minutes until the play started, but luckily Seth didn't appear until the second act. Livvy found Milo a costume and ran through the lines and stage positions with him, but he hardly needed to listen; he knew everything off by heart. How had he let this happen to him? Never, never in his whole life had he wanted to act in a play in front of hundreds of people.

He wondered idly whether Beth had had an inkling that Zack might let her down, and that was why she had asked Milo to go through his lines with him. Where was she? Of course, out front, where he should be, sitting next to that friend of the author, what was her name, oh never mind. Everyone was rushing about; he watched them through a haze. His eyes were sweating. He saw Guy's mouth open and shut but couldn't hear what he was saying. Alice had to go, she was in every scene, but she squeezed Milo's hand and kissed his cheek and wished him good luck. He sat in a daze while Livvy whispered to him. *Breathe, breathe.* Halfway through Act One, his stomach heaved. Livvy whipped a bucket out of nowhere and he emptied his lunch into it. She patted him on the back and redid his make-up.

Act One finished. It was time. *Breathe.* Alice came in for a costume change and her brow furrowed at the sight of him. 'Milo, it's going to be OK. I'll be out there with you. Just talk to me, OK, like we did when we practised my lines? Don't look out at the audience – talk to me, focus on me. Can you do it?'

He nodded and was sick again.

Someone pushed a plastic cup of clear liquid into his hand and he tipped it into his mouth. It burnt his throat, but felt good. He smiled and dragged himself up. Someone else pushed him to the wings and he listened for his cue. *This is really happening*, he thought. *Bollocks.*

Afterwards Beth thought with relief, *That could have been much, much worse.* Milo was a little wooden at first, and needed a prompt when he looked out into the audience early on and panicked. But he warmed up and relaxed, and played the part of Seth to perfection. He growled and grunted and strutted and smouldered. It was spectacular. Guy put it all down to the tequila. Backstage, the cast finished the bottle and Mr Gifford turned a blind eye. They ran screaming down the corridors to the sixth-form common room and drank a couple of beers together.

Waves of people came up to Beth and Milo to congratulate them and slap them on the back. Milo was grinning, enjoying every minute of it, but still looking a bit spaced out.

Livvy was chatting to some people from Zack's house and came back to where the group was sitting. She looked nervous. 'There's something fishy about Zack's story. Someone overheard him on the phone to his supposedly ill mother; he didn't sound worried, he was buzzing, they said.' She hesitated. 'Sure you want to hear this?' she asked Beth, who nodded, her mouth set. 'Well, shortly after that phone call, he was spotted climbing into a flashy motor and a couple of fourth-year girls asked him what he was doing. He told them his mother was having a party and this talent scout from America was coming and wanted to meet him.'

There was a silence from Beth as she let the news sink in. Her boyfriend and leading man had nearly scuppered the whole play. He was selfish and thoughtless, and had lied. He wasn't even brave enough to come and tell her himself. Everyone waited, holding their breath, for an explosion.

Beth shrugged. 'It's kind of funny, don't you think? That it happened to Zack like it happened to Seth in the play?' She found that she really didn't mind as much as before. She was still angry with him and thought less of him, but as Milo had been so fantastic and everything had worked out in the end, she didn't want to ruin the party by having a massive sulk.

At ten o'clock, the bar closed and everyone wearily made their way towards their houses. Milo took Livvy and Beth back to Norcombe House and set off for the cottage.

Beth called after him, 'Will you be all right? Wouldn't you be better staying in Casterbridge House tonight?' She had never seen him drunk before; he was swaying and his hair was all messed up, and he couldn't wipe the grin off his face.

'I'm not *that* drunk. Look, see.' He walked straight along a line painted on the road. 'I'm far from sober, though, very far from it, so I'm going home to sleep off my hangover in peace.'

They said goodnight, and Livvy and Beth signed in to Norcombe House. Then Beth changed her mind, grabbed something she'd been saving up from under her bed and quietly slipped out of the door before it was locked. Livvy would let her in their bedroom window later.

A little way into the woods, she caught up with Milo, crashing through the undergrowth.

'Shhhh. Don't make so much noise,' she shouted. She wasn't entirely sober herself.

Milo laughed. 'What are you doing out?'

'Ta-da.' She opened her coat to reveal the bottle of champagne. 'It's warm, but I thought we should celebrate. Yes?'

'Yes.'

They tramped on a bit and couldn't decide where to go.

'Your place?' suggested Beth.

'Wouldn't you rather be outdoors tonight? How about the secret garden?'

It was almost a full moon and the air was still warm. Milo fetched a couple of blankets from a small shed in the far corner of the garden and they lay on their backs, looking at the stars and propping themselves up on their elbows every now and again to swig the champagne straight from the bottle. They talked about everything except Zack. But now she was away from the others, she couldn't help thinking about him and her eyes filled with tears. Ridiculous, feeble girl; she couldn't seem to hold them back. 'Do you want to talk about him?' said Milo softly.

She brushed the tears away. 'How could he do this to me? He's making me cry – *me*. He's so selfish. I know it turned out OK...'

'Better than OK, wasn't I?' said Milo, pretending to have hurt feelings.

'Yes, yes, better than OK, you're amazing, blah blah. But

what am I supposed to do now? The worst bit is, he didn't even have the decency to come and find me and explain about the agent. How can I be pleased for him now, if he gets a big break, when I know he ditched me and left me in the shit?'

'It's just how he is.'

'Don't say, "I told you so."'

'I wasn't going to. But you have to understand this about him – he's totally selfish. He's also very impulsive, like a little boy really. He wants something, he takes it. Doesn't stop to think what it means to other people. I've seen this sort of thing with him over and over again.' Milo paused, like he'd said too much. He frowned. 'I don't like the way he behaves, and he knows it, so we keep our distance from each other now.'

'Now? How *do* you know him so well?'

'Don't know if I should say. Ages ago I promised him I wouldn't tell anyone.'

'Oh, come on, please,' she wheedled, taking another swig of the champagne.

'OK, well, I suppose I don't really give a shit about keeping his secrets safe when he's been such a knob. Don't tell him I told you, but he was actually born in Weatherbury.'

'London Boy? I don't believe you.'

'It's true. Scout's honour. His mum and dad – not the duke, not his real dad – they were on holiday on the coast when she went into labour with him. There was this cottage hospital in Weatherbury back then, my mum used to volunteer there, and that's where Zack's mum gave birth to him. My mum remembered because Zack's mum was such a pain in the neck. Of course, later, it turns out that the duke went to The Island and so Zack's name was put down. It's why Madame Smythe never comes to any school events; she can't bear to remember the awfulness of giving birth in the middle of nowhere.'

'But why does Zack find that so embarrassing? It was just a mistake of geography.'

'Well, after that experience, Madame Smythe was never to be seen out of the city. But her husband, he was a doctor in London, and he loved the countryside so he spent as much of his holidays at various places on the coast near here – Studland, Lulwind, Kimmeridge. He used to bring Zack down and they spent a part of every school holidays here with us.'

'Wait – with you?' Beth was astounded.

'Yep. Dr Smythe used to take the two of us fishing. And he was a massive rugby fan. He taught us both how to play, and we watched club matches together. Zack and I were like brothers. He was a great laugh, a complete show-off, but nice. Used to get us into trouble, and I'd get us out of it with my angelic face...'

'Are you talking about your best friend... is this the one you told me about? You said you ran away to his house. Zack? Zachary Smythe was your best friend?' Beth's mouth was open. 'I can't even picture this. How is this possible?'

Milo shrugged. 'We were little kids. This is when we were eight, nine years old. Dr Smythe gave my parents the idea of me applying to the school too. My mum took a full-time job here as a music teacher and my dad as the groundsman. That way they got a reduction in the fees.

'Anyway, Zack was at a posh prep school in London and he started acting more and more conceited. He found out about his real father, and he behaved awfully to Dr Smythe, who left around then – he'd had enough of his wife and son treating him like dirt. He went to Africa to work for Médecins Sans Frontières. By the time Zack came to The Island, the year after me, he was this whole new person. He told me not to hang around with his friends, which was fine by me, and he made me swear I'd never tell anyone we'd been friends.'

'Or what?'

'Or nothing. I wasn't that bothered if he wanted to hide it from everyone.'

'That's incredibly sad and also incredibly funny.'

'Yah, isn't it indeed?' Milo did such an accurate impression of Zack that they both laughed until their cheeks hurt.

'I am so drunk,' giggled Beth, 'I feel like I could do anything now.' She snuggled in closer to Milo and put her arm over his chest. For someone so large and solid, he was surprisingly soft and warm. 'This place is lovely. You won't ever tell anyone else about it, will you?'

'No. And you? You can keep it a secret from Zack?'

'Absolutely. He'd probably only want to come here and…' She tailed off.

She felt Milo tense, but his voice stayed level. 'It's OK, you can say it, you know.'

'I don't really want to talk to you about it.'

He said slowly, 'Fair enough. But are you OK? I mean, I'm not going to get all heavy about it again. But he hasn't… made you do anything you didn't want to, has he?'

'No, God, of course not.' She dug him in the ribs. They were silent for a few minutes and Beth caught herself thinking – *Has he?* She lay mulling it over, the thought drifting through her like a dream, and she gave in to her tiredness and fell asleep.

Milo felt her body relax against his and her breaths become slow and even. At one point she half woke, and she sighed and whispered, 'I wish we could stay here forever, Milo.'

He whispered back, 'I wish you would stop messing with my head, Beth.' But she was well away.

The next morning, Milo was woken by Beth shaking him. She stretched, shivered with cold and checked her watch.

'Half six. I have to get back to my house before they notice I didn't sleep there.'

'Mmmm?' Milo took a few moments to realise where he was. His throat was dry and his mouth tasted of champagne. 'Why are my eyes throbbing?' he groaned, holding his hand against his forehead. He turned his face away from Beth so she wouldn't smell his breath.

'Because you're a lightweight. Come on, let's go.'

They left the garden and Milo locked the gate.

'Ah, I nearly forgot to tell you. I didn't want to worry you before the play, and then I forgot last night, what with all the extra... um... acting I had to do. But Edward told me that Zack said something very strange to him a few weeks ago. He said something about your family being 'interesting'. Did you tell him about your mum and dad?'

Beth frowned. 'No. You're the only one that knows. But his mum was giving me weird looks at half-term. Shit. Why would he say that? D'you think he knows?'

'Maybe. Or maybe he's bullshitting. Are you seeing him in the holidays?'

'Yep, well, he's supposed to be coming down to Cornwall next weekend. Livvy, Mel and I are staying in a flat near the beach and Justin Ravensdale and Zack are coming for the second week. If I don't decide to tell him to take a long walk off a short pier, that is.'

Milo suggested that she should try to suss out what he knew and didn't know. He told Beth he'd be in Cornwall too; he and Justin were representing Weatherbury Hall at a schools' rugby training camp in Truro from Monday until Saturday and at the end of the week a squad for the South would be selected. They said a hurried goodbye and Beth ran off.

Milo trudged down to his cottage and collapsed into bed, sleeping peacefully and dreaming less peacefully for the rest of the morning.

That evening, Edward rang to ask him a favour. His parents had hired a horsebox to bring Caspar and Gilbert back to Bodmin; could Milo drive the horses on his way to rugby camp? They would of course pay him. Milo badly needed the money – he was missing a week's work for the rugby camp and it would save him the train fare – so he took the job.

'But why aren't you keeping the horses at school any more?'

'Bonnie wants to ride again, which is a big step forward. And I've had the worst school report of my life, my parents are going ballistic. No riding for me next term, because of A Levels.'

Milo thought that Edward sounded strangely upbeat, like he didn't even care any more. What was going on with him?

'Are you…? This isn't about Beth, is it? I mean, why have you had such a bad report?'

'Beth? No. Well, I suppose, I must admit, it knocked me sideways when I got back from Berlin and she was with that creep. But I guess I always knew she didn't love me. I mean, she never promised me anything. It's my fault.' Only now did his voice crack with misery.

Poor Edward, thought Milo, *he's really taking this hard. After what happened with Bonnie, it's not fair that he has to go through this again with Beth. Bloody Zack, he doesn't deserve Bonnie or Beth.* Milo tried to give Edward words of encouragement, but he felt like he'd made a bit of a hash of it. At the end of the phone call, he made the arrangements with the horsebox and hung up, feeling pretty miserable himself.

Beth also had a phone call that evening. Zack called to apologise for his desertion and explained that it had all happened so quickly, he hadn't had time to come and find her. She listened in silence and only half believed what he was saying.

'Beth, babe, she works for Aaron Spelling, you know, *Charlie's Angels*. She's one of his casting agents. She was talking to me the whole night about a new TV show set in a high school in Beverly Hills. She really thinks I'm right for it. I'm so sorry I did a bunk, but this was big time for me. Please forgive me. I'll make it up to you, I promise.'

Any time, any time now, thought Beth, *he's going to ask about* Cold Comfort Farm. *How did it go? How am I? Aaron Spelling, my arse.* She listened until he ran out of steam.

'I'll think about it,' she hissed, 'but don't hold your breath.' And she slammed down the phone.

Chapter Seventeen

Beth picked up Livvy from her family's farmhouse early the next morning and together they drove to Exonbury station, where Melanie was waiting for them. They had two weeks booked at a little flat in a village called St Emit on the north Cornish coast. Beth had grudgingly agreed to let Zack come after another grovelling phone call and more promises to make it up to her *in any way*, which she had to admit she was looking forward to.

Mel was in a good mood that day, kissed them both hello, slung her bag in the boot and, when Livvy called shotgun, squashed herself into the back seat of the Beetle. There were no seat belts in the back and the handle that wound down the window on the front passenger side had broken off, but luckily the window was only a tiny bit open so the breeze wasn't too bad.

'What are you going to do when it rains?' said Melanie.

'Get wet, I suppose,' replied Beth.

'This car is a Pile of Shit,' said Livvy.

'I resent that. There is nothing wrong with this car. Well, only the window and the seat belts and the fan. But apart from that, it's perfect.'

Before they reached Bodmin Moor, Beth saw a signpost for Truro, where Milo would be next week, and also for Bodmin, where Edward lived, but took the turning to St Emit. It reminded her of that dream of the maze she'd had at half-term. They got lost when Livvy's map-reading took them too far along the A39, and as they approached the coast it started to rain, but they were all in good spirits, singing along loudly to the songs on Radio 1, the only station that played in Beth's car, as the knob was stuck.

Six days later, Beth was having a dismal holiday. It had been raining on and off, the clouds racing across the sky, chased by a cold wind. She, Livvy and Mel were bored and at each other's throats. They'd all been drinking and smoking too much, because there was nothing else to do except watch children's daytime TV or play *Monopoly*. And she hated to admit it, but she missed Zack and the way he told her she was beautiful and made her laugh. She was still angry about the play, but she couldn't hold a grudge, not when he had been so sweet on the phone. He had told her he wanted to apologise properly to her, and then went on to explain some of the things he wanted to do to her by way of that apology. She was glad he couldn't see her blushing.

She woke up late, and was surprised to see that the sun was shining. There was a note on the kitchen table from Livvy and Mel, saying they had gone windsurfing and telling her the name of the beach, if she wanted to come later. They hadn't wanted to wake her, she had looked so *peaceful and sereen*. Beth chuckled. She wasn't sure if Livvy did it on purpose to wind her up, or if she really was that bad at spelling.

Beth changed into her bikini, T-shirt, shorts and flip-flops. She headed into town and followed the low wall that separated the road from the beach until the houses thinned out. The wall ended and she turned towards the sea, walking through the dunes on a path surrounded by grasses and flowers, pockets of air cooling and warming her skin. She passed a small shop selling drinks and surf equipment and then found an out-of-the-way beach, almost empty except for someone walking their dogs and a couple of kids playing with a ball.

She took off her shorts and T-shirt and went for a swim. The water chilled her skin and cleared her fuzzy head. Afterwards, she dried herself off with her towel, then lay on it and let the sun do the rest. The sand was cool as she dug her toes and fingers down into it. She closed her eyes and the sun shone red through her eyelids. Her skin soaked up the heat and, to the faint sound of seagulls squawking, she fell asleep again for a little while.

She was woken by a ball hitting her leg and sat up, sleepily looking at it lying on her towel. Two young boys rushed up, both with bright blond curly hair and freckled faces. The older one, about eight years old, stopped and the smaller one collided with him.

'Hello. Who are you?' asked Beth, laughing as they rubbed the sand off their faces.

'I'm Luke.'

The little one piped up, 'And I'm Han. Are you Princess Leia?'

His older brother corrected him. 'Duh. I've told you before – Princess Leia is made up. There's an actress, that means another lady pretending to be Princess Leia.' He turned back to Beth. 'Are you the actress who's Princess Leia?' he asked, his eyes wide and serious.

Beth laughed. 'No, I'm not. Anyway, I don't want to be Princess Leia.' She breathed in and out of her mouth loudly. 'I am Darth Vader. I will destroy you with the power of the dark side.' She stood up and unsheathed her lightsabre. The boys screamed with fear and delight and attacked her from both sides, until all her limbs had been cut off and she lay dying in Luke's arms.

She showed them how to build a sandcastle of the *Millennium Falcon*. As they were finishing, the boys' mother approached them from the surf shop. They made her close her eyes and then they revealed the sandcastle to her.

'Hi, I'm Emily. Thanks for playing with the boys. We were going to get some lunch. Would you like to join us?'

They headed back up to the shop and Beth sat in between the two boys, opposite Emily and her husband Jimmy, who ran the shop. He had the same bright curly hair as his sons, and the three of them reminded Beth of smaller versions of Milo. In the afternoon, they played some more until Emily called the boys in to go home. Beth sat for a while with a Coke, reading her book and watching the sun slowly sink in the sky. She wondered how Milo was getting on at the rugby camp; today would be the last day.

Her thoughts were interrupted by a tap on the shoulder. A boy, about fifteen years old, crouched down beside her and pointed to two surfboards and two wetsuits behind him.

'Hi, I'm Joel, Jimmy's son. He's sent me over to ask if you'd like a surf lesson.'

'Emily and Jimmy have another son?'

'Ah, you met my brothers? Emily's actually my stepmother.' He had a kind, shy face with a wide grin. 'Did they make you play *Star Wars*? I always have to be the baddie.'

'I like being the baddie. Much more interesting. Yes please for the surf lesson.'

They spent the next hour in and out of the waves, during which time, more and more surfers kept arriving, calling and waving hello to Joel and Beth. Finally they all dragged themselves out of the water and someone built a campfire. Joel pressed a bottle of cider into her hand. Someone else produced sausages and bread rolls. Another kid turned up with a ghetto blaster and, as the sun's rays weakened and sank on the horizon, they sat around chatting and eating and listening to music. A joint was passed around and Beth listened to them all talking about their holiday jobs in bars and restaurants; as lifeguards and surf instructors. She felt so blissful by the fire, sitting next to Joel, pressing their goosebumped legs together to keep warm. He put his arm round her, but it didn't feel threatening, it was more of a friendly hug, and she didn't shrug him off. She thought to herself, *I could be anyone here. I am anyone. And they accept me and they like me.*

'Who are you here with?' Joel said quietly.

'I'm sharing a flat in St Emit with a couple of school friends, this week and next. My boyfriend's supposed to be coming down tomorrow, from London.'

'What's he like?'

Beth thought for a moment. 'Umm... I'm not sure how to describe him. He's... funny. Well, actually, not really funny, more like sarcastic. He's...' She was struggling to find the right words. 'He's... just different. He makes me feel good.'

'D'you mean he's good in bed?' laughed Joel.

'Yes, I suppose I do.' Beth was laughing too.

Later, Joel gave her his sweatshirt and, when she started shivering, offered to walk her back to her flat. At the door, he kissed her cheek and said to bring her friends down to the beach tomorrow. She let herself in, blinking in the harsh light. Sitting on the sofa were Zack and Justin.

'Oh, hi, you're here. I didn't know you were coming tonight,' she said.

'Where have you been? It's pretty late,' said Zack.

'Just on the beach, there was a party. Where're Livs and Mel?'

'Asleep. They let us in earlier; they had no idea where you were. Who have you been with?'

'Nobody, just some friends I met today.'

'Then whose is that?'

Beth looked down at Joel's sweatshirt and was glad her sunburn hid her blush. 'Someone gave it to me because I was cold.' She was tired and not as glad to see Zack as she'd thought she would be. All her mellow happiness from the day and evening on the beach was melting away. She wanted to crawl into her bed alone and drift off to sleep. 'Look, I'm beat. I'm going to bed. See you in the morning, OK?'

She caught a look that Zack and Justin exchanged as she passed the sofa on her way towards the bedroom. When Zack came in later she didn't even hear him; she was fast asleep.

The following morning, she woke early and made everyone breakfast: coffee, orange juice, bacon and fried egg sandwiches, whistling along to a tune on the radio. They sat around, Melanie and Livvy raving about the windsurfing, saying they had to go back and do it another day next week.

'How was rugby camp, Justin?'

'Shite. I spent the whole week dodging out of the way of a load of hairy ogres. Talk about the Missing Link. These guys are freakishly huge. Farmer West did well though, he's made it into the squad for the South of England. Except for yesterday, he got knocked out cold.'

'What?' yelled Beth. 'What happened?'

Justin glanced at Zack and shrugged. 'He got kicked in the head by a chap about twice the size of him. He was out for about ten seconds and needed a few stitches. No big deal.'

'Jesus, why didn't you fucking tell me last night?' She was frantic; Milo had already had concussion last year from falling off the ladder. What if this was more serious? She stood up from the table, looking for her keys. 'I have to go and see him. Where is he?'

'Truro hospital. Why bother? He'll be on his way home by now.'

'Beth, don't be such an idiot,' chipped in Zack. 'I've just arrived, you can't leave now.'

'Wanna bet?'

She drove as fast as she could to Truro and followed the signs to the hospital. Furious and upset, she parked her car haphazardly and sprinted towards the revolving doors of the casualty entrance. As she did so, Milo stepped out into the sunshine. He was wearing a blood-spattered T-shirt and faded blue rugby shorts; had a black eye from earlier in the week, which was various shades of purple and yellow; was looking pale; and his whole head had been shaved. She ran up to him and put her arms around him. He gave her a bear hug and a puzzled smile.

'You gave me such a shock. I would have come earlier. Are you OK? You look like a sheared sheep.' She walked around him and saw a red, raw stitched-up scar about five centimetres long at the back of his head. His scalp was pale and he had a tan line where his hair used to be.

'You should see the other guy. What are you doing here? How did you know?'

'Justin told me. He and Zack arrived last night at St Emit. Can't you stay out of trouble?'

'I'll try my best, Mum.'

Beth elbowed him in the ribs and he blanched.

They decided to get a cup of tea, after which Beth would take Milo to the station for his train home. As they turned to leave, they saw Edward Markham emerging from the hospital. He had a few bunches of flowers in his arms and a small suitcase. He looked bewildered to see them there.

'Edward? Is everyone OK? Is Bonnie OK?' asked Beth.

Edward had tears running down his face. 'No, she's not,' he whispered. 'She tried to k… k… kill herself.'

'Oh my God. Why?'

Edward gazed at Beth as if he was trying to work out who she was. He turned to Milo, who was looking shocked. 'She got a visit at home yesterday. From… from… Zack.'

'Zack? Why?' What was Edward going on about? Beth looked at Milo, who had a strange, sad expression on his face.

'What's this got to do with Zack?' Her heart was thumping in her chest and there was silence. The truth dawned on her. 'Do you mean to say that Zack... and Bonnie...?'

Edward nodded. He looked down at the ground but caught sight of Beth's watch and grabbed her wrist. 'He gave you this? *You walk in beauty*? Is that the inscription? Typical of Zack to misquote Byron. I told you, he's bad news. He fucked my sister' – Milo and Beth winced; they had never heard Edward swear before – 'and now he's fucking you. He's made her ill, she's anorexic and yesterday he secretly arranged to visit her, and when we found them together, my father chucked him out and called the police. Bonnie took some pills. She's had her stomach pumped. He's evil. I told you this already. You didn't listen to me. It's too late.'

'I... I'm... there must be some mistake. Zack?' Beth couldn't think clearly. 'How did you know the inscription on the watch?' But before he replied, she already knew what he was going to say. Her heart froze.

'He gave it to her last year. I found it and gave it back to him, in January. He passed it on to you. You fell for that one, didn't you?' Edward's voice was harsh and cruel, and Beth felt like he'd taken her legs away from under her. 'I hope you've been using protection. Unlike Bonnie.'

'OK, that'll do for now, thanks, Edward,' Milo said quickly, taking Edward's arm and leading him away to his car. Milo helped him put the flowers and the case in the boot, spoke to him through the window and watched him drive away. He came back to Beth and put his arm around her shoulders.

'You knew?'

Milo nodded.

'Why didn't you tell me?'

'I couldn't tell you about Bonnie; she loved him and wanted us to protect him. We promised her.'

Milo pointed to a patch of grass and they walked over and sat down opposite each other. Beth leant her head forwards onto his shoulder and cried as he tried to soothe her, rubbing her back and stroking her hair. She looked up at him, her eyes stinging and snot running from her nose. She wiped it off with the back of her hand and rubbed her hand on the grass.

'I'm sorry, Beth.'

'Don't be. I'm the idiot who doesn't listen to anyone. I thought I could handle him. I thought I was going to be the one, you know, the one to calm him down. All along it was Bonnie.'

Milo was tearing out clumps of the grass beside him. 'I'm not sure that's true. I don't think anyone will ever calm him down. He only wants what he can't get. He can have you,' Milo looked away from her, embarrassed, 'but he can't have Bonnie. So he wants her. It's that simple with him. He's a bastard. I hate his fucking guts.'

Beth looked up, alarmed at his bleak voice. 'Because of me?'

'Because of you and Bonnie and all the other ones.' He paused and looked at her. 'What are you going to do now?'

'I don't know. I feel so stupid.'

'Listen,' sighed Milo, 'I'm going to give you a pep talk now.'

'A pep talk?'

'Yep. Ready? You are the bravest, most adventurous person I know. The way you live your life, it's amazing. Don't let this stuff with Zack change that. It's a setback. He's not worth it.' He raised her chin with his hand and she could see in his eyes that he was strong and that he believed in her.

She gulped and wiped her face again, smiling a wobbly smile. 'Yeah, you're right, Milo. Fuck him.'

'Fuck him,' he shouted.

'I did!' she shouted back, and there was a moment's silence before both of them roared with laughter.

'So, tell me, what are you going to do now?'

'Back to the beach, dump Zack, have a lovely holiday with my friends, go back to school, ignore him and get on with my life.'

'Good girl. Do you want me to come with you?'

'No.' She put her sunglasses on, lit a cigarette and stood

up. She brushed herself off and took a deep drag and exhaled. 'Come on, or you'll miss your train. I'm going to need to buy a new watch, too.' She held out her hand to him to help him up, and looked at him, smelly, crumpled, tired, beat up and bald. 'Thanks, Milo.'

'No problem. I'm not just a pretty face, you know.'

When she'd dropped him off at the station, promising to call him later, she felt less brave than she'd made out. While she drove, she thought about Zack. She'd been so crazy about him, but why? He was seriously attractive and the way he made her feel when he was with her was unlike anything else. She recalled her conversation with Joel and couldn't really find anything else about Zack that she liked. He wasn't easy to talk to, was always sarcastic and dismissive. He couldn't hack it when she tried to speak about books; just said it bored him. One of his favourite sayings was *Ignorance is bliss*. Some of his opinions on school, parents and life in general, which she'd found so amusing at first, were starting to grate – he was one of those people who didn't have much to say, just kept repeating the same things over and over. She got the feeling he was always trying out for some part with her, like he had to prove how good an actor he was. Close-ups, raised eyebrows, penetrating looks – it was like he was in a soap opera, and not a very good one. Also, he had a very loose relationship with personal hygiene.

By the time she reached the coast, the low sunshine was shimmering on the sea, blindingly bright. She checked the flat first, but it was empty. Maybe she should walk down to her beach from yesterday; see if Joel and the others were there before she had what was going to be a very unpleasant encounter with Zack. But in the garden at the front of the first pub she passed, she saw Livvy waving at her, sitting at a table with Melanie, Justin and Zack.

'Milo OK?'

'Yep, fine, I dropped him off for the train home.' Beth made a grim face at Livvy and startled her. 'Zack, I need a word.'

'Sounds serious.' He took a long drag on his cigarette, blew a smoke ring into the air and waited. 'Well, what is it then? What's the story?'

'Alone.'

He made a bored face, took a sip of his drink and pushed himself up from the table. He picked up his packet of cigarettes and looked at her. Eyebrows raised. 'I'm all yours, babe.'

Beth turned away from him and walked towards the sea, sitting on the beach wall about fifty metres from the pub and staring in front of her, trying to stop her hands from shaking, until he sat down beside her.

'We're finished. You need to leave the flat tonight, go back to London.'

'You're not making much sense. Why exactly are we finished?' He drank from his bottle again.

'At the hospital, Milo and I bumped into none other than Edward Markham. He was visiting his sister.' She let this sink in. 'Edward had some interesting things to tell me about you and Bonnie. He also told me that this,' she took off her watch and dropped it in his lap, 'was originally a present from you to her. So basically, you can fuck off if you think I'm going out with you, since you've lied to me from the moment you met me.' She swung her legs around and jumped down from the wall onto the road.

He turned to face her and said in a strangled voice, 'Beth...'

Be strong, she thought to herself, but when she turned around, there was such an anguished look on his face, her heart melted.

She took a step back to him and he said, 'What's... wrong... with Bonnie?'

Beth totally lost it. She screamed at him, anything she could think of, about how he was a miserable, lying fuckwit with no brain and a tiny dick and smelly feet, and a philistine and a Neanderthal, and how she hated him and never wanted to see him ever again and hoped he'd die.

In the pub garden, everyone had stopped talking to listen to the ranting girl. When Zack, shoulders hunched, finally got up and walked away from her, Justin turned to the group on the table next to theirs and said, 'She's such a sweet, quiet girl, don't you think?'

Beth sat alone on the beach wall until she couldn't see Zack any longer. She was still shaking and felt like crying. But she fought it back and walked over to the table. There was silence as Livvy, Justin and Melanie stared at her.

'Right, so who wants a drink? My round.'

'I'll help you.' Livvy stood up and they went into the pub. Beth ordered four beers and five tequilas, slamming one and leaving the empty glass on the bar before she carried the tray back outside. Their table was empty. Melanie and Justin had legged it.

'Oh well, all the more for us, then,' said Beth, and she and Livvy sat down, with the feeling that most of the other people sat at the tables were looking at them, and started drinking everything as quickly as they could. While they drank, Beth filled Livvy in about what had happened with Milo and Edward at the hospital and what had made her fly off the handle at Zack.

'So it's over?'

'Of course it is. It was all bullshit anyway. Everyone – including you – warned me what a cocksucker he is.' She blinked back the tears. 'Let's not talk about him; let's get smashed and go down to the beach, see if Joel and everyone are there.'

'Who's Joel?'

'Oh, you're going to love him. So cute. Really gorgeous surfer dude.'

They bought some cans and another bottle of tequila from the supermarket, and staggered down the deserted path to the beach. They could already hear the music and smell the smoke from the fire. Everyone welcomed them, and Beth sat on a log over the other side of the fire from Joel, next to whom she had positioned Livvy. But only half an hour later, Joel crouched down behind Beth, put his hand on her shoulder and asked her if she was OK.

'Never better.'

'Livvy told me about your man. Sorry.'

'Ah, him. Don't be sorry, he was a fuckingloser.'

'But good in bed?'

'Yeh. Plenty more fiss in the shea, though. Fiss in the shea? S... oops, I may be a bit hammered.'

Joel sat down beside her.

'Nonono, you should stay with Livvy, she likesh you.'

Joel grinned and pointed towards Livvy. 'She's got a funny way of showing it.'

She was getting off with another boy. They giggled.

'She told me that you think I'm cute.' Joel looked into Beth's eyes.

She looked back, tempted for a moment, but looked away. 'I do. But... I don't know. You remind me of someone else. Someone... a friend. I think it would be weird. I wouldn't want to mess that up. I know I'm notmaking mushsense.'

'No big deal.'

He was still cheerful and sweet. Beth was so relieved she hadn't hurt his feelings that she smiled and tried to put her arm around him, but ended up falling backwards off the log. She and Joel collapsed into giggles and he lay back on the sand with her, looking up at the stars.

The rest of the evening passed in a blur. There may have been some skinny-dipping, and she and Livvy eventually made their way up the road to the flat. It was empty and dark, and they collapsed into bed.

They slept through until midday the next day, and when

both had swallowed many Alka-Seltzers and drunk some strong black coffee, they ventured out towards the village to buy Cokes and chocolate. Beth felt tired and sick but knew that she had done the right thing, chucking Zack. They had another day at the beach, hired some boards and wetsuits from Jimmy, and Beth tried to teach Livvy how to surf. They ate fish and chips for dinner and met the group from the beach at the pub.

From then on, they had a fantastic holiday. The sun shone and they surfed every day, finishing in the evening with beers and barbecues, their skin glowing from the sun and the salt. Livvy was a great hit with the locals, but Beth held back, relieved to be Livvy's sidekick for once, and nobody made a move on her. It was clear that Joel was crazy about her, but he took her lack of interest in good grace, and all the other boys kept their distance out of a sense of friendship to him.

On Thursday morning, Livvy and Beth, relaxed and freckled, wandered down to the village shop for their morning sugar fix, picking flowers from the hedges on the way and putting them in each other's hair. They saw some friends clustered around the shop door, holding and reading a newspaper. Livvy went inside while Beth tapped someone on the shoulder to see what the big story was. Many pairs of eyes stared at her as one of them turned *The Sun* towards her and she found herself staring at her own photo with a screaming headline: *Tragic '70s Car-Crash Supermodel Daughter ALIVE!*

Beth felt sick. She grabbed the paper and, ignoring the shouted questions, ran back to the flat and slammed the door behind her. The phone was ringing. She ignored it. She skimmed the story but she knew what it would say anyway – and as she read it a second time, she knew with absolute certainty that this story had come from Zack. The photo on the front page was the one she had given him in the winter and there were quotes from *close friends* or *school friends* that could only have come from him. James' book, *Ten Lives*, was quoted, and they had found other photos of Beth's mum. Everything was laid out there on the pages, her whole life: Anne and James, Melchester, Weatherbury Hall. This was the day she had been dreading for so long. It was happening.

Livvy came rushing in and found Beth staring straight ahead, tears coursing down her cheeks. Livvy was so confused and concerned about her that Beth felt it was only fair to explain the whole story and why she'd hidden it from her best friend. The phone kept ringing and Beth told Livvy to ignore it.

'But it could be Anne, or James.'

Beth knew that Anne was in Sydney at a friend's wedding – she wouldn't have seen the story yet. James didn't have the number here and in LA it was the middle of the night. Nobody had the number except…

'Milo,' she whispered.

She grabbed the phone and heard his voice. Thank God. He offered to get the train or hitch-hike down, but she knew how much he needed to work and told him that Livvy was there with her. He told her it would be OK, but to stay where she was and not go back to Melchester; they would work out where she lived, and there had already been an interview on the local news with some bloke called Steven Dean or Dean Stevens from her old school. She was best off staying in Cornwall where nobody could find her for now.

Milo promised to call later, and Beth hung up. Zack knew where she was – and so did Justin and Melanie. Surely they wouldn't be so cruel as to tell the press about the flat in St Emit? But Livvy wouldn't put it past them. She made a call to her brothers and asked them to find out where Zack was, and she called Tab, instructing her to get hold of Melanie.

Livvy went into overdrive. She spread the word in the village that nobody should let on that Beth was here, at least until Saturday when they planned to make a break back to Wessex. Livvy also stocked up on food at the supermarket, and they spent the rest of the day talking to friends on the phone, watching the news and smoking too many fags.

Beth was worse than useless. She tried to concentrate on what was happening but couldn't follow what Livvy was saying. Eventually Livvy packed her off to bed, where she lay shivering. Through the wall she could hear Livvy on the phone, asking questions and giving directions. She thought she heard Milo's name, and also Mr Toms' and Edward's.

The following day went much the same way. Livvy left Beth alone in the ringing silence of the flat, and returned with a whole stack of newspapers, which all carried the story. It was on morning TV and now they had someone outside James' flat in LA.

'It must be a slow news day,' remarked Livvy. 'Here's the plan. Tomorrow, we're driving to Milo's house, so that on Sunday we can get back to The Island without being spotted. I've spoken to Mr Toms. He says, once we're on school property, the press will have to leave you alone. He's already contacted the editors of all the tabloids to warn them that, otherwise he'll prosecute for trespassing. Tomorrow afternoon, he's coming to Milo's cottage with Mr Markham, who wants to talk to us about Zack. He's in the deepest of deep shit.'

Livvy still hadn't managed to get any new information from Tab about Melanie, who wasn't at home and wasn't with Justin, or at least that's what Justin was saying.

'Why are you bothering with Melanie and Justin?' asked Beth.

'Because of his parents.'

'What about them?'

'You don't know? Justin's dad is editor-in-chief and his mum is the society columnist for *The Sun*.' She frowned at Beth. 'You really didn't know that? You can't tell Justin anything – it always gets back to his parents sooner rather than later. If I'd known about your secret, I would have told you all this earlier.'

'So you think that Zack gave the story to Justin, or Justin's parents, because I split up with him? For revenge?'

'To be honest, I'm not sure that's everything. It's not really the sort of thing Zack would do. I mean, no offence, but I think he's more upset about Bonnie being in hospital than about splitting up with you. Wait… let me think… Edward called Milo and Milo gave him the number for here. Edward told me that Zack's had a restraining order put on him, because he tried again on Saturday night, straight after he'd left here, to find out where Bonnie's rehab is. So… that would have given him time to get back up to London, if he went to Justin's house straight away… Shit, shit, shit. Something's not making sense. I've got to talk to Mel. She's the one who can tell us what Justin and Zack did. Where are you hiding, Melanie?'

Later that evening, Tab called. She had finally tracked down Melanie and had convinced her that she should spill the whole story. Livvy listened to Tab, nodding and making little huffing noises. When she got off the phone, she poured herself and Beth a glass of wine.

'So, Mel's been a total bitch, but she has redeemed herself. Apparently she wasn't your greatest fan because you ruined her chances with Milo – another piece of information you have neglected to tell me about, thanks for that – and Justin hates Milo anyway, because of the rugby thing.' Livvy took a breath and sipped her wine. 'But Mel's poured her heart out to Tab and admits she's screwed up big time. She's dumped Justin, by the way. Says he gives her the creeps. She told Tab that Zack has known about your parents for ages – Mel wasn't sure exactly when he found out, but she said that Zack's mum recognised you from some photo… Anyway, Zack kept it to himself, because he knows how indiscreet Justin is.

'But on Saturday night, Justin drives Zack and Mel home and on the way, Zack makes him stop off at the Markhams' and the whole story about Bonnie comes out, including that she tried to do herself in last week. Justin takes Zack home and calls his parents with the scoop – *Daughter of Cabinet Minister Suicide Attempt* – and Zack overhears him on the phone. He flips out, but it's too late. So Zack makes Justin take him to his house, where Justin's mum is already writing up the story. She refuses to stop unless... Zack gives them something else. Something better.' Livvy stopped.

'He gave them me?'

'Got it in one. Justin's parents weren't exactly convinced, but then Justin persuaded them it would be a better story. Lots more glamour and mystery and no chance of getting sued. Mel didn't know anything about it; she's shitting herself that she's going to get into trouble at school. And she's sorry that it's happened to you.'

Beth's head throbbed. She left her glass of wine standing on the kitchen table and went to her room. She tried to go to sleep but everything kept running through her head. Zack had betrayed her. How could he hate her that much? She heard Livvy on the telephone, a soft knock on her door, a whispered goodnight. Beth waited for another hour, until she was sure Livvy was asleep, dressed and left the flat.

She wandered through the deserted streets, catching her reflection in a fish-and-chip shop window, and stopped to look. There was nothing in herself that she recognised. She only saw one thing – her mother. How could she have lost herself so quickly? Was that all anyone else would see? Was this how it was going to be from now on, forever?

She passed a phone box and thought longingly of Milo. She wasn't sure how late it was, she didn't have a watch any more, but thought it was past midnight. Could she call him now? Would he be asleep, or sitting up, worrying about her? She opened the door of the phone box and stepped inside, breathing in the stale smell, and picked up the receiver. She dialled 100 to reverse the charges but when the operator answered, she lost her nerve and hung up. How was Milo going to help? Nobody could help her now. She felt so lonely.

She started walking again, in the direction of the little beach but following the path further, as it curved up above the sea and along the cliffs. She barely knew where she was going, but found an old bus stop that looked out onto the dark ocean on the other side of the road, and sat on the slatted wooden bench. She curled up after a while, trying to keep warm, shivering in her thin coat and pushing her hands up into her sleeves. Through the night she stayed there, too tired to move, too restless to sleep.

Birdsong woke her in the morning and a solitary car drove past, a song blaring out of its open window and fading away. She sat up and rubbed her eyes, her head pounding and her shoulders aching. She had to face the journey back to Wessex today, and then school tomorrow.

Her holiday felt like it had happened a long time ago, or to another person. It detached itself from her and floated away. At the thought of what her life would be like from now on, a weight settled all over her, as if someone had covered her with a heavy blanket.

Beth's eyes searched along the coastline to the east, towards the faint glimmer of the sun rising from between the dark cliffs. The sea, which had been a fun and shiny toy for her and Livvy to play with last week, now looked treacherous and gloomy.

She heard footsteps on the road and slunk out of sight into the corner of the bus stop, not wanting to be seen by a stranger. But it wasn't a stranger; it was Livvy. Beth called her name as she passed, but her voice came out as a raspy whisper. Livvy turned around at the sound and enveloped Beth in a hug.

'Oh, you gave me such a fright. I woke up this morning and you weren't there. I didn't know where you'd gone. I've been searching for ages; so have the others.'

'The others?'

'Don't talk if it hurts. God, you're freezing. Here, I brought you another jumper.' She gave Beth Joel's sweatshirt. 'Joel and everyone. Come on, we have to get you back before Jimmy and Emily call the police. Only… we can't go back to the flat. Justin or Zack must have told them where we were staying.'

Livvy took Beth's hand and led her back towards St Emit, turning off the High Street and knocking on the door of a caravan parked in a side street. A girl called Rachel, whom Beth recognised from their evenings at the beach, opened the door and ushered them inside. Rachel gave Beth a cup of tea and she nearly fainted with hunger and gratitude when a bacon sandwich appeared on a plate in front of her. Livvy whispered something to Rachel before she disappeared, and Beth sat eating and drinking, her throat hurting and her eyes bleary with lack of sleep. Rachel gave her a blanket and made her lie down on the fold-out bed. All the time she was dozing, she heard the door opening and closing and the hushed voices of people coming and going.

It was time to leave. Livvy had their bags packed and ready in the car.

'Joel's been an absolute hero. He told the journalists that were camped outside the flat that he'd spotted you in a café in Wadebridge. They gave him fifty quid for that information. So they all hotfooted it to Wadebridge and Joel nipped inside the flat and packed our bags for us and got your car keys. We need to leave now before they discover the scam. Let's go.' Livvy hugged Rachel and pointed Beth to the car, giving her a large pair of sunglasses and a New York Yankees cap.

'What are these for?' croaked Beth.

'It's a disguise, dummy.'

'But if they see me wearing these, they'll know it's me, it's so obvious.'

'OK, don't wear them. I thought it was very *Blues Brothers*, that's all. Now get in the car. I'm driving. Let's hit it.'

Beth did as she was told, although, she thought sulkily, Livvy was enjoying herself with the cloak-and-dagger routine more than was strictly necessary. Too weak to argue, she put on the cap and glasses, settled herself into the passenger seat and rested her head to the side facing the window. She watched the sea disappear into the distance, feeling like she was on the crest of a wave that was going to smash her life as she knew it into millions of tiny pieces.

The truth were loud. It couldn't get much louder.

The rain began as they joined the main road, and Beth stuffed a dirty, sandy towel into the gap in the window. She watched the central reservation flash by through steamed-up windows. Her head dropped and jerked up again. Livvy stopped at the services near Ivell to fill up the car with petrol and she bought Beth a pack of Anadin Extra and a carton of Ribena.

'No Coke?' rasped Beth.

'It's rich in Vitamin C. Drink up.'

At lunchtime they arrived at Milo's cottage and Beth directed Livvy to the shed behind the lane. The door was unlocked and a note from Milo said he'd be back from work when it was dark. Livvy ran Beth a bath and heated up some soup.

At two o'clock, Mr Toms arrived with Mr Markham. Livvy had lit a fire and the room was far too hot – it was making Beth feel groggy and sleepy. Mr Toms asked Livvy to repeat what had happened with Zack, Justin and the Ravensdales, which she did with painstaking attention to detail, quoting sources and referring to notes.

Mr Toms said, 'Elizabeth, as you know, I was unfamiliar with the situation concerning your parents. I respect your decision for that to remain a secret. But now we have to look at the facts together and decide on the best course of action. Mr Markham contends that Zachary Smythe's behaviour has threatened the privacy of his family, the welfare of his daughter and his own reputation and career in the government. Is there anything that you would like to add to these points?'

Beth shook her head.

'Zachary has not behaved very well towards you,' said Mr Toms. 'I understand that you two are... were... in a relationship. Is that correct?'

She nodded.

'And he has revealed your secret, that you had kept for fifteen years, and you have nothing to say about it?'

Livvy interrupted. 'Sir? She's lost her voice.'

'Yes, thank you, Olivia, I was aware of that.'

Mr Markham leant towards Beth. He looked tired and old. 'You shouldn't have a sense of loyalty to him.'

'No,' she whispered. 'But you should.'

Mr Markham leant back. 'Why on earth would you say that?'

'Because Zack has done the only thing he could think of to save Bonnie, to show her and you how much he loves her. At first I thought he hated me. But then I realised, he doesn't hate me. He loves her. Nothing else matters. For once, Zack has thought about what his actions might mean to someone other than himself. He chose to protect her future, probably hoping that that future will involve him. It's the first time he's ever behaved with any sort of responsibility or loyalty to another human being.' She stared at them all with defiance and turned back to Mr Markham. 'You should *thank* him.'

'Zachary will not be returning to Weatherbury Hall next term,' explained Mr Toms.

Livvy said, 'You should expel Justin. It was his fault; he was the one who blabbed to his parents. Without him neither story would have been printed.'

'We are expelling Justin for the culmination of a series of offences, this last one being a serious breach of trust. Zachary has been suspended from school for the offence which he committed with Bonnie last year, because they both assured us that that offence occurred outside the school and in the school holidays, but his mother has made the decision to remove him from the school permanently.'

It was all decided, despite Beth's refusal to blame Zack. Mr Markham shook her hand and left. Mr Toms asked Beth if he could take her to the school san, but she said she was feeling well enough and was just tired.

'Then I will take my leave. I'll see you both tomorrow, and I hope to put all this unpleasantness behind us with the new term. You'll be safe here at school.'

When he'd left, Beth collapsed on the sofa with Livvy. They turned their heads to face each other, resting their cheeks on the back of the sofa.

'Don't cry. It's going to be OK. You'll see.'

Beth's sobs rose from somewhere deep in her body, making her shoulders tremble and her face crumple.

'You've been so brave. The worst is over now. He's not coming back.'

'But don't you see? The worst bit is about to start. I have no life left. Everything I wanted is gone. Even he's gone.' She gulped and shook her head, her hair falling over her face. 'I had this dream about Zack, ages ago, that he and Edward and Milo and I were in this awful maze; I was trying desperately to get out, and he helped me. Zack. I chose him to help me above Edward and Milo. I know it's silly, but I really thought that dream meant something, that... I dunno, the maze was going to kill me. And Zack was the one to save my life.'

Livvy thought about this for a while. 'Did you ever think that perhaps you weren't *supposed* to get out of the maze? That taking Zack's way out was wrong? That you were meant to be there all along?'

'But it was horrible and dangerous.'

'If the maze was your life, let's say, then it was really Zack that was the danger. He was the one who wanted to take you away from your life, or take your life away from you.'

'Livvy, you are wise beyond your IQ.'

'So they say.'

Beth fell asleep with her head on Livvy's shoulder, snoring softly through her blocked nose, and didn't hear Milo come in later. With him was James, who had flown back from America as soon as the story broke. Milo carried Beth up to the spare bedroom and the three of them spent the evening talking about her, the past and the future, which began tomorrow.

Chapter Eighteen

On Easter Saturday, when Beth had dropped Milo off at Truro train station, he watched her car disappear around the corner before leaving the station himself. He had no money for a train ticket and wasn't very good at fare-dodging. He'd tried it once, had sat in his seat sweating and panicking, unable to think up an excuse should the ticket collector do his rounds. He couldn't face that again.

He'd made a sign to hold, with *MELCHESTER* written in large letters, and stood at the entrance to the first main road he found. He felt like shit: his head was throbbing from the knock at rugby camp, he was exhausted and woozy, the beating sun was making sweat dribble down his back. With his shaven head and scar, he knew he looked like he'd been in a fight. A fight with a lawnmower. His stomach was twistingly empty and he smelled of hospital – a smell that reminded him of all those times he'd visited his mum before she died.

He was worried about Edward, who was in bits, and Beth, who had her own problems with Zack. The damp patch on his shoulder where her tears had soaked through his filthy T-shirt was starting to dry now. He was about to return to the train station – nobody was ever going to pick him up in this state – when a lady in a maroon Ford Cortina pulled up. She wound down the passenger window and shouted at him.

'How old are you?'

'Eighteen.'

'Why is your head shaven?'

'I was in an accident yesterday.'

'What kind of accident?'

'Playing rugby. Someone kicked—'

'Say no more. Climb in.' She opened the door for him, grabbed his bag and threw it onto the back seat. 'Oof. Just wanted to check you weren't a weirdo, that's all. I'm heading to Havenpool; can you get another ride from there?'

Milo admitted that he lived in Weatherbury. He had thought it would be easier to get a lift to Melchester.

'Well then, that's marvellous – I'll drop you off at your door. So tell me about your rugby – were you at that schools' training camp at Truro College? Nasty head wound you've got there. What does the other fellow look like, hahaha…'

She didn't stop talking for three and a half hours, about the weather, the state of the roads, the recession, how Thatcher was on her way out, her rose garden, how dreadful junk food was – she just went on and on. Milo replied politely whenever he could think of something relevant to say, staring out of the window at the fields and trees flashing by, his legs in their shorts sticking sweatily to the plastic seats. When they stopped off at the services, he drank from the tap in the men's loos, he was so thirsty and hot.

Milo was supposed to work with the school groundsman that afternoon, but he took one look at him and said, 'Get yourself home, you daft fool. You look a shambles. Get some kip and for pity's sake have a wash. See you tomorrow.' If the weather was fine, he'd be on the mower, and if it rained, they had work to do in the boathouse.

After a good night's sleep, Milo felt like a different person. It was another warm, dry day so he had an easy time sitting on the mower. He listened to some tapes on a Walkman he'd borrowed from the lost property box while he mowed the cricket outfield, the athletics track and the perimeter of the sports pitches.

In the evening, the whole grounds staff, some of whom were Milo's old friends from the village primary school, went to the Buck's Head pub together. The landlord was famously relaxed about underage drinkers from the village, but had no truck with the 'posh-school kids', who, if they dared to cross the threshold of his establishment, were served watered-down drinks at twice the normal price. He made an exception for Milo, who watched them all get drunk, sipping his one beer, laughing when they called him Kojak and challenging them all to beat him at darts, which nobody managed. He even won some money on the fruit machine, so he bought his round without having to dip into food money.

All week he worked from dawn to dusk. He'd be more than two hundred pounds richer by next Saturday, which wasn't really enough to see him through until half-term, but it would have to do. He would have to get the phone cut off and eat every meal at school. He couldn't remember the last time he bought new clothes. And he didn't have a clue how he was going to pay his poll tax bill; even twenty per cent of it was going to be a struggle. He thought of asking Mrs Toms or even Beth for help – a loan until the summer, when he could work for eight straight weeks – but he was too proud.

Was it really only one year ago that his dad had killed himself? His mind wandered back to last Easter, when, with his dad, he'd been doing the same work at The Island: dismantling the rugby posts and the football and hockey goals and packing away the winter sports equipment; preparing the boats and boathouse for the summer, as well as mowing, rolling and lining the cricket pitches and grass tennis courts. Every day, Milo, who was good with horses, had mucked out, fed and exercised the three horses that had been left at the school by the pupils. For him, it had been a normal Easter, albeit without his mum. For his dad, it had been the last few days of his life.

All year since then he'd worked flat out, trying to keep up with his schoolwork, rugby training, the play and his paid work. He felt a tinge of resentment, and not for the first time, that his dad had left him in this mess, not caring enough about his only son to stick around. Had he felt that Milo was one burden too many to bear? Milo would never know the answer to that question. So he pulled himself together and put these thoughts aside, knowing there were plenty of people his age who had a lot less than he did. At least the cottage was mortgage-free.

On Thursday, when he turned up for work, the groundsman gave Milo a copy of *The Sun* with a scowl.

'That's your girl, int it?'

Milo frowned as he scanned the story.

'She in trouble?'

Milo nodded.

'I can't spare you, we've got too much to do.'

'I'll call her, that's all. Then I'll work through my break.'

The groundsman watched as Milo sprinted to his bike. He was a grumpy middle-aged man, with only this job and his pretty nineteen-year-old daughter to be proud of in his life. He hated the privileged, spoilt kids at this school, every last one of them, except for Milo, whose dad had been a mate of his, and who worked twice as hard as any of his other lads. Also, Milo had never, not once, tried to lay a finger on the groundsman's daughter, unlike all the other boys in the village. Real, proper gentleman. Right soppy about this famous girl, though; that stunt he'd pulled with the bulbs, it was as clear as daylight Milo had done it, although he never owned up to it. That soppiness, reading books and all, came from his mum. Too much education, that woman. Although the groundsman did envy her collection of Beatles LPs.

Milo was desperate to speak to Beth, but either the number she'd given him was wrong or she wasn't answering. He tried again later in the morning and spoke to her at last. She sounded like she'd been crying, and his heart twisted for her. He was secretly relieved that he didn't have to go and fetch her; it would have been a disaster for his precarious finances. Livvy would cope. Milo tried not to be envious that Beth would need a lot of consolation and that his arms would not be the ones to give her that. He pushed this selfish thought out of his mind.

That afternoon, Mr and Mrs Toms found him painting the cricket boundary with the line-marking machine. When Mrs Toms had got over the shock of his missing hair, they explained to him that they needed to get in touch with Beth, but there had been no answer from her aunt in Melchester, so Milo gave them the number of the flat in St Emit.

Exhausted at the end of the day, he called again and spoke to Livvy. She filled him in on what she'd managed to glean from various school friends who lived in London. He told her that when they left Cornwall, they should come to his cottage.

On Friday he had no choice but to go to work and let everyone else sort out the mess. He was handed the newspaper again; there weren't that many new details, only a few more quotes from so-called friends and more photos of Beth's parents. More background stuff. That meant they hadn't found Beth yet. If she could make it back to The Island, then maybe the story would fizzle out, as the story about her parents had done in 1974.

He had at least persuaded Livvy to bring Beth to him tomorrow, so that she would be somewhere unknown to the press, but close to The Island. One day, then he'd see her again. He couldn't wait to talk to her, to comfort her and to scrutinise her eyes, her face for minuscule clues as to what she was thinking. He got a call from James, who was at Heathrow airport, wanting to know where Beth was, desperate because Anne had gone AWOL in Australia and he was out of his mind with worry. Milo advised him to stay in London that night and gave him his address for the next day.

He tidied the spotless cottage and made the bed in the spare room, leaving the Swatch watch he'd bought for Beth for her birthday by the side of the bed. He wanted to write something witty and unforgettable on a note for her, but he was too nervous and tired to think of anything.

Saturday: at work at the stables, he saw Mr Markham arrive at the school, recognising him from the TV. Milo watched him and Mr Toms as they drove off through the rain to his cottage. Which meant Beth was already there. Mr Toms hadn't said anything to him about what was going to happen to Zack and Justin, but he hoped with all his heart that they would be chucked out, the pair of them, and that he would never see them again.

Three hours to go; two, one, half an hour. Done.

He raced to the bursar's office to give him his time sheet and collect his wages, rode his bike like the wind down the main driveway, skidding in the rain and the dark until he finally saw the lights of his cottage, arriving at the same time as James was knocking on the door. James looked rather startled to see him, but they shook hands. Milo saw James glancing up at his bald head, so to reassure him, he turned around, pointed at where he thought the scar was and said, 'Rugby injury.' When he turned back round, James was looking slightly queasy.

His heart hammering, they stepped inside together and Livvy motioned for them to be quiet. There Beth lay, flushed cheeks, long lashes brushing bruises under her eyes, her hair falling in dirty strands over her face, beautiful, hurt and fast asleep.

'Can you carry her up to bed please, Milo?' whispered Livvy. 'Blimey, what's happened to your hair?'

Chapter Nineteen

On Sunday morning, Milo woke at dawn. He had tried to persuade James to take his bedroom, as Beth and Livvy were sleeping in his spare room, but James had insisted that the sofa would be perfectly satisfactory. Milo hadn't known what to expect when he met James; Beth hadn't talked about him much. Perhaps somebody sophisticated and eloquent – or a bit scatty like Anne, or determined and stubborn like Beth. But James was reserved and so soft-spoken that when he asked them about Beth, Livvy had to ask him to repeat himself several times. Milo thought that James might have been surprised that Beth had a friend like him, a big, scruffy, beaten-up rugby player. So he showered in the morning, found some clean clothes and tried to make himself look presentable.

James was fast asleep on the sofa, but stirred as Milo made coffee.

'Sorry to wake you. Did you sleep well?'

'Not really, but I took the liberty of borrowing a few books from your shelf. It's the jet lag, you see. Are the girls up yet?'

'One of them is.' Livvy trudged down the stairs in her pyjamas, yawning and stretching. 'The other one's out for the count.'

'What's the plan for today, Milo?' said James.

Milo looked at Livvy, hoping she would take charge.

She turned to James. 'Well, just practical things, really. You and I should go back to Melchester and pack Beth's bags for term. Anne won't be back until the middle of next week, is that right? Beth wasn't sure.'

'I'm afraid I'm not sure either.'

'Billy and Jake, my brothers, are arriving this afternoon with my stuff and I'd like to go up to school then. I want to find out what everyone's saying and sort a few things out. Milo, this morning, you can do that thing you do with Beth to stop her freaking out' – James raised his eyebrows questioningly, but was ignored by Livvy – 'and then James, you should drive her up to school at bedtime – not before – so she doesn't have to face too many people until tomorrow morning. Mr Toms is making some sort of announcement in assembly tomorrow, something about how we need to all pull together and stiff upper lip, you know, that sort of thing.'

James looked impressed and slightly overwhelmed.

Livvy continued, 'I'll just shower and then go and get us all some breakfast and today's papers. Let's leave her to sleep for as long as you can bear it. I know you're both dying to see her, but she's knackered and fluey and apart from that, she's the same sulky, difficult, recitent Beth that we know and love.'

'D'you mean reticent, Livs?' said Milo kindly.

'Yes, that too.'

They did as they were told, both Milo and James glancing upstairs when they thought they heard a sound. When Livvy came back with croissants, milk, bread, jam and a jumbo carton of orange juice, they tucked in and pored over the papers to try and find the relevant stories. Beth had been relegated to the inside pages now, so they enjoyed reading out some of the statements they found ridiculous.

'They're starting to make stuff up now; this is good, they have nothing new,' laughed Livvy. 'Listen: *A school friend of Beth Sauveterre/Atkinson recalls how she took part in a fashion show arranged at school, and what a natural she was.* That's utter crap – Beth refused point-blank to do the fashion show.' She chuckled. 'Now I know why.'

It was nine o'clock when they heard floorboards creaking upstairs. Livvy poured a cup of coffee and slid it towards Milo. 'Here, you take it up to her.'

Milo shook his head and slid it to James. 'She won't want me to see her yet, before she's showered and dressed.'

Livvy and James smiled knowingly at each other and James stood up to take the coffee. They heard some excited squeaks and a lump came to Milo's throat when he thought he heard sobs.

Livvy patted his hand. 'It's probably a good idea for her to do as much crying as possible today, so it's out of her system. She's going to need to go back into Ice-Queen mode tomorrow.'

'D'you think?' Milo was at a total loss. How was Beth going to manage to do all the things that Livvy and Mr Toms and every other person in the world expected her to do? It was like acting – in front of an audience every day, always being watched and never being able to let down your guard. Milo got why Beth had been so daunted by the prospect of being mega-famous.

James came down the stairs and gave them both a weak smile. 'Beth wants us to leave straight away to fetch her clothes from home. If she's already thinking about her appearance, well, that's a good sign.'

'That's no sign at all; she never stops thinking about her appearance,' pointed out Livvy.

'Unfair,' shouted a hoarse voice from upstairs.

Livvy and James made tracks and Milo was left alone to wait for Beth. She took ages in the shower, so he put on a record to pass the time. What on earth was he going to do with an agoraphobic, bad-tempered, flu-ridden girl on a rainy day?

When she came down the stairs, he stood up, but thought that looked ridiculous, so he sat down again. He scratched his neck and smiled an apology at her, trying to swallow that lump in his throat. He was doing this all wrong.

'It's OK, you don't need to make a big deal of it, you know. I'm not going to break.'

Good. Excellent. Bolshie Beth, I can cope with that, thought Milo. 'Hungry?'

'Bit.' She yawned. 'Where are the others?'

'They've gone to Melchester to pack for you. We have all morning; what do you want to do?'

'We don't really have much choice but to stay here, do we?'

'Well, I did have an idea… eat some breakfast and I'll tell you about it on the way.'

Beth shrugged her shoulders and ate slowly, staring out of the window at the rain. Milo went to fetch the car and she climbed in with a blank look on her face. She didn't ask where they were going. She didn't seem to care.

As they drove south towards the coast, the rain hammered on the roof of the car. Milo had wound up the window using a monkey wrench before they left. They parked in a deserted car park and climbed down some steep stone steps to a pebbly beach that curved round in a bay, with rocky cliffs on either side enclosing it partially from the sea, and white chalk cliffs rising up behind the beach. They were the only people crazy enough to come to the seaside on a day like this.

'Why are we here?' she sniffed.

Milo shrugged. 'Might be the last time you get to leave school for a while. I thought you'd like it here.'

She shielded her eyes from the rain and shivered. 'Yes, wow, great. Now can we go home?'

'This was Dr Smythe's favourite beach.'

'I don't want to talk about him.'

'You don't have to. I'll talk, you listen. We came here during the last summer holiday we had, just before I started at The Island. Zack was a strong swimmer, but he was only ten years old. He was horrible that day, sulking and arguing. Dr Smythe and I went to get ice creams from the café up at the top of the cliffs, and when we came back, we saw Zack in the water, way out near the entrance to the cove, where the currents are strong. He was obviously panicking. Dr Smythe dived in, but Zack was too far away. Luckily, a rowing boat came around the cliff and dragged him in, otherwise he would've drowned.

'When Dr Smythe asked him why he had gone swimming alone, even though he knew full well that it was dangerous, he just shrugged his shoulders and said, "My real father says I can do anything I want with my life. I wanted to swim. So I did."'

Milo looked at Beth, the sound of the waves crashing on the shingle in front of them.

'And the moral of this story is…?'

Milo turned towards the sea and she followed his gaze. They couldn't see the horizon because of the rain and the mist.

'Umm…' He rubbed his hand over his head. 'Not sure, really. I suppose I wanted to tell you that Zack is…'

'…a selfish prick? Yes, message received and understood. Now can we go home?'

'Not yet.'

She groaned. 'Is this going to be another pep talk, Milo? Because I don't need it.'

'Come on, let's get out of the rain.'

There was a café at the top of the cliffs. Beth hesitated, but Milo assured her he'd called ahead; the cousin of a friend of his was working today. They pushed the door open and a bell tinkled. The café was warm and muggy, with a radio playing in the back, and no other customers.

'Hi, Claire,' said Milo to a girl a few years older than them who emerged from the kitchen behind the counter.

'Hi, Milo. Did you reserve a table?'

They looked around at the empty tables and both laughed.

'This is Beth.'

'Pleased to meet you. Having a rough time?'

'You could say that.'

They sat down at a Formica-topped table near the steamed-up window and Milo ordered tomato soup and a cup of tea for both of them. They could see the waves crashing on the beach and the dark clouds like a ceiling, with a lighter layer of rain underneath, streaming down into the water. At first, they ate and drank in silence, staring out of the window.

Eventually, Milo spoke up. 'How're you feeling?'

'Don't want to talk about it.'

'Maybe it'll help.'

Beth gave a harsh laugh. '*You* want *me* to talk about my feelings? You, who never talks about anything?'

'There's not much to talk about.'

'God, it's like you're not even human. In the last few years, you've lost your mum and your dad. You're barely eighteen, you live alone, you have no living relatives, no money. Your dad committed suicide, for fuck's sake. You never talk about it, you never cry; you never get angry. How can you be so... stoic?'

Milo sighed. 'I do get sad and I do get angry.'

Beth looked sceptical.

Milo sat back in his chair and took his time to search for the right words. 'I miss my mum every day. She was such a lovely person. I miss her so much it hurts.' He thumped his chest. 'Here. It hurts here. I'm starting to forget what she looked like. I have to look at a photo sometimes.'

Beth was silent.

'I guess you'll never have that problem.' Milo put his hand to his head, rubbed his scalp and closed his eyes. He continued in a low voice, 'I am angry with my dad. Whenever I think about what he did to me, it makes me want to punch someone.' He felt so lonely telling her this, even with her there. 'The question I keep asking myself is, *What could I have done differently?* Maybe if I'd talked to him about Mum, maybe I could've stopped him... I was so useless. Do you ever have that dream where you're driving through the night, you don't know where you are, you're running out of petrol and you can't find your way home... everything seems so scary and out of reach. Have you ever had a dream like that?'

'Something similar.'

He didn't say anything for a while, and then, 'I know I let him down.'

'You did not. It's not your job to sort out your parents. You were a child.'

'Well, I'm not any more. As you've noticed, I have no money and no family to help me. So I decided, that's it, I have to help myself. I have to get on with my life. And you know, I am lucky.'

'Lucky? How?' Beth snorted.

'I have the cottage. I have The Island. That school, it's paradise for me. I try not to imagine what my life would have been like if I didn't have it. You know, I have some friends in the village; they aren't as lucky as me. My mate Scott – his brother's in jail, for GBH. Another friend of mine, Karen, she has six younger sisters and brothers. Their dad left last year and her mum has two jobs, so Karen has to get the children fed and put them to bed in the evenings. She has no time to do her homework. A guy I was at primary school with – Andy, you know him; he works in the kitchens at school? – he earns three quid an hour. He hates his job, but it's that or the dole. None of these people are as lucky as me.'

'Or as me?'

'Look, I know it's a steaming pile of shit at the moment. I don't envy your life. For me, the tragedy is over. For you, it's just starting. So, the way I see it, you can either sit around sulking about it or you can make a plan and get on with your life. It could have been worse, you know.'

'How? How could it have been worse? My boyfriend lied to me and hung me out to dry, I've got to spend the rest of my life in the public eye, nothing I ever do in my career or my life will be my own, I have no privacy, I won't know who my friends are. You'd have thought that losing my parents when I was a baby would have been enough, but now... now I lose myself too.'

'I'll tell you how it could have been worse. You've got James and Anne. You've got friends who knew you before you were famous. You've got a brain. You've got money—'

'I told you, I don't want the money.'

'Oh, don't be so self-pitying.'

Beth looked up at Milo, her eyes wide with surprise.

'Money can buy you lots of practical things that will make your life better. It will buy you privacy and protection and power. So don't start being a poor little rich girl. It doesn't suit you.'

'Jesus, don't hold back, OK? I get it.'

'And you know what else? You're lucky that you look like your mum. Not just so that you'll never forget what she looked like.' Milo looked at her, a smile forming over his lips.

'What, then? What's so funny?'

'Well, have you seen the pictures of your dad? No offence, but he was no oil painting.'

Beth rolled her eyes.

They drove back to Weatherbury in silence, listening to the radio. A news report came on and Beth tensed. Milo turned up the volume. The top story was still Beth, but it was all the usual rehashed information. Nigel Dempster was interviewed, but said very little that hadn't been said already. Milo shrugged and turned the volume down again.

'We could really do with another Watergate now, to take you off the top spot. Or a nuclear war or a famine. As many people suffering as possible, to ensure your personal happiness.'

From Beth, not a flicker of amusement.

Livvy and James were already at the cottage. Livvy had lit the fire again and she put the kettle on, while Milo opened a cupboard to find the teabags. He frowned at her.

'What's all this?'

'We bought a few essentials, as a thank-you for your hospitality.'

'Essentials? You've bought half the supermarket.'

There were packs of tea, coffee and cocoa, tins of baked beans and spaghetti hoops, Pot Noodles and Weetabix, crisps and biscuits. Livvy grabbed some Hobnobs and handed them around to everyone.

'See – hospitality.'

There was a knock at the door and Guy poked his head round it.

'I thought you'd all be here – anyone need a lift up to school in this delightful weather? Hello, sir, you must be the famous Uncle James; honoured to meet you, big fan of your work. Loving the new look, big man. And hello... Mademoiselle Sauveterre.'

Beth, who was sitting on the sofa clutching her tea, turned her head to give Guy a look of pure loathing and looked away again.

Guy winced theatrically. 'Not ready to joke about it yet?'

Milo gave his bag to Guy, pushed him out of the door and said he'd meet him at school later. Billy and Jake arrived to collect Livvy and before Milo could head them off, they had danced round to the sofa and plonked themselves either side of Beth. She did her best to ignore them.

'Can I have your autograph, Sauveterre?'

'Very funny.'

'Will you go out with me, now that you've split up with Zack? I promise I'll be a *model* boyfriend.'

Milo interrupted. 'Leave it out, BJ.' But the corner of his mouth twitched.

'Argh! It's Frankenstein. What the fuck... excuse my language, sir...'

While Billy and Jake ran over to Milo and were stroking his bald head and introducing themselves to James, Beth stood up and strode over to the stairs.

'Don't go, Sauveterre.'

'Sod off and leave me alone. And you halfwits – Frankenstein *made* the monster, so Milo is not Frankenstein, he's Frankenstein's monster.' And she stomped upstairs.

Once Billy, Jake and Livvy had gone, Beth came back downstairs and they ordered a Chinese takeaway for dinner. She sat silently, pushing the food around her plate, while James and Milo talked about LA and what James was going to do now. He had to go back, he said, next week at the latest, but he would return to England by the end of the summer term and maybe he, Anne and Beth could go away together, somewhere remote, where they wouldn't attract too much attention. It sounded sensible to Milo, but he couldn't help thinking that not seeing Beth for eight weeks was going to be hard for him.

Beth went outside into the garden to smoke a cigarette.

James watched her close the door behind her and said in a resigned voice, 'I didn't tell Beth, I didn't want her to get more upset about this boy, but my agent had a call from his agent.'

'Which boy?'

'This Zack Smythe. His agent called me about the film we're making of *Ten Lives*. He thought Zack would do well for the part of my brother-in-law.'

Something in Milo's brain clicked. 'When was this? When did the agent call?'

'Umm... let me see... in the winter, a while ago.'

Milo frowned. 'Before or after Christmas?'

'Why? Does it matter?'

'Sort of. Well, not really, I suppose. But Zack told me that he auditioned for *Cold Comfort Farm* because he wanted to pull... I mean, go out with Beth. But if the agent called you before then, before they got together, maybe it was the other way round – maybe all he ever wanted was to get the part in your film.'

'But why would he ruin his chances by selling the story to the newspapers?'

'Zack's not very good at seeing things through. I've never known him plan ahead for more than one day. Perhaps his mother was masterminding this.'

'You talk like it's an international spy ring.'

'Sorry, I don't mean to get all dramatic on you. But Beth's still hurting about him, even though he's been so awful to her. She still believes that at some stage, even if it was only early on, he really did love her.'

James thought about it. 'And you think, maybe he never did?'

Milo shrugged. 'I suppose it doesn't matter either way now.'

'So you're not going to tell her?'

'Would you?'

James was silent for a moment. He looked at Milo with a sad smile. 'You'll look after her?'

'I don't think she wants me to look after her.'

'But you will anyway?'

'Yes. I will anyway.'

Beth came back in and Milo stood up to clear the remnants of the meal. He took a long time – he wanted to delay the moment when he had to leave.

She moved across to the kitchen counter and cleared her throat. She was fiddling with her hair. 'Um. Thanks for trying to cheer me up today. It really helped. I mean, you know, it was actually crap, but I appreciate what you were trying to do.'

'You gonna be OK tomorrow?'

'I reckon. Save me a place at breakfast? Seven thirty.' She

pulled up her sleeve and showed him the Swatch watch. 'I won't be late.'

'You'd better not be. There are plenty of very punctual girls who would like to sit next to me.'

'Oh yeah – with that hair, you'll be beating them off with a stick.'

Their eyes met and Milo felt a weight lifting off him. Guy would be proud: Beth was trying to joke about it. She was strong; she was going to be all right. And he would be by her side. Even if it was just for breakfast.

Chapter Twenty

'So, Milo's going to do the rounds early tomorrow morning. Guy, BJ, Henry and he will go from Casterbridge House up to Shottsford House to talk to Edward and Finn. I've already seen Tab, Sav and Susanna, plus Mel.'

Beth lay in her bed that night, half listening to Livvy.

'We go to breakfast together, we sit together, we do everything together. These are the only people who are allowed to know how upset you are about Zack. For everyone else, just show them your Ice Queen face. As far as they're concerned, nothing's changed, same old, same old. They'll soon get bored and the whole thing'll blow over.'

'If you say so.' Beth was grateful to Livvy for taking over, but couldn't muster up any more enthusiasm than that.

Breakfast in the dining hall was busier than usual, especially for the first day of term, when most of the school usually preferred an extra half-hour in bed. People slowed down near their table, had a quick look at Beth, and moved on. She sat wedged between Milo and Edward, and everyone at their table was distractingly rowdy. Billy and Jake had them all in stitches over how they got sacked from their holiday jobs teaching little rich kids how to sail – they'd got steaming drunk one night and were still drunk at work the next morning. Billy had been sick over the side of the boat and Jake had fallen in the water, more than once. The little kids had thought it was hilarious but some of the parents had – for some reason – got the hump. The tables around theirs were hushed, listening in on the stories to see if they could pick up anything about Beth. They soon gave up.

'This is so much fun,' whispered Henry to Milo. 'Are we going to do this every day?'

Livvy instructed them to meet in half an hour so they could all go together to assembly. While they were brushing their teeth in their room, Livvy told Beth that Zack was at a tutorial college in London.

'What's a tutorial college?'

'Like a crammer.'

Beth looked puzzled.

'No? It's a sort of day school – basically, they take anyone, mostly kids who've been expelled from other schools. The parents pay huge amounts of money to get their disgraced children through their exams.'

'I wonder why Zack bothers? All he ever wanted to do was act. Why is he even taking A Levels?' wondered Beth aloud.

'Ah, that'll be the duke. He only pays his allowance if Zack gets his A Levels, that's the deal.'

'Must be some allowance.'

There were six knocks on the door – three slow, three quick.

'Oh, for God's sake, come in. Why is everyone enjoying this so much?'

'Only me,' said Tab in a melodramatic whisper. 'Is everyone ready for stage two of Operation Ice Queen?'

Beth sighed and picked up her rucksack. Livvy and Tab followed her out to where the others were waiting. As they walked down the road to the main building, Guy pulled her aside.

'How're you doing, Kryptonite?'

'Never better, Robin.'

'Robin? I think you're mixing up your superheroes and their sidekicks.'

'I think you're mistaking me for someone who gives a shit. What do you want anyway?'

'Fancy a little something to calm your nerves?' He opened his rucksack and pointed to a small, half-empty bottle of tequila. Beth shook her head wordlessly.

They walked to the theatre for assembly and took their seats, to nudges and whispers. Beth stared ahead of her, her face blank. The headmaster gave a speech about the start of term, exams and how important it was for fifth- and sixth-formers in particular to knuckle down.

'And, as you will all doubtless be aware by now, there has been some media interest in one of our pupils.' He paused. 'We have a rule at Weatherbury Hall that will be strictly enforced – that every pupil here has a right to a normal education, no matter who they or their parents are. Any pupil who breaks this rule, who talks to the press or gives a statement, will be most severely punished. Two pupils who have already fallen foul of this will not be returning to Weatherbury Hall – Justin Ravensdale and Zachary Smythe.'

There was a gasp from the audience, and Beth looked around, bewildered.

Livvy whispered, 'Not everyone knew who sold the story.'

They listened as Mr Toms rambled on about other events in the term, including the election of head boy, head girl and prefects for the following year. Beth tried to listen but she was getting so many dirty looks, she felt her fragile composure draining away. As soon as assembly was over, flanked by Livvy and Mel, she hurried towards the exit. Beth looked left and right and all she could see was girls shaking their heads, some of them weeping and all of them looking up at her as she passed, giving her daggers. This was all she needed. An army of snivelling, love-struck schoolgirls, hating her.

That day and the next, and the day after that, and every day following, all eyes were on Beth as she mimicked being normal: always on time, homework finished, not a foot wrong, not a hair out of place. Sleep, classes, choir, sport, meals, common room, sleep and start it all over again. And again. And again.

When she was alone in her room, she would curl up into a ball on her bed, make herself as small as she could, and let her imagination rove. She missed Zack, even though she knew she shouldn't. His hands, his skin, his eyes, the way he looked at her, it was all seared onto her brain. When she closed her eyes, she could feel his hands all over her, pushing back her hair as he covered her with kisses. She knew, like Milo had said, that she should grow up and get over it, but she couldn't hold it together all the time. He didn't understand.

When Livvy was there, Beth would take off somewhere, into the woods or, if it was raining, into one of the bathrooms, stuffing a towel under the door and smoking furiously until she felt sick. She pushed her food around her plate at mealtimes, taking little bites every now and again so that nobody would notice and make a fuss.

She signed up for cross-country running as her summer sport, so she wouldn't have to train in a team. She ran as fast as she could, the ground tumbling away under her feet, gravity pulling her legs out into long strides. When she was sure she'd left the others behind, she would find a place to hide until they ran past her, and sat, smoking and thinking. Sometimes the route took in October Hill, where Milo had taken her on New Year's Day. She sat and stared at the changing cloud shapes in the sky and the patchwork fields, cut across by hedges and country roads, leading to the sea. Reluctantly, she hauled herself up from the cold ground and staggered back to school in last place.

She knew she should be grateful for the tight group of friends who spent as much time as they could hanging out with her. But all she wanted was to be alone. Either they irritated her with their constant worry about how she was coping, or they made a big drama about being her bodyguard, with secret signs and codes between them, none of which interested or amused her in the slightest.

Livvy was certain that she couldn't have kept her secret for much longer, and tried to explain to a sullen Beth how she had been living on borrowed time.

'I reckon you had until Speech Day, tops, before anyone recognised you. Look, I'll show you what I mean.' She held up her copy of the School List, which had the names and addresses of every pupil and teacher at the school. She pointed at names on the page and moved down it. 'This guy's parents are publishers. Her dad is a theatre producer. His mum is an opera singer and her dad is something in TV. Her dad is an actor, you know that already. The Markhams: politician and artist. The Ravensdales: journalists. Another actor. A designer. An ex-rock star. That's the kind of people who send their children to this school. They're arty, they're sometimes famous, they're all the same age as your mum and dad. There are very few nurses and car salesmen and social workers who can afford to send their children here. It's not that kind of school. So all it would have taken was for one of these parents to have seen you at Speech Day, and then the game would have been up.'

'Fine. Whatever you say. The truth were loud.'

'Exactamundo! Oh, right, I see. But yes. You know I'm talking sense.'

'I said fine. Just drop it, OK? You're only going on about it because you're pissed off I didn't tell you about my mum and dad before.'

225

Livvy looked hurt. 'That's not true. But while we're on the subject, you know, you don't talk to me about anything. You don't tell me anything important. I thought we were supposed to be friends.'

Beth curled up on her bed with her back to Livvy. 'I'm not used to having friends.'

'Well, get used to it then.'

The person with whom she could most relax was Edward. He matched her mood and preferred to keep away from the crowd. They played chess or went for walks down by the river. He never asked her about her parents and wasn't bothered by their glamour or fame, probably since his parents were also glamorous and famous. He did tell Beth that his mother had already known who she was. She was an artist, he explained, and had been part of that same in-crowd at the same time. When she first met Beth, she had seen the resemblance to her mother and had wondered whether Beth was the missing baby. She hadn't been nosy enough to ask, and hadn't told Edward, preferring to wait until Beth elected to tell them herself. Beth held everyone else at arm's length, including Milo.

Milo watched them together and didn't like to intrude, hoping that Edward might be able to bring more comfort to Beth than he ever could. He never thought of them as a couple, because they were too silent and cheerless with each other. It was more likely that Edward saw Beth as a substitute for his sister. Milo thought that Beth might be able to do him some good, too.

Every so often, he managed to persuade them to join the group, even if it was just for a quick drink on a Saturday night at the sixth-form common-room bar, or to come and watch a school cricket match. He was trying to hold it all together as best he could, but he had a feeling that Edward wasn't spending much time revising and Beth was merely going through the motions.

He spoke to Anne and James often on the phone, but could only reassure them that Beth wasn't going off the rails.

Once, on the phone to Anne, he read some graffiti on the phone-box wall – *Delilah is a bitch*. He'd heard a group of younger girls talking about 'Delilah' but didn't know anyone who had that name in the school. He asked Alice if she knew who Delilah was.

She looked sheepish. 'You really don't know?'

Milo shook his head.

'It's Beth. Everyone in the lower years hates her—'

'Yes, I know, because of Zack. Which is really unfair, by the way. But I don't get it – why Delilah?'

Alice laughed, half amused and half ashamed. 'It's not all because of Zack. Look, who did Delilah get her claws into?'

'Samson.' Milo was still puzzled.

'You still don't get it? That's very sweet, how modest you are. Come on, think – how did Delilah steal Samson's strength?'

Milo caught up. He blushed. He was Samson, with his shaved head. 'That's so stupid. I got them to shave my head in hospital when they stitched me up. It was nothing to do with Beth.'

Alice shrugged. 'You know what they say: why let truth get in the way of a good story?'

A few days before A Levels and GCSEs began, Milo heard his name spoken by a group of people gathered around the main school noticeboard. He stopped, then walked closer, wondering what was happening and why he was involved.

'Congrats, West.'

'Hey, Milo, nice one.'

Two younger girls giggled and blushed, then scurried away, nudging each other.

Of course – it must be the announcements for next year's prefects, sports captains and such. The committee dinner had been last night, Edward had told him. They'd made the final selection based on the school election – each pupil had a vote. Milo must have been re-elected captain of rugby.

As he approached the noticeboard, more and more people congratulated him, slapping him on the back, shaking his hand, making a big fuss about it, which was strange, because no one who was 1st XV captain in the lower sixth would ever be a surprise for the position in the upper sixth. He checked the list, starting at the bottom. There was his name, with the other team captains. His eyes travelled up the list, heads and deputy heads of houses, and finally, almost at the top, he found his name again. His eyes moved to the left and he had to double-check because he'd been made head boy. He stood there staring at the notice, not believing it. He thought that perhaps it was a joke and that someone would come along soon to take down the notice and put up the real one.

At last it sunk in. It was another few minutes before he could rouse himself to check the list again for his friends' names. Susanna, Henry and Livvy were prefects, but Beth's name was not on the list. Milo knew she wouldn't be bothered about it, but he was bothered for her. He ran his hand through his short hair, growing back at last and covering his scar, annoyed about the pettiness of everyone at the school. To the majority of the girls, especially below sixth-form level, Beth was the reason why their hero and heart-throb Zack had been kicked out. Never mind how many times Milo explained, with steadfast loyalty towards her, that it was Mr Markham who had insisted, Beth had never said anything against Zack, and he wasn't expelled anyway, his mum had taken him out of the school; it seemed that the truth would never be more important than the story they wanted to believe.

Milo saw Edward walking out of the library and asked him if he had time for a game of chess.

'Not today, I've got a German oral practice session. But congratulations, for head boy I mean. I'm so glad it's you.'

'What happened with Beth? Wasn't she even considered for anything?'

Edward looked annoyed. 'I argued her case at the committee dinner, but they can't consider anyone who hasn't got the votes from the rest of the school. It's a flawed system. Still, I don't suppose Beth is that bothered, is she? As she hates the limelight so much. See you, and well done again. Couldn't have happened to a nicer man.'

Chapter Twenty-One

Edward's A Levels – English, history, politics and German – were due to start the following week and he was totally unprepared, having done little or nothing since he got back from Berlin. He had a place at Cambridge to read law, conditional on at least three As, but he was a long way past caring about all that any more. Why, again, had it been so important to him? What did it matter?

The one thing he found he could really focus on was Beth. Zack was gone – the restraining order, the expulsion; he'd never be able to harm her or Bonnie again. What a blessed relief to be rid of that lowlife. Now Edward had a chance to keep the girls safe and that was all that mattered. Eventually, Beth would forget Zack and might – just might – come to see that it was Edward whom she really loved. He bought her presents and wrote her letters. He kept a diary to record his feelings about her. Late into the nights, he wrote stories about their future life together, imagining them somewhere far away from the people who wanted to do them harm and the places that meant nothing to them. *Beth Markham*, he wrote in these stories. *Edward and Beth Markham. B. M.*

He dreamt that she loved him and that she wanted him as much as he wanted her, disturbing dreams that sometimes morphed into violence. After he'd been woken up by a nightmare, he stayed awake all night, writing down what he had dreamt, hoping that if it were on the page, he could make it leave his head.

He spoke to Bonnie often, on the phone and also long, rambling conversations in his head. He spoke to her when he was alone, which was almost all the time, telling her about the mundane details of his day. In his head, Bonnie was riding, reading, recovering, a little happier every day. He couldn't remember what she'd really said and what he'd made up. He didn't care. It was all Bonnie anyway.

The Island became an alien place to him. He rushed from building to building, afraid to be outdoors for too long, sticking to the same routes, seeing threats in the faces of all the pupils and the teachers. He disliked the dining hall, but if Beth or Milo were there he would sit with them and if not, he would find a place alone, at a table near a wall, with his back to the room.

On the evening before his exams began, his mother called to wish him luck. She was looking forward to him being home for a while, when they were over, before he went up to university. They spoke about his eighteenth birthday, which was a week after the end of term, and she asked him if he'd like to have a party. She and his father would go with Bonnie to Scotland, so he could use the house without them 'cramping his style', and he could travel up to Edinburgh on the train the following day to meet them. At first he thought it was a terrible idea, but he remembered how he and Beth had enjoyed their weekend at his place, before everything started to go wrong, before he went to Berlin, before she and Zack got together. He thought, if she came, and Milo, and it was a fun party, with good music and lots of friends, that Beth would be sure to relax with him and let herself be persuaded that they were right together. So he said yes, and his mother sounded relieved.

'Try not to let things get on top of you, darling. You sound so tired.'

He and the other upper-sixth-formers, including Billy, Jake and Finn, started their exams, and Edward ransacked his brain, clutching at ideas he thought he'd read and learned a lifetime ago. His pen moved across the paper, line after line, words forming and reforming in his head and melting onto the pages in front of him.

And so it went on, day after day, the same routine, and he smiled and nodded when people asked him how it was going, and the leaden feeling inside him grew until he felt so heavy, he had to drag himself out of bed in the mornings.

A package arrived from his mother with the invitations for the party, professionally printed. She was hiring a catering service and a DJ. *All taken care of*, she wrote. *Hope your exams are going well; this party will be something to look forward to.* Edward handed out the invitations to everyone in his year, plus the group of Beth and Milo's friends from the lower sixth. Almost everyone accepted – it was the first time Edward had ever had a party. They were curious to see the home of the Foreign Secretary and wondered if Bonnie, the mysterious sister of their soon-to-be-ex-head boy, would be there.

On the day that Edward finished his final exam, he scraped back his chair from his desk, walked past the other desks in their neat rows and followed the rest of the pupils out of the sports hall into the bright late-morning sunshine. He felt like there should have been some sort of a fanfare, a crowd of cheering well-wishers waving flags and holding up banners saying *CONGRATULATIONS, EDWARD MARKHAM.*

There was nothing. He felt deflated and empty as he looked at the backs of the others as they jumped and screamed with joy, throwing bags, notes and files into the air.

He didn't know what to do with himself. He wandered down to the school post office to see if Bonnie had written, but there wasn't a letter from her, so he drifted towards the tennis courts behind the main school building. He watched a couple of games and lay back on the grass slope, wondering what was going to happen next. Not just this afternoon, which stretched yawningly in front of him, but tomorrow, and the weekend, and the summer holidays and the rest of his life.

This time last year he'd been so sure of his future. Now he saw it only in the vaguest and dullest way, like a mist had descended and obscured what had been the clear path ahead. His head felt scrambled and he couldn't unscramble it. Was this normal? It didn't used to be.

The sun thrummed onto his head. The grass was damp and cool beneath his shirt. He sat up with a start and remembered that Beth had asked him to stop by her room after the exam. Quick; he mustn't on any account miss her. He scrambled back up the slope and walked briskly up the hill towards her house. He knocked on the window, but neither she nor Livvy were there. As Edward cursed in disappointment and anger at missing a chance of spending time with Beth, a piece of paper on her desk caught his eye. He could read his name written on it in large purple letters. He hurried round to the front door of Norcombe House and sprinted to Livvy and Beth's room. It was a note to him with instructions and a map.

The map showed the way to Greenhill Bridge. Milo had told Edward about this place, but it was outside the school's boundaries so he'd never been. It was upstream of the school, about half an hour's walk through the woods and along the river. Underneath the bridge was a weir where you could swim and plenty of shade and hiding places. He wasted no more time, taking the path into the cool, dappled woods.

It was a good map and he had no trouble finding the right place. When he drew nearer he could hear voices, so it wasn't only Beth, Edward thought with regret. When he emerged from the woods, he saw BJ, Livvy, Henry, Guy, Milo and Beth lying on the grass. There were rucksacks and a couple of towels, some Tesco shopping bags and a guitar. They shouted hellos and made room for him between Livvy and Beth.

'How did your exam go?'

'How does it feel to be finished?'

'Where were you? We waited for ages.'

'Did you see Melanie or Susanna and Finn? We lost them.'

He shrugged, shook his head and smiled, relaxing and forgetting the tension of the exams. Billy lit up and passed round a joint. Edward had never tried marijuana before, so he watched Billy and Livvy when they took a drag and when she passed it to him, he took it and raised it to his mouth.

'Ed – are you sure?' Beth whispered to him. Everyone was staring at him, amazed. Milo had frown lines across his forehead.

'Well, I'm not really head boy any more, am I?' Edward put the joint in his mouth, pressing it lightly between his dry lips. His heart beat more quickly as he breathed in the dry, bitter smoke filling his mouth, and swallowed it. He gave a splutter and smiled. 'I don't feel anything.' He passed it on to Beth.

'Sometimes you don't, the first time.'

Everyone had a drag except for Milo, who passed the joint straight on to Melanie, who had arrived with Susanna and Finn. Milo walked over to the river and retrieved a six-pack of beer which he'd hidden last night between two rocks in the water, one of which he opened and the rest he passed round. Edward shared with Beth, enjoying the cool liquid trickling down his parched throat and the feeling that his lips were where hers had been a few seconds before. When the joint came round to him a second time, he felt his head lighten as he breathed in. It rippled through him gently and his shoulders relaxed as he exhaled.

'Oh.' He lifted his head up towards the cloudless sky and leant back on his elbows.

'Lovely, isn't it?' said Beth, lying down next to him.

'Lovely.' He closed his eyes and opened them again as his head span. 'Better with your eyes open.'

They finished the first beer and drank another. Beth was humming a tune, and someone asked her what it was.

'Sing it for us, will you?'

'Only if Milo plays the guitar.' She sat up and turned her face to him with a sly smile.

'What? West, can you play the guitar?'

He blushed. 'I told you not to tell anyone.'

Edward felt a pang of jealousy. How come Beth knew so much about Milo? What other secrets did they have?

'Why isn't Beth allowed to tell us?'

Milo shrugged.

Beth was laughing – the first time Edward had seen her laughing for ages. 'It's because he thinks he looks stupid when he plays.'

'OK, this is why I don't tell you stuff,' muttered Milo.

'Oh, come on, big man, you can't look any more stupid than usual,' said Guy.

Milo was shaking his head. 'Cheers for that.'

Everyone was doubled over with laughter.

'What does he look like, Beth?'

'Well, he just sort of looks very... concentrate-y.'

'Is it a bit like this?' asked Guy, putting his tongue out of the corner of his mouth and screwing up his eyes.

'Yes. Just like that. How did you know?'

'Oh, because that's how he looks when he's in class.'

'And when he's working in the library.'

'And when he's deciding what to eat.'

'And when he's masturbating,' added Guy.

Milo said, 'I'm going for a swim.' He took off his T-shirt and shorts, leaving on his boxer shorts, which were grey and had clearly seen better days.

Melanie stood up. 'I'll come too.'

There were whistles and shrieks of delight, but Milo ignored them all and strode into the cool water, lying on his back in the middle of the river and letting the current carry him downstream. Melanie sat on the bank in her underwear with her legs dangling into the water. Jake and Guy crept up behind her, lifted her by the arms and threw her in, jumping in themselves and splashing her as she spluttered and swore at them. The others started stripping off to their underwear. They all had tan marks around their necks and upper arms and legs. Soon Edward and Beth were the only ones left on the blanket.

'You not going in?' she asked him.

'I will if you will.'

'I need a wee first.' She stood up, stretched and walked towards the trees.

Edward caught up with her. 'I'll come and guard you.' She gave him a funny look, so he said, 'I'll look the other way, promise.' He turned his back and watched the river as he heard a stream of liquid hitting the ground.

She moved around the tree and leant her forehead against its rough bark. 'Thanks. Pissing in the great outdoors is not my favourite thing. Sometimes I wish I was a boy.'

Edward turned to her and fastened his eyes on hers. 'I never wish you were a boy,' he said softly, and moved closer.

'Don't, Ed.' She looked sad and shook her head. 'Not here.'

'Where, then?'

'No, I didn't mean that. I mean I don't want you to kiss me.' She moved around him, taking off her T-shirt as she walked, throwing it on the pile of clothes, hopping out of her skirt and running towards the river in her plain white bra and knickers.

There was a pause as almost everyone turned towards her, the girls wishing they looked like her, the boys wishing they could, just once even, get their hands on that perfect, lithe body. Edward's gaze moved from Beth over everyone and landed on Milo, who lay in the water staring fixedly up at the cloudless sky.

The moment of quiet was broken as, with a splash, she jumped in.

They dried off in the sun. Edward smoked more and felt a languor in his body and a fuzzy happiness in his brain. The sun was seeping through his closed eyelids and into every pore of his skin, drying and warming him. He sighed with pleasure. He sat up slowly and looked around him. Beth was lying on her side next to Livvy, talking to her in an undertone. Henry was reading a magazine. Susanna and Finn were sitting opposite each other, playing cards. Billy and Jake were having an arm-wrestling contest on a dead tree branch, bleached white by the sun, with Guy adjudicating. Milo was sitting on the riverbank, talking to Melanie, who was leaning back on her hands, face turned up to the sun, eyes closed. As Edward watched, Milo leant towards her and kissed her neck. Edward glanced at the group – nobody was looking that way except for him. Melanie turned her face to Milo's and kissed him on the mouth. He shifted his body awkwardly nearer to her and Edward could see that the kisses were getting quicker, more urgent. Milo stopped and looked down at the river. Melanie dipped her face and asked him something. He nodded his head.

Edward checked to see if anyone else had seen the kiss. They were all doing exactly the same as before. Had he imagined it? He heard a splash and Milo was in the river again. Melanie came back and lay on the blanket next to Finn and Susanna, with a small smile on her face.

BJ and Guy hurtled across from the woods, sweating and jostling each other.

'We're bored. Wake up, everyone. Let's play Truth or Dare.'

'What are you, thirteen?' complained Livvy.

But Susanna and Finn put down their cards and everyone sat up.

Milo came over from the river and shook himself all over them, like a wet dog. He parked himself next to Melanie and handed out more beers. 'What's going on?'

'Truth or Dare.'

Milo raised his eyebrows. Edward caught a sideways look from him to Melanie.

Billy said, 'I'll start. With… you, little sis.'

Livvy groaned.

'Truth or dare?'

'Truth,' she said resignedly.

'OK.' Billy rubbed his hands together. 'Have you been all the way with Henry?'

'Oh God, you really are thirteen. Why does this always have to be about sex? No, I have not fucked Henry, you perv. Your turn. Truth or dare?'

'Dare.'

'Jump off the bridge into the water.'

Milo started to object that the water wasn't deep enough, but Billy sprinted to the bridge, vaulted over the railing and splashed into the water.

'Too easy,' he shouted. 'Whose turn now?'

Jake asked Susanna, 'Truth or dare?'

'Truth.'

'Have you and Finn ever had a threesome?'

'Why, are you offering?'

Finn spurted beer out of his nose and everyone cracked up.

Susanna asked Edward, and to everyone's surprise he said, 'Dare.'

'Who are you and what have you done with Markham?' said Guy.

Susanna whispered something to Finn, who nodded and fell back laughing. 'Strip off.'

'Wh… what?'

Susanna shrugged. 'I've always wanted to see a naked head boy.'

Edward looked around. 'Be very afraid, Milo, your turn next.' But as he said it, he was already taking off his shorts. He took a deep breath and pulled down the elastic on his boxers. The girls screamed with embarrassment and Edward stood there with his arms held high above his head until someone told him to put it away. He got dressed again and sat down, elated and red in the face. Livvy was whispering something in Beth's ear, giggling.

'My turn. Milo – truth or dare?' asked Edward.

'There's no way I'm getting my kit off. Truth.'

Edward blurted out, 'Who would you rather kiss, right here, right now – Beth or Melanie?'

There was a heavy silence. Edward's eyes darted to Beth, who was trying to smile. Around the circle, he saw Milo frown and flash a glance at the river. Milo turned back towards Edward, who dropped his gaze. Everyone was waiting, holding their breath.

Milo twisted to Melanie and kissed her, gently holding the side of her head. The kiss went on for ages, and everyone was screaming with laughter and whooping.

'When you choose "truth" you're only supposed to say the answer, not *do* it.'

Milo and Melanie broke apart. She was grinning coyly, and Milo kept his eyes only on her.

The atmosphere had changed. Edward was appalled at himself. Why the hell had he said that? Milo had always been a good friend to him, but Edward had just put him in the awkward position of either hurting Melanie's feelings, which he was too kind to do, or lying about his feelings for Beth, which he was too honest to do. Edward sat on the grass and wished with all his heart that he could disappear.

Milo was seething. He hadn't meant it to happen, that kiss by the river, but he'd felt drunk and he liked Melanie, and knew she liked him, and she was pretty, and she was there. Obviously Edward had seen them kiss, and how could he have asked the one question that would really put him on the spot?

Beth couldn't get her head around what had just happened. It was too much to process. All she knew was that when she saw Milo kissing Melanie with such obvious passion, her heart went cold. She tried to catch his eye, but he wouldn't look at her.

The others could only guess at what was going on. Something was certainly strange between Milo, Edward and Beth, but more importantly, big news – Milo had kissed Melanie. Livvy and Susanna were swooning because it had been so strong and romantic. BJ, Finn, Henry and Guy couldn't believe that Milo had been so... dynamic.

They packed up their stuff and headed through the woods towards school, each person holding back the branches for the next one. Sunburnt and spaced out, they peeled off towards their separate houses, calling their tired goodbyes. As Finn was walking Susanna up to her house, they heard quick footsteps behind them and Jake tapped her on the shoulder.

'I'm leaving tomorrow. Any chance of that threesome?'

Chapter Twenty-Two

'Right, thank Christ for that,' said Livvy the following day. 'I've been waiting for years to get rid of my brothers.'

She turned to Beth, who was still waving at the taxi with BJ and Edward in it. Other upper-sixth-formers milled around, climbing into cars, saying goodbyes, some crying, some whooping with joy.

'Let's spend the afternoon having a beauty session. Sav's got this crazy wax from Kenya, we can wax our legs, and I want to do face packs, pedicures, the lot. Are you up for it?'

Beth was sad about Edward leaving, but after he'd tried to kiss her again at the river, and after all that kissing between Milo and Melanie, it would be good to spend some time alone with the girls.

'Sure, sounds lovely. Is Mel coming?'

'I asked her, but she said she was busy.' Livvy wiggled her eyebrows and left unsaid what they both knew – that Mel was more than likely with Milo.

Beth thought of his cottage, of October Hill and the secret

garden. If he really liked her, these places would become Mel's places. There it was again: that pang in her heart. Like someone had hit her with a sharp metal object.

There were four weeks until the end of term. Bowing finally to the pressure from Livvy and the other girls, Beth began to relax and enjoy herself more. She felt safe at The Island. Mr Toms had stuck to his word and there were no more stories in the press about her or her family. James and Anne wanted to take her away over the summer, to a place they'd found on a remote beach in Thailand, which they were going to rent for the whole of August. But Beth thought of St Emit, of Joel and his gang of locals, and knew that they'd have more fun there, surfing and playing hide-and-seek with anyone who got too nosy. She wrote Joel a letter, care of the surf shop, and he wrote back, saying he knew the perfect house to hire; they'd set it up and make all the preparations. He couldn't wait to see her and his sweatshirt. She began to count the days.

It wasn't that Beth had forgotten about her predicament and about Zack. But as the days trickled by, she thought less and less about him and what he'd done to her, and began to gain some perspective. Milo was right: it could have been worse. She sometimes had a fleeting memory of something Zack had said, a touch or a look, but these moments became fewer and easier to bear.

It was difficult for her to travel up to London for the English A Level theatre trip to see *The Tempest*. In the coach she fretted about meeting Zack. Henry had been assigned to look after her as he was in her English set and he tried his best to calm her down.

'Beth, my darling, there's no way in the world you'll see him. With ten zillion people living in London, why would you bump into him?'

'Because he's still doing English A Level and *The Tempest* is a set text. So of course, just my luck, he'll definitely be there tonight. Anyway,' she shook her head and looked out of the window, 'it's not only him. I haven't been in a crowd of people since Easter. What if someone recognises me? I should have stayed at school.' She sighed. 'Let's talk about something else. Let's talk about the lovely Livvy.'

It was Henry's turn to sigh. He was silent for a moment before he spoke in a low voice. 'I'd rather talk about the lovely Milo. That Kiss at Greenhill. Let's talk about that.'

Beth blinked. 'Are you saying what I think you're saying?'

Henry turned to her and fastened his gaze on her. 'I am. At least, I think I am. I adore Livvy, she's like a sister to me. But when I dream about That Kiss, which I think it's fair to say we all do, I dream about Milo, not Melanie. And the way he was as Seth. Mmm. So sexy. Do you know what I mean?'

'Henry, this is huge. I had no idea.' She gripped his hand, and he squeezed hers back.

'Neither did I, really.'

'Who else knows? Why are you telling me?'

Henry shrugged. 'No one else. I figured you know how to keep a secret. Plus, if there's anyone who understands unrequited love with regards to Mr West, it's you.'

'I don't know what you're talking about. You've got completely the wrong idea. I've never been interested in him like that.'

'OK, lady, you keep telling yourself that.'

Beth harrumphed, turned away and stared out of the window. She had thought about that kiss, she'd listened to Livvy describing every minute detail of it to Tab and Sav. Like something out of a film, the way Milo's soft and yet strong hand touched Melanie's face, kissing like nobody else was there, like they were the only two people in the world. Since then, Mel had been walking around school with a dazed look on her face, spending every minute by his side, the two of them – nicknamed 'Milonie' – disappearing off together whenever they could.

Beth thought about all the times she'd been alone with

Milo, when he'd tried to tell her how he felt about her, and how dismissive she'd always been. She'd made him promise to leave her alone, she'd flirted with his friend and gone out with his nemesis, and – big surprise – he'd told her that he wasn't interested in her any more. There were times when she saw him looking at her and she thought, *He still loves me*, but she couldn't be sure it wasn't wishful thinking.

Wishful thinking? What on earth was she going on about? She was being ridiculous. Nothing was ever going to happen with Milo. He was her friend. Her solid, decent, kind, loyal friend. After she'd run out of adjectives and to take her mind off Milo, she tried to imagine Henry snogging him, and started giggling.

'What? What is it?' demanded Henry.

'I'm… I'm…' She was doubled over with laughter and had tears in her eyes. 'I'm trying to imagine' – she hiccupped – 'you seducing Milo.'

'Don't make me regret I told you.' But he couldn't help joining in. 'Seriously though, how am I going to tell Livvy?'

'She's a big girl. We'll think of something.'

The only other drama that evening was onstage – there was no sighting of Zack and nobody recognised Beth. When the coach got back from London it was past midnight. Beth slid into bed quietly, but Livvy was wide awake.

Livvy sat up and turned on the light by her bed. 'You will never guess what.'

'What?'

'We were in the common room tonight and the TV was on; nobody was watching it really because all the boys were talking about sport and all the girls were talking about shopping, you know—'

'Livs, get to the point, will you? I'm knackered.'

'OK, well, anyway, bam: on the TV screen, there's Zack's face – and he's on *The Bill*!'

'What do you mean, *The Bill*? As in—?'

'As in the rubbish cop programme, yes. He was an extra in it, he had literally one line. We were all sitting there, mouths open. Honestly, we were wetting ourselves. It was so… desperate. I wish you'd seen it.'

'He probably did it to get his Equity card.'

'Yeah, well, he can keep telling himself that.'

Beth cheered up when she saw him on *The Bill*, and she had to agree with Livvy, it was really lame. One of the fifth-formers had taped it and let Livvy borrow it from her. Beth had no idea whether the big-break American TV show had all been a crock of shit, but this was about as far away from Beverly Hills as you could get.

After her conversation with Henry on the coach, she tried to put thoughts of Milo out of her head completely. He was the same Milo as ever, but with a spring in his step. It was all paying off, his hard work at school and his positive way of seeing things. He was going to have one hell of a university application form next year – he was a scholar, rugby captain and head boy. Beth did notice, however, that he was looking thinner than she'd ever seen him. At mealtimes he shovelled as much food as he could into his mouth, and Beth wasn't the only one to notice.

'Whoa, big man, not eaten for a week?' asked Guy, looking at Milo's tray, piled with plates of food.

'Hungry,' mumbled Milo.

'Too much sex, my friend.' Guy winked at Melanie, who was sitting next to Milo. She rolled her eyes. Milo glared at him but didn't stop eating.

Melanie said in a low voice to him, 'Are you staying at the cottage tonight? I could sneak down later…'

Milo shook his head and gulped down a mouthful. 'Told you, can't stay there at the moment. Electricity's on the blink.'

'That's OK, we can keep each other warm.' She squeezed his leg. He pulled it away from her.

'No. It's too big a risk. If I get chucked out of here, that's it for me. Don't ask me again. Ever.' His voice had risen, and everyone was listening. Beth saw him quickly glance up at Guy with a grim look on his face. Melanie had tears in her eyes.

Guy pushed himself up from the bench. 'After you've licked that plate clean, you coming for a run?' he said to Milo.

But Milo shook his head again, finished eating and turned to Melanie. He asked her something quietly, she nodded, and they got up and left together.

Guy sat down again. 'Trouble in paradise.'

Beth tried to hide the smile that was creeping onto her lips. Especially when she looked at Henry and he was doing the same.

She received a letter from Edward, who was at home with Bonnie and their mother and the horses. The letter was strange, full of disconnected sentences, random thoughts and too many exclamation marks. Milo also had a letter, but he wouldn't show it to her.

Two weeks until the end of term. Beth, Anne and James would go to Cornwall on the first day of the holidays, and everyone had an open invitation to stay with them. On the nights before and after Edward's party there would be a full house – the Roses, Finn and Susanna, Henry, Guy and Tab were all booked in.

Milo was going to stay at Edward's house. Edward had written to apologise for the way he'd behaved at the river. He was so angry with himself, he wrote, and begged for forgiveness. He hadn't been thinking clearly and it would never happen again. Milo forgave him immediately.

Mel wasn't coming to the party. After her involvement in the fiasco at Easter, her parents had told her she had to get a holiday job, so she was au pairing for some family friends who were spending the whole summer on Sardinia.

Milo was relieved. He'd told Melanie he wouldn't sleep with her at school and she had tried everything to get him to change his mind, sulking, cajoling and flirting. Some of the things she told him she'd do to him made him break out in a sweat. But he wouldn't budge. He got the feeling that the minute she got him on his own outside of school, she would be unstoppable.

Guy thought he was off his rocker. They were cycling no-hands down the main drive, sharing a packet of crisps.

'A girl, quite a hot girl actually, wants to shag you. She'll do anything you want, she's so dirty, and you refuse. *What are you on?*'

Milo shrugged.

'I can't understand you sometimes, Milo. Are you even of the male species?'

'Why don't you shag her, if you think she's so hot?'

'I said "quite hot". I'm not stirring your cold porridge.'

'But I haven't... umm... stirred her porridge,' said Milo, wincing at the words.

'So, in summary: you won't shag her, even though she's gagging for it, and she's your girlfriend, but you think I should...?'

Milo gave him a despairing look and conceded, 'I'm confused about why we're having this conversation.'

'Join the club.'

Milo didn't really know what to do about Melanie. She was a nice girl, and he liked kissing her a lot and he liked talking to her a bit, but he didn't feel there was much more to it than that. Considering that he'd started it all, with those kisses at the river, he felt pretty bad about ending it with her. So he let it carry on, and he thought maybe he could write her a letter in the holidays or let it drift into nothing. It wasn't much of a plan, as Livvy would say, but it was all he could think of.

Milo's plans for the holiday, apart from the party, were the same as ever. He had four weeks' work at The Island and two weeks at Melchester Racecourse. Mrs Toms had set up some work experience for him at a veterinary surgery in Melchester. He might get a few shifts in the Buck's Head if he asked the landlord, who was an old friend of his dad's and the man who had taught Milo, as a child, to swear. Milo had by this time nearly run out of his Easter holiday money; he'd had the phone and the electricity cut off, which he thought he could do without for the rest of the summer. He was very relieved that he could start earning again and vowed to be more careful next year, and not go buying watches for people, and he'd have to hitch-hike everywhere. He'd had a piece of luck, because the groundsman offered to buy his mum's Beatles records off him and he'd made five hundred pounds. He had been gobsmacked when that sum had been mentioned, and although he was sad to lose half of his mum's music collection, he was desperate for the money and told himself not to be sentimental about the records.

In the last week of term, all anyone could talk about was the holidays. On the Friday, all the upper-sixth-formers were due back at school for Speech Day, at the end of which everyone else would leave, so that the school was empty for everyone but the upper sixth for the Leavers' Ball.

On Thursday afternoon, Beth found a note pushed under her door. She opened it and read:

Dickon requests the presence of Mary at ten o'clock.

She went to bed as usual and later crept out of her window, which Livvy closed behind her, giggling and whispering, 'Don't do anything I wouldn't.'

'It's not like that,' insisted Beth.

'Then why are you wearing perfume?'

Beth ignored her.

'And lipstick. I want to see all that lipstick still on your lips later.'

When Beth arrived at the walled garden gate, she knocked gently and heard Milo's footsteps on the gravel before he opened it, filling the doorway, and ushered her inside. In the middle of the grass square, he'd spread out blankets and had brought food and a bottle of wine. There were even a couple of candles. She smiled.

'Mel busy tonight?'

'No idea. I've never brought her here.'

'How come?'

'I promised you, this place was only for us. Plus, she'd probably only want to come here and...'

Beth scowled at him. She wandered over to the blanket and lay down on her front. 'Just because you're head boy and you're finally getting laid, it doesn't mean you should become all big-headed, you know. It doesn't suit you.'

He sat next to her. As he did so, he brushed her leg with his arm. 'I'll keep that in mind. But, for the record, I'm not... um... getting laid.'

Beth sat up and pretended to be busy pouring wine into two plastic cups. Her hands were shaking. She was so relieved, she could have cried. What on earth was going on with her? She couldn't understand why her heart was beating so fast. Her palms were sweaty and she nearly dropped the wine.

She was on the point of turning up her face towards his, when he said, 'Anyway, enough about that. Are you looking forward to Edward's party? How are things with him, d'you reckon?'

Edward. He wants to talk about Edward. Of course. She turned around to Milo and handed over a cup, afterwards lighting a cigarette. One of her hands was next to his on the blanket; their little fingers were millimetres away from each other.

'Umm. I don't really know. He'll probably be OK, now that his exams are over; it'll do him good to be at home. He said in his last letter that Bonnie's doing really well too. They're even thinking about asking if she can come back to The Island for her sixth form.'

'Can I ask you something? I'm not being nosy, or trying to hassle you...'

'Once again, Milo, please spit it out.'

'Has he… have you… you know?'

'Mmm, not at all nosy, then? No, Milo, he hasn't and we haven't. I won't and he isn't. We're not and he never will be.'

Milo scratched his ear. 'Well, that's good to know. I think.'

'I… if you must know, I had a conversation with him before he left school. He's sort of… I think he's under the impression that I'm going to succumb to his charms at his party.'

'And are you?'

'I just told you, I think in a very clear and concise way, that I won't.'

Milo thought about it. 'I'm glad Zack's gone. And I'm glad Edward's gone now too, in a way.'

He reached across her to pull some crisps out of a bag and she breathed in his smell, of sweat and soap and something minty. Her heart started thumping again. She clenched her fists.

'You know, you once told me that you weren't interested in having a boyfriend. Do you remember?'

She nodded and smiled.

'You know what I think? Zack was bad news, and Edward, well, he's crazy about you, but he's kind of intense. I think…' he looked her right in the eyes, thickening the air between them, '…next year you should try to stay single. What do you think?'

The air deflated. *Wrong, wrong, wrong. Smile harder, nod, don't give it away.* 'Yes, good idea. Excellent idea. I'll do that.'

Not far off, outside the garden, they heard a whirring and grinding sound. They looked at each other, confused, and Milo put his finger to his lips. Beth stubbed out her cigarette. They crept to the door and slowly opened it, peering out into the darkness in the direction of the noise. They couldn't see a thing.

'What's going on? Is it something to do with Speech Day?' she whispered.

'Beats me.' He shrugged his shoulders. 'I've got a bad feeling about this. It's nothing to do with the grounds staff.' He mulled it over and glanced at the blanket with regret. 'I hate to say it, but I think we should call it a night. There's something about this – it's dodgy, I know it is, and when one of the teachers hears what we're hearing, we should be safely tucked up in our beds.'

Beth helped him pack up the rest of their picnic. They left everything in the shed and scarpered back to their houses.

In the morning, they had lessons until lunchtime, after which Speech Day would begin. But there was a rumour going around that something was happening on the sports fields, so at breaktime Livvy and Beth wandered down with a large crowd towards the cricket pitch. They saw it from half a mile away. Someone had made a beach volleyball court, complete with net and pristine sand, on the grass next to the road, where every car that passed would see it. There was a banner proclaiming that the beach volleyball tournament would begin after the speeches.

'I don't get it,' said Beth. 'Since when was there a beach volleyball tournament?'

'It's a prank.' Livvy stared in wonder at the sight.

'But why? What is the point of that?'

'There's no point to a prank. The point *is* the prank.'

'Livs.' She waved her hand in front of Livvy's glazed-over eyes. 'I'm terrified to ask you this but... do you know who did this... prank?'

Livvy nodded very slowly. 'This has got BJ written all over it.'

'No it hasn't, that would've been too obvious,' shouted voices behind them. 'Hello, little sis. Hello, Atkinson.'

Chapter Twenty-Three

Milo spent the first week of the summer holidays supervising the clear-up of BJ's beach volleyball court, which had been a big hit on Speech Day with parents and pupils alike. Mr Toms – who had raged about it in private – had taken his wife's excellent advice and pretended to the parents that it had been planned as an official part of Speech Day. Milo hadn't complained about the extra work, as he directed the diggers and trucks that Mr Rose had sent from his farm. Billy and Jake had been jubilant about their prank. It had taken weeks of planning and Milo suspected that Mr Rose had been involved as well. Nobody would ever forget it, which was exactly the effect they wanted, and they'd got away with it because of Mr Toms having to save face.

Milo had been called up to the stage to receive his head boy badge, handed over by Edward, and had worn the new suit that he'd bought in Melchester with his Beatles money. Edward had shaken his hand proudly, Guy had whooped loudly, Beth and Livvy had hugged him, and Mrs Toms was in floods of tears.

The morning after the Leavers' Ball, BJ had stopped off at Milo's cottage. They were grey-skinned underneath their suntans and Milo plied them with coffee, worried that they were still drunk and about to drive home. But he couldn't stop them – they had another party to get to, and one every night until Edward's party, the day after which they were going Interrailing around Europe for the summer. It had been an awesome night. Edward had been so smashed that they'd had to stop him from taking off all his clothes in the middle of the dance floor. He'd woken up in the morning on the roof of the school and didn't know how he'd got there. Milo knew two people who might have been involved.

The day before Edward's party, Milo hitch-hiked to Bodmin station, where Edward picked him up, as they'd agreed. Edward was on good form. He was more relaxed than Milo had seen him in ages, since last winter in fact. Bonnie was looking well, a little thinner and paler than he remembered her, but happy. They had dinner and Mrs Markham was kind and effusive about Milo becoming head boy. Everyone had an early night. Milo slept late and by the time he woke up, Mr and Mrs Markham and Bonnie had already left for Scotland.

The day of the party was swelteringly hot. A heat haze rippled off the park and Edward and Milo spent the morning lazing in the shade in their shorts. Mid afternoon, when the caterers arrived, they tried to help but the manager told them to go away and relax, as they were getting in the way, so they went back to the shade and played chess and drank a cold beer. Edward was starting to tense up again. Milo could see he was distracted and beat him easily and quickly, again and again before Edward gave up altogether.

'What are we supposed to be wearing tonight?' asked Milo, half asleep on the dry, brown grass. He couldn't even be bothered to open his eyes, he was so hot.

'Nothing. We should wear nothing. Birthday suits.'

Milo groaned. 'Not that again. It's becoming a habit with you. The Naked Head Boy. They'll write a story about you in *Viz*.'

At the rented house in St Emit, Beth searched through all the clothes in her wardrobe and decided on a short skirt and a black top with spaghetti straps.

'What are you wearing black for, in this heat?' said Livvy, in a sundress. She was flushed and sweating, but looked gorgeous, thought Beth fondly. 'Not that you don't look like an angel, as usual,' continued Livvy. 'This is going to be such a fab party. I can't wait.' She lowered her voice. 'D'you think I should sleep with Henry tonight?'

Beth smiled lovingly at her friend and said, 'Um, Livs, we need to talk...'

Edward paced through the house with the catering manager, checking that everything was in the right place, picking up things and putting them down again, finding fault when it all looked perfect. There were long tables and benches set out on the patio and the doors and windows to the house had been flung open in the hope that a non-existent breeze would cool it. From the kitchen drifted smells of delicious food. The living-room floor had been cleared for dancing and the DJ was setting up. Outside, bunting and strings of lights had been hung on every tree. There were kegs of beer and champagne bottles cooling in large tubs of ice.

Milo had a cold shower, changed into shorts and a clean white T-shirt and wandered downstairs as Edward was coming up to find him. Milo noticed that Edward's hands were shaking.

'Help me choose what to wear, will you, Milo?'

He followed Edward upstairs and thought he could hear him muttering to himself, 'What will she like, what's her favourite colour, what did she say that time...?'

Up in his room, Edward rummaged around and pulled out all his clothes and dumped them on the bed.

Milo smiled. 'It looks to me like a pair of khaki shorts and a white shirt is the way to go.' Those were the only colours that he had, over and over again. 'Are you OK? Looking forward to tonight?' They could hear the DJ practising in the background.

'Yes, yes, I think Beth will like it.' Edward looked up at Milo. 'Have you spoken to her? Did she say anything at the end of term?'

Milo didn't know what to tell him.

Edward went on, 'You know her well, she's your friend. What would you say are my chances with her? I can't stop thinking about her. I really think she likes me, what do you think?'

'I—'

'Of course, I know you liked her too, but you're with Melanie now, so that's all OK with us now, isn't it? I think, if Beth likes all this' – he waved his hand in the direction of the music – 'I think it could be tonight, do you think…?'

'Don't get your hopes up too much, OK? It's not exactly been an easy time for her lately.'

'Yes, yes, I know all that, but she's such a good girl. She knows it's right. She must do. It's all coming together.'

At Waterloo station, two boys were standing on the platform, waiting for the train to Exonbury.

'Sure you're not coming?' asked one.

'No, it's a waste of time. Look, are you sure this is a good idea? Why not blow it off? Bonnie probably won't be there anyway.'

'I'm going. At least Beth'll be there.'

'What do you think's going to happen with her?'

The first boy shrugged. 'We'll see. She's still hot. Perhaps she's been missing me.'

'You're deluding yourself.'

'Well, it's worth a try.' The train pulled up at the platform and Zack climbed on. 'You know how I like a challenge, Justin.'

The St Emit group was ready to leave for the party. Billy and Jake were wearing only shorts and flip-flops. Guy's pockets were bulging with packets of condoms; he had to take them all out before he could even sit down. Finn and Susanna sat either side of him in BJ's car. Henry, Livvy and Tab went in Beth's car. Livvy had been knocked for six about Henry, but once she got over the shock, it all made sense and she was even pleased about it. It had frustrated her on several occasions that Henry hadn't fancied her as much as she did him. Now she knew why.

'So,' she said, rubbing her hands together as they drove towards Bodmin, 'Who else is coming to the party? I feel like lurve is in the air tonight.'

They went through the names of all the boys they knew, and Henry wanted to give them all marks out of ten, so that kept them busy until they turned into the Markhams' driveway. Edward got nine, because he was so handsome and was the host.

'Wait, we forgot about Milo. What score does he get?'

Beth, Henry, Livvy and Tab all shouted together, 'Eleven!'

Edward and Milo heard the first few cars and taxis arriving, and Edward bounded downstairs to welcome everyone. He stood at the bottom of the stairs and said, 'Thanks for being such a good mate, Milo. I really appreciate it.'

Milo smiled awkwardly but didn't reply.

'Things are going to be great from now on. Nothing's going to go wrong.'

Chapter Twenty-Four

It was a legendary party. A party that was talked about for months and years afterwards. There was enough champagne to make every single person sick, but no one was. There were new couples made and old ones unmade, but no fights and no tears. The heat was stifling, but the DJ mixed in segments of songs about rain – *I Wish It Would Rain*; *I Can't Stand the Rain*; *It's Raining Men* – that signalled it was time for everyone to run outside and cool down under the lawn sprinkler.

There was a feeling at that party that anything could happen.

About an hour after the St Emit group had arrived, a line of taxis snaked up the driveway: the guests from the London train. Sleeping bags and rucksacks were dumped upstairs, champagne bottles were popped, outfits admired, all with the maximum of noise and spectacle. Milo watched quietly as people who'd seen each other only last week greeted each other as though it had been years. He slipped into the kitchen to see if he could find a beer and got chatting to a very pretty waitress. There was a tap on his shoulder.

'West, sorry to interrupt.' A friend of Milo's from the rugby team was standing behind him, grinning at the waitress. 'Thought I should give you a heads-up. It might be nothing, but on the train, in a different carriage, a bunch of us thought we saw Zack.'

Milo's thoughts snapped away from the girl. 'Zack? On the same train?'

'Yup. We thought it was strange, given what he did to Atkinson, but maybe…? Did Markham invite him?'

'No, no way. Not possible. Sure it was him?'

'Fairly. Maybe he was on his way somewhere else. We didn't see him change at Exonbury.'

Milo mused over this information, and whether he should tell Edward or Beth. He decided it had to be a coincidence – after all, everyone else on that train was already at the party. And Edward would surely have told him if he'd invited Zack.

The pretty waitress left to hand out drinks, so Milo wandered through to the patio and watched the dancing for a while. Beth was on the dance floor with Edward, deep in conversation, oblivious to everyone else. He had his hand on her lower back, and his other hand was on her bare shoulder. The sun was sinking and the heat was going out of the day. Milo shivered and put down his beer. He didn't feel like drinking it any more.

He sat chatting with some of his rugby friends about their plans for the summer and beyond. When someone suggested playing Truth or Dare, Milo excused himself. He saw Jake, or it could have been Billy, disappearing into the darkness at the edge of the garden with Susanna and Finn. Someone had started a food fight with the pudding and the catering staff had retired to the kitchen. Milo caught his waitress' eye and shrugged apologetically: she would have to clear it up later.

He found Beth sitting on the stairs, with people coming and going around her. Her eyes were glittering, her hair sweaty and dishevelled and her eye make-up smudged. He sat down next to her and she put her arm around him. She smelt of perfume and cigarettes.

'Hey there, you. How's it going?'

'Good,' she hiccupped. 'Taking a break from dancing.'

'With Edward?'

'Uh-huh. He's very hyper.' She turned to him and gave him a wonky smile. 'You know, Milo, I am very drunk and I can't think too straight, but... what? What are you looking at...?'

Milo was staring at the front door, not believing his eyes. The music was thumping in the next room but there was a deathly silence in the hallway, as everyone stopped talking and turned to the door.

'Hello, Atkinson. You're a sight for sore eyes.'

Milo stood up, feeling the heat rise in his face. He took a step down, meaning to go to Zack and punch his lights out, but felt someone tugging at his shorts. He turned to see Beth scrambling up the stairs. At the top, almost out of sight, she waved frantically for him to follow her. The hallway at the top of the stairs was dimly lit, but he could see that she was pale and shaking.

'What's he doing here?' she hissed.

'He's gatecrashing the party,' murmured Milo in disbelief.

'Yeah, I gathered that. Where the fuck is Edward? Not that he's in any state to help.' She took his hand and pulled him along the corridor until they found an empty bathroom. She locked the door behind them and sat on the edge of the bath. 'I have to get myself sobered up. I can't deal with him otherwise.'

Milo nodded.

She washed her face and tied her hair back. 'Need coffee. Food. Then I'll be OK.'

Milo showed her to a back staircase that led to the kitchen, where they sat amongst the bustling waitresses and catering staff and ate anything they could get their hands on and drank strong black coffee. They sat for a while in silence, Beth not needing to say, *Please help me get through this*, and Milo not needing to say, *I'm here for you.*

'I thought we'd seen the last of him.'

Beth shook her head. 'I always had a feeling that I'd see him again. Even if it was just on the TV, or at some party...' She pressed her lips together and raised her eyebrows. 'Shall we?'

They emerged from the kitchen to find Livvy, her face creased with concern. 'I've been looking for you. Do you want to leave?'

Beth shook her head. Livvy hooked her arm into Beth's and the three of them walked through the living room into the dark garden, and onwards until they reached a group sitting under a tree strung with garlands of lights. Milo knew Zack would come and he did, his hair shining in the lights of the house behind him. He slowed down when he saw them and sat on the dry grass. There were a few raised eyebrows and surreptitious glances to see how Beth was handling it, but nothing else was said.

Milo sat in silence and wondered if Beth felt anything for Zack any more. She didn't talk to Milo about him, for obvious reasons. *Damn him, why can't he just stay away? Was it always going to be this way, as Beth suspected? And where the hell is Edward?* Milo was ready to do whatever Beth wanted – to force Zack to leave, for example, and he knew Guy and BJ would pitch in – but he was taking his cues from her, and she was sitting by his side, giving the impression that everything was normal.

At one stage Zack ambled off and Milo saw him dancing inside the house. When he came back, he looked looped. He sat cross-legged directly in front of Beth and stared at her, his head cocked to one side. Milo felt Beth tense beside him.

'Everything all right, Zack?' said Livvy.

He ignored her. 'Atkinson, I see you're wearing that skirt of yours that I like so much.'

'It's actually Annabel's skirt.'

'Well, well, wouldn't you know? You two always did have the same taste.'

Beth rolled her eyes. 'It's such a pleasure to see you again. What are you doing here? Did you come all this way just to bait me?'

'No, I came all this way to see you. Don't you miss me?'

'Yes, terribly. I miss the way you cheated and lied. And the way you sold me out. I pretty much can't live without you.'

'Look, I'm sorry about all that. I made some mistakes. But everything's cool now. Maybe when you're next in London—'

'I'll be sure to call you if I ever need anyone to fuck up my life for me.'

Zack shrugged his shoulders and gave it up as a bad job. He turned away from Beth as if he wasn't bothered and lit a cigarette.

Someone muttered, 'Nice try, Zack.'

Later, the catering staff cleared the food, empty cups and bottles from the house and the DJ played his final songs. It was two o'clock in the morning. Most of the guests had traipsed upstairs and collapsed into their sleeping bags, or fallen asleep on the lawn or on benches in the garden.

Milo yawned and said he'd check up on Edward, who was bound to have passed out on his bed. He wondered if his own bed in one of the spare rooms was still, by some miracle, unoccupied. Beth decided to try her luck in Bonnie's room. As they made their way upstairs, dead on their feet, Milo heard shouting outside the open front door. They paused in the darkness at the top of the stairs, eavesdropping on the heated conversation. When he realised it was Edward and Zack, Milo moved to intervene, but Beth laid her hand on his arm and motioned for him to sit and listen.

He couldn't hear any specific words, but both boys sounded angry. Beth touched him on his hand and mimed going to bed;

she looked pale and she could hardly keep her eyes open. Milo stood up and turned with her to go upstairs.

He heard a car door slam and the noise of scraping gravel. His eyes snapped up to Beth's. If that was Zack leaving, whose car had he taken? They both turned and headed downstairs to talk to Edward, but outside, neither Edward nor Zack were anywhere to be seen. Milo squinted through the darkness and saw a car disappearing through the trees, and in the interior light he saw the shadows of two heads. Milo reeled. What were they doing together?

'Jesus Christ,' said Beth. 'Which of them is driving? The drunk one or the high one? What shall we do?'

Milo was trying to think. Should they follow them? He was sober, he could drive Beth's car, they could catch up with them and flash their lights, maybe get them to pull over. Part of him wanted to leave them to it, to go and crawl into his bed and ignore the problem. But then again, this was Edward, his friend, doing something reckless and dangerous, and he and Beth were perhaps in a position to help him. Milo decided.

'Let's go after them. You got your car keys handy?'

She ran to fetch them, and Milo drove off quickly in the direction they'd seen the lights vanish. It was all narrow country lanes with high hedges around here, and he really had to concentrate through his tiredness to negotiate the curves in the unlit road. He wound down his window for some fresh air. Beth was silent, sitting on her hands, staring straight ahead of her.

They came to a crossroads and he didn't know which way to go, since he hadn't seen Edward's car since they'd started following him. It was like they were lost in a maze. He could be driving around all night. As Milo was turning the car around to go back to the house, he heard a screeching noise and a loud bang.

'Shit. No.' Milo swung the steering wheel in the direction of the noise and slammed his foot down. He turned a curve and saw Edward's car, lights blazing, wrapped round a tree to the side of the lane. Bursting out of his door, ignoring Beth's cries, Milo pelted towards the driver's side. There was white blossom falling from the tree, covering the car and the ground like snow, and Edward, dazed and rubbing his shoulder, was climbing out, muttering and blinking, not seeing Milo as he shouted at him, 'Are you OK? Are you all right?'

Milo looked back at the Beetle. Beth was out of her door and running towards Edward's car to the passenger side. With one quick movement, Milo vaulted over its concertinaed bonnet and saw in the windscreen a circular smash, splayed-out streaks like cracked ice. *It can't be. Got to get there before her*, hands together, grab the passenger door, wrench it open, a scream, he stumbled at the sight of Zack, sitting back in his seat, his face streaked with red, his neck at a strange angle, the inside of the windscreen covered in blood.

No... no... no. Milo froze. He stood, his eyes unable to look away, his body unable to move. He heard Beth's voice from far away. She was shouting at him, but what were the words she was saying? She took his shoulders, shook him and turned him towards her.

'Milo. Milo. Listen. You've got to do what I say. Drive back to the house, call an ambulance. Then find Livvy, wake her up. Tell her what's happened. She'll know what to do.'

'W... what? What do I do?'

'Listen: house, ambulance, Livvy. Say it after me.'

'H... house, Livvy, ambulance.'

'Good enough. Go. Take Edward.'

'What about you? You should come too.'

'*No*. I'm staying here. I...' She looked at the car. 'I'm staying here with Zack.'

'Shouldn't Edward stay here too? If it's the scene of a... crime. Or something.'

'Take him with you, Milo. Look at him. Take him back to the

263

house; he'll be safe there until the police arrive. Do what I say. Now. Please.'

Milo staggered towards Edward, who was hovering near the car, touching his shoulder and still muttering to himself, '...just wanted him to leave... wanted to get him away... away from us... leave us alone...'

Milo grabbed him without a word and led him to the Beetle, pushing him inside and slamming the door. He had to put Edward's seat belt on for him; he was sitting, staring ahead, his mouth moving. Milo started up the engine and reversed until he could turn in a wider section of the lane. As he drove back to the house, struggling to see the road through the black spots that obscured his vision, he regretted that he had left Beth alone at the crash. He didn't have the faintest idea what else to do, other than what she had said, but he did know that he wanted to stay with her.

At the Markhams', he opened Edward's door, holding his arm to help him out of the car, then sat him on the front doorstep and ran to the phone. In a haze, he called 999 and answered the dispatcher's questions, hung up and went to find Livvy. The house was quiet, and even Milo crashing and banging around every room, turning on lights, didn't rouse any of the sleeping guests. In the distance, through the open windows, he heard sirens. At last he found Livvy and shook her awake.

'Livs. Please, wake up. There's been an accident,' he spluttered through his tears.

'What?' Livvy was awake immediately. 'Beth?'

'No, she's fine, Edward too. It's Zack. He... I think he's...'

She looked at his face. 'Shit. Have you called the police?'

The sirens had stopped in the distance, but there was the sound of more cars pulling up on the gravel outside. They ran downstairs and saw two police officers, one male and one female, at the door. While Milo stumbled towards the door to meet them, he could hear Livvy on the phone with Anne, giving her the address.

They explained to Milo that an ambulance and another

squad car had been sent to the scene of the accident. They took him outside to where a third officer was talking to Edward. Milo tripped on the front step and someone steadied him. He pulled his arm away and managed to turn his head before he was silently sick. They sat him down and asked him some questions. He heard words: *fatality... windshield impact... not wearing seat belt... driving under the influence.*

Livvy crouched down beside Edward and put her arm around his shoulders. She said gently, 'Hey. Where are your parents staying tonight?'

Edward didn't answer. He didn't move.

Milo said, 'They're in Edinburgh. I don't know which hotel, but they left a number by the phone. It should be by the phone.'

Livvy disappeared inside with the policewoman.

Milo started crying again. He felt an arm round his shoulder. Livvy. She knew what to do.

'Anne and James are on their way. Edward's mum and dad too, they'll be back as soon as they can. Don't worry, everything's OK now.' She soothed him and stroked his back as the sobs racked his body. All he could see when he closed his eyes was the motionless face of his childhood friend. There had been too much death in his life.

He thought, *When will this ever end?*

Beth had watched Milo drive off into the night. She moved towards the car and put her arms around Zack. Although shards of glass were sticking into her and she felt the skin on her face tear, she felt no pain. She hauled him out of the car and sat on the ground with his head in her arms as she stroked his hair and waited.

Lights and noise broke through the night. She stayed where she was, on the grass, by the car. Shapes ran towards her, arms took him from her, she heard them ask her name, they helped her to stand. She opened her mouth and the last thing she knew, the ground came rushing up towards her.

Chapter Twenty-Five

When Beth came to, the first thing she noticed was how quiet it was. No sirens, although they were in an ambulance. She looked at the ceiling. Not to her right, where the other stretcher was. She felt calm, like someone had poured icy water into her body, and she felt no pain, even though they told her she had cuts from the glass on her head, her arms and her hands. She reached her arms up above her. They had blood on them.

At the hospital, nobody hurried; there were no doctors and nurses hurtling along corridors shouting instructions, no one screaming with pain or grief. They took her to a room, examined her and cleaned her wounds. She waited for the pain to come. She waited to feel something. She followed their instructions and answered their questions.

She waited.

Anne arrived. Muffled voices in the corridor; someone said her name. Both of her names.

She waited.

Anne drove her back to the Markhams'. She sat in the kitchen, where she and Milo had sat together a few hours ago, *Help me get through this*, more questions, people moving towards her and away from her, sounds and voices and lights. They took her in a car as the light of dawn was seeping up all around her, entering her eyes and forcing her to close them.

When she opened them again, she was in a bed. Livvy, red-eyed, was asleep beside her.

She heard faint cries. Someone was having a bad dream.

When she woke again, Livvy was gone. She sat up and felt woozy. Anne was there, James too, and they helped her. She washed and dressed in the clothes they gave her, like a child. She ate and drank what they gave her. The phone rang and rang off again.

'Where is everyone?'

Gone home; their parents came to collect them.

'Milo?'

He's here. But he has to go later today. Would you like to see him?

'Yes.'

She folded herself into his arms and felt his tears wet on her head. *I'm here.* She wondered why she wasn't crying.

He had to go back to work. He'd see her next week. For the funeral.

'Funeral?' she repeated.

Milo left. Beth slept again, before Anne and James took her back to Melchester. She wanted to see Milo again, to ask him a favour. They drove her to The Island, where she spent a few hours in the audiovisual department.

Anne and James offered to drive Milo to the funeral, but he already had a lift. He said goodbye and went back to work.

It would be the first time that Milo had ever been to London.

Part of the road outside the church had been cordoned off: the police had warned James that it was a scrum of journalists, photographers and TV cameras. Beth closed her eyes and took a deep breath, opened the car door and kept her head down. Through the flashing and shouting, enclosed in Anne and James' arms, she ran to the church door. Inside it was blissfully quiet. The church had been decorated with anemones, Madame Smythe's favourite flowers. The pews filled up with friends from school and people Beth recognised from Annabel's house. Justin was there, but not his parents. Madame Smythe and the duke were smartly dressed but ashen and gaunt.

Milo arrived with a middle-aged man, tall and solid like he was, with grey hair and sad eyes. They sat in the pew beside Beth, nearly at the back. Milo gave her his hand.

Don't leave me.

I'm right here.

When it was her turn, Beth stood up unsteadily from her seat. The walk to the front took aeons and every step was the most painful thing she had done in her life. She regretted asking Madame Smythe if she could speak at the funeral now; she couldn't remember why she'd wanted to. Her footsteps on the tiles echoed in the hush of the church. She swallowed but there was no moisture in her mouth. Her breaths in and out were ragged and jumpy. Her head ached. The words stuck in her throat.

'I… I wanted to show you what I remember of Zack. When I was with him, he… he… he was so different, he was so special. He had his own kind of life that he wanted to live, and it shone out of him. Zack didn't believe in dwelling on the past or planning for the future. He shouldn't have died now, not before he could show us what kind of a person he was really going to become. I… I'm sorry, I'm not making any sense today.' She sobbed tearlessly and felt so alone up there, with everyone looking at her.

She turned to the projector and pressed the play button.

Wish You Were Here began to play and pictures of Zack faded in and out on the screen. Stills that Beth had taken of him and film she'd made of him talking, walking, smoking, laughing, acting, scowling, lying, sitting, breathing, living. She stared as the song played out his life and she felt her eyes, sore and throbbing, threatening tears. Her legs buckled and she found Milo's arm under hers.

Five minutes later, it was over. That was all she had to give and it was over. Milo led her out of the church, she felt like the ice had melted, and she gave in to her tears.

At James' flat afterwards, Milo introduced them to Dr Simon Smythe. He had worked in Ethiopia in the refugee camps and then moved to Nairobi, where his ex-wife had called him for the first time since he'd left England to tell him about his son's death. He hadn't known that Milo had lost his parents.

Beth could see that Dr Smythe was becoming increasingly troubled as Milo described his life. He was quiet as they ate dinner and the following day he took Milo back to Weatherbury in his hire car, while Beth and Anne stayed with James in Clapham.

'The press are having a field day,' said Anne to James on the evening after the funeral, after Beth had gone to bed. She sighed as she read the newspapers in front of her on the table. 'What on earth are we going to do? This story's not going to die down for lack of information. The Foreign Secretary's son kills the son of the Duke of Wintoncester, who's the ex-boyfriend of Beth Sauveterre.' She swore and put her head in her hands.

'It will die down. Markham has resigned; they're talking about an ambassadorial posting, possibly Berlin. We need to get through the summer and keep Beth out of the way. Perhaps go back to Cornwall, or Thailand?'

But in the morning when they suggested the plan to Beth,

she refused. She wanted to go back to Melchester. St Emit and Thailand were 'too far away'.

'Too far away from what?'

Beth said she didn't know.

And so they drove back to the little house in the Cathedral Close. Beth walked up the stairs and opened the door to her room. She sat down on her bed and looked around her. What she wanted more than anything now was to stay there, alone.

So she did: for every day of that long, hot summer, she locked herself away in silence. She thought about Zack and how she'd shouted at him on the beach wall and told him she hoped he'd die. In the evenings she came downstairs and sat in the garden, and she was haunted by the thought that everything Edward had done had been her fault. She couldn't sleep at night, lying in her bed and staring at the ceiling, remembering the ambulance and the hospital and how they took Zack away from her to the morgue. She hid everything away in that room and that garden because the words wouldn't come out right and she was afraid of what those words should be. Silence was easier.

Chapter Twenty-Six

Milo was never alone in the weeks following the funeral; Dr Smythe saw to that. He drove Milo back to the cottage and stayed in the spare room. Every day they kept busy, driving to the coast, hiking along the footpaths that criss-crossed the Wessex hills, fishing on a boat Dr Smythe borrowed from an old friend in Knollsea. Sometimes they talked about Africa and Dr Smythe's work in the refugee camps there; sometimes they talked about Milo's school life; sometimes about Zack, sticking to their memories of the old days; sometimes they didn't talk at all, but enjoyed the companionable silence, the warm, salty smell of the sea and the bright colours of the sea and the land reflected in the sunshine.

On the evening before Dr Smythe's return to Kenya, they sat in the cottage garden, side by side, grilling sausages on a makeshift barbecue.

'I've asked Mrs Toms to stop by every now and again, see how you are,' said Dr Smythe, staring into the fire.

'Check up on me, you mean?' But Milo said it cheerfully.

Dr Smythe gave him a guilty smile.

Milo said, 'You don't have to worry about me. I'm fine. I've been through worse.'

'You shouldn't be alone.' When he looked at Milo, he had tears in his eyes, and it wasn't the first time Milo had seen him like that.

Milo thought, *Perhaps it's you who shouldn't be alone.*

Dr Smythe said, 'I've been thinking. I'm going to move back; get a job near here. I've been meaning to settle in Blighty again.'

'If you're sure.' Milo waited. He thought he knew what was coming.

'I'd like to help you more. You shouldn't have to work all hours and worry about earning enough money to feed yourself. I want to give you some money to tide you over, get you through school and university.'

'That's very kind. But I'll pay you back when I start earning.'

'So, a loan?'

'A loan.' Milo took his outstretched hand and they shook on it. 'Thank you, Dr Smythe.'

'Let's stop all this "Dr Smythe" now. Simon will be fine.'

'OK. Thanks.'

Dr Smythe – Simon – paused, as if he was deciding whether to say more. 'You've really been through the mill these last few years. I'm proud of you. A lesser man would have crumbled.'

'Like Dad, you mean?' It just slipped out; Milo hadn't meant to sound so resentful.

'Your dad had his own demons. But you're different. Stronger. More like your mum.'

'He took Mum's death hard. Harder than I did, apparently.'

Simon shook his head sadly. 'It's more complicated than that… it's important for you to know that your dad's suicide wasn't a reflection of how he felt about you.'

'I'm not sure I agree with you. We both missed her; only he left me to deal with it. I was seventeen years old.' Milo jabbed the fire with the stick he was holding, sending up sparks into the semi-darkness.

'No. That's not the full story. You probably don't remember because we kept it all away from you. Milo, listen. This is important. You need to know that he wasn't a well person, his whole life. He'd been suffering from depression before you were born, way before your mum died.'

'What?'

'He'd always struggled. This is what I'm trying to tell you. Those times I used to come down to Wessex and take you and Zack off for the day – our camping trips, the rugby matches, all of that...'

'What?'

'There were times before then, that he'd tried to take his own life.'

'What?' Milo wished he could stop saying, 'What?' but he couldn't seem to process what Simon was saying. 'How did I not know this?'

'Your mum didn't want you to see him like that. I helped out as much as I could until he was back on his feet.' Simon looked at Milo. 'I thought you ought to know. You couldn't have done anything. It wasn't your fault.'

It wasn't my fault. Slowly those words arranged themselves in Milo's frozen brain, until they were the only things he could see. *It wasn't my fault.* He stared at Simon, his heart hammering, feeling the words and the thoughts solidify. *It wasn't my fault.* Milo put his head in his hands and felt relief rush through his body and tears burn his eyes. All this time, he'd tried to figure out what exactly what he'd done wrong and the answer was nothing. *It wasn't my fault.*

'Milo, was I right to tell you? Are you going to be OK?'

Milo straightened up and nodded. 'Yes. Definitely. I'm going to be OK.'

Thanks to Simon's loan, Milo didn't have to work through the summer holidays for the first time since he could remember. Twice a week, he did his work experience at the vet's practice on the outskirts of Melchester.

On the other days he went to visit Beth, who refused to leave her house. He had tried taking her out for a walk one evening, but a young girl approached with an autograph book and smiled sweetly at her. As Beth reached out her hand to take it, the little girl said, with tears in her eyes, 'I'm so sorry that people you know keep dying in car crashes.' Beth turned on her heel and stormed back inside the house, leaving Milo to apologise to the girl and her mother.

At least Beth agreed to see him – she wouldn't even open her door to Livvy, who called Milo after work one day and begged him to do something.

One day he and the vet paid a call to Yalbury Farm, which had a riding stables, run by the farmer's wife. Mrs Durnover was fretting because her groom had broken his arm and was out of action for at least four weeks. Could Milo fill in? He couldn't, but he told her he knew someone who could.

When he knocked off work he drove to Melchester and found Beth in her usual spot in the garden. She was so thin, she looked more like her mother than ever, frail and washed out but hauntingly beautiful. She often forgot to wash her hair these days and was wearing an old, faded pair of jeans and a baggy T-shirt. She had a book on her knees, but Milo noticed that she hadn't read much of it since last week.

'I've found a holiday job for you.'

'I can't. People stare at me and say stupid things.'

'You'd have to get up at the crack of dawn.'

'You know I'm not a morning person.'

'It's on a farm, out in the middle of nowhere.'

'Sounds charming.' She scowled at him.

'The pay is pitiful.'

'Well, you're really selling it to me.'

'It's with horses. Grooming, mucking out, feeding, exercising them when they're not being used for lessons. Will you think about it at least?'

'If I think about it will you bugger off?'

'Nope.'

'You're so annoying. Seriously, Milo, I don't think I'm ready.'

'You'll never know unless you try.'

She shook her head, giving up. 'OK. You win. I'll think about it.' She sighed and went back to picking a scab on her arm. 'When would they want me to start?'

Milo grabbed her thin wrist and looked at her watch. 'Mrs Durnover is expecting you in… about eleven hours.'

She blinked. 'What? Don't tell me you've already told them I'll do it?'

'Uh-huh.'

'What the…? You can't do that, Milo.'

'I just did.'

In the morning, she followed the directions Milo had given her and arrived at Yalbury Farm at 6am. She could imagine from Mrs Durnover's expression how she must look – even though she'd washed her hair last night and tried to eat something. She looked frail and tired. She felt frail and tired.

But once Mrs Durnover had shown her what to do and left her to it, her exhaustion melted away, and for the first time since Edward's party, she forgot about Zack, about everything but saddles and bridles and stirrups. The horses were beautiful and stood patiently as she tried to remember what Edward had taught her. She loved touching them, their warm flesh under their silky coats that she brushed until they were glossy. Three hours later, all the horses were gleaming and ready for their lesson. At the end of the day, she worked on each of them until her arms ached so badly she could hardly drive home.

When Milo called at eight o'clock that evening she was fast asleep.

Beth worked to blot everything out. Her appetite returned and she wolfed down the meals she was given, because they no longer tasted like cardboard. The colour returned to her cheeks, her hair shone and when she rode the horses, she felt the nearest to happiness that she thought possible. She cut off several pairs of her jeans and wore them to work, with old T-shirts and trainers. She wore her hair in a thick plait down her back, no make-up, chipped nail varnish and the NY Yankees baseball cap on backwards. Not a single one of the kids who came for riding lessons or their parents recognised her.

She still cried herself to sleep some nights. She still had bad dreams. She thought about Zack and Bonnie and Edward and blamed herself for the whole mess. If she hadn't come along, everything would have been different. Zack and Bonnie would have found a way to be together and Edward would have been safely on his way to Cambridge University.

When Zack had died, she'd felt like she was swimming underwater. Everything around her was quiet and dark. The water was pressing on her and none of her senses worked properly. She couldn't hear her own heart beating. She couldn't feel her own skin. But she wanted to stay submerged because if she rose up to the surface of the water, the horror of what she'd caused would be there and she couldn't face it. It was too big.

Time was abstract and enormous; a day seemed like a month and a sleepless night like a year. But when she started working at Yalbury Farm, there was something about those horses that trickled into her senses. They were so alive, it was frightening. When she touched them or smelt them, it flooded through her and warmed her. At night, when she closed her eyes and thoughts of Zack loomed, she reached out and touched the horses and felt their heat and their softness, and she drifted off to sleep. Mrs Durnover had been kind and sometimes told her to slow down a bit, take one horse at a time. That was how she got better: one horse at a time.

She had a visit one evening from Milo.

He dumped a cardboard box on her bed and said, 'I've got good news and… weird news.' He sat down next to her. 'Mrs Markham came to the cottage. They've been trying to get Edward committed to a psychiatric hospital, and Zack's mum and dad have agreed to support that in court instead of a prison sentence for him.'

'Wow. That's so kind of them to do that.'

'Yeah, so Mrs Markham is hopeful that Edward will be able to put it behind him and concentrate on getting better. If that's possible. They – the Markhams – are talking about going abroad, perhaps next year, or as soon as Edward can be discharged.'

Beth felt a tiny twinge of hope. It was possible, surely it was.

'And the weird news?' she said.

'Mrs Markham was clearing out some of Edward's school things the other day and found this box with your name on it. She asked Edward, and he said he wants you to have it.'

'Why didn't she bring it to me herself? Doesn't she want to see me?' *She blames me for what's happened with Edward*, she thought.

'It's not that she blames you. It's more like she thinks you wouldn't want to see her. Because her son killed your… killed Zack.'

Beth stared at the box. 'What's in it?'

'I don't know, I haven't looked. Neither did Mrs Markham. It's for you.'

With trepidation, Beth opened the lid and they saw piles of letters, books, photos and packages. She reached out and picked up a piece of paper. It was a letter Edward had written to her from Berlin and never posted, dated the 21st February. Another written the following day, then two more the week after that.

There were letters he'd written all the way through March and April and a diary he'd filled with stories about Beth, how he loved her, how it felt to kiss her and what she looked like naked. Beth felt queasy as she read it. She flicked through the pages and read her name and Bonnie's as Edward confused the things he'd said to them. There were poems and presents, the watch he'd given to her for her birthday, jewellery, twelve faded red roses, unopened boxes of chocolates, the map she and Milo had drawn to Greenhill Bridge, newspaper cuttings from Easter, and scrawled over everything, *Beth Markham, B. M.*

Milo and Beth looked through everything and she could see that he was getting more and more worked up. It was all sick, the product of a sick mind, and she felt only pity for Edward and her overwhelming and relentless guilt. All of it, it was all her fault. She waited for Milo to ask her whether any of it was true and knew, because she knew him, that he would never believe a word of it. How lucky was she, to have his unbreakable loyalty? If only she believed in herself as he believed in her. She let him take the box away to make a bonfire of it in his garden.

Milo carried on visiting her every day. Sometimes, when she was having a bad day, she took it out on him, snapping at him or ignoring him. He apologised if he thought he'd said the wrong thing. She complained that she couldn't read any more, and he offered to read to her. She griped that she looked and smelt terrible every day after work, and he went upstairs to run her a bath. She took it out on him and he listened, or soothed, or smiled, or hugged her, whatever she needed. When they were alone she told him about her nightmares and how Zack's face haunted her. She said a word she could never in her life remember saying to anyone, ever: sorry.

The start of the new school term was looming. Everyone else had been sure that Beth wouldn't want to return to The Island, but Milo knew she would want to be there and he knew why, because he felt the same way. At The Island they felt safe.

Term started and Beth threw herself into the routine and felt comfortable with the curfews and the rules that she had found so restrictive last year. She wanted to direct another play and was constantly in the AV department editing films that she'd made. They were all so busy with piles of homework and university applications that there was no time to dwell on their grief.

Milo began writing his application, and had intended to write Bristol Uni as his first choice, as well as Liverpool and Edinburgh. Simon persuaded him to apply for Cambridge as well. He had never even considered Cambridge, but Simon and Mr Toms were optimistic. Simon had also written to an old rugby friend of his who lived in Queensland, who offered Milo a job on his sheep farm for July, August and September next year, after he'd finished A Levels and before he went to university. Milo was tempted; he had never been abroad and the money was good, which meant he could pay Simon back earlier than he thought.

Beth had always planned to go to an American college, USC or NYU, but was having second thoughts. James tried in vain to find out what had changed her mind. She couldn't explain it; she'd thought about it non-stop through the summer and she knew she wanted to stay in Britain. She visited the NFTS in Beaconsfield and applied only there. Everywhere else was 'too far away'. James gritted his teeth and said nothing. He was splitting his time between London and LA, and Anne was getting itchy feet again and was talking about travelling around South America. But Beth, young, adventurous and with her whole future in front of her, didn't want to go 'too far away', a phrase that was starting to get on James' nerves.

Beth was surprised at herself too and she found herself wondering what had changed. She knew she was a different person from the one who'd arrived at The Island just over a year ago. She felt like she'd grown up so much since then, when she'd only been interested in how people saw her and how attractive they found her. She had behaved so badly towards Edward and had deserved everything she got from Zack. When she heard about Milo's plans, especially about Australia, she tried to be happy for him, but failed miserably. She tried not to be selfish, but it was no good.

She was in the AV department one afternoon, editing a film she'd made of the boys – Milo, Guy and Henry – and she was messing about with setting it to a song. The clips of Milo were the best; he was ignoring the camera as she'd told them all to do, whereas Guy and Henry kept on thinking it was funny to speak directly to it. She cut out most of the footage of them. The song she set the film to was *Here, There and Everywhere*, and after an hour or so she was pleased with the result. She sat back to watch it.

She was unaware that Guy and Livvy were walking past, or that they heard the song and looked through the window. They nudged each other and watched the film too. Milo was smiling shyly, talking to Guy, putting his arms round his two friends, telling a joke and playing the guitar with his back to the camera. There was some footage from a rugby match, and also of Milo standing on a hill with a view of the sea.

They crept away. Livvy's eyes were wide with surprise.

'Did you know?' she whispered, even though they were out of earshot of the AV room.

'Know what?'

'That Beth… is in love with Milo?'

'Beth is in love with Milo?'

'Oh, come on, don't be thick. Did you not just see that film? Do you not understand anything about girls?'

Guy, who had been concentrating on his own appearance in the film, caught up. He beamed. 'Yes. Oh yes, yes, I see what you mean. Oh wow. This is great. This is… are we allowed to tell him, Livs?'

She shook her head. 'No, absolutely not. She has to do it herself, in her own time. What if Milo doesn't love her back?'

Guy stared at her, dumbfounded. 'Not… love… Beth… back. Do you not understand anything about boys?'

Chapter Twenty-Seven

The first Saturday of half-term was Milo's nineteenth birthday. It was also the day of the grudge match against Sherton Abbas school, and Beth had been banned by Mr Shepherd from watching. Fine by her; she had other plans.

She had arranged to pick up Milo from his cottage that evening, and while the whole school was at the match, she did her hair and make-up more carefully than usual and chose her favourite skirt and blouse. It was still too early, but she couldn't think of anything else to do to fill the time, so she set off and, as she walked through the woods to Milo's cottage, it started raining, the drops splashing through the trees that were losing their leaves. Before long she was soaked through, but she didn't mind.

It was running through her mind like a train, everything that had happened with Edward and Zack. And Milo. If she tried to picture herself next year, in ten years, in thirty years, all she could make out in that uncertain future was that she wanted him to be there too. She never wanted to be without him.

She started to panic.

Jesus, is that what this is? Is it all about Milo? Has it always been about him? I don't know. I've screwed up everything: I screwed up when I hurt Edward and then I did it again when I was with Zack.

It's no good.

I'm no good.

But with Milo I could be good. Milo is pretty much everything to me. I love him. What? I love him? I love Milo? I do, I really do. I love Milo.

She sat on a tree stump and hid her head in her hands. If she could have, she would have climbed under it. For the first time in her life, she was properly terrified.

She didn't know how long she stayed like that, but she was starting to shiver, and then it came to her: *Fear is good, fear is real.*

There was this: *If I want him, if I don't want to lose him, I have to do something about it. Now.*

After the match, Milo had showered and changed into an old pair of jeans with holes in one knee, and a T-shirt underneath a red checked shirt that Beth had once described as 'not as awful as your other clothes'. She'd said she was coming by at six o'clock on her way home to Melchester. He heard her knock and open the door. He didn't even look up from his book.

'Hi. Hey, you're early. How is that possible?'

She didn't answer as she stepped inside the open door.

Now he looked up. 'You're dripping on my floor. Is everything OK? Are you OK? What's wrong?' It was her face; Milo hadn't seen her like this for ages. He sprang up from his chair and crossed over towards her.

She stopped him in his tracks with her hand. 'I'm OK,' she whispered. But there were tears rolling down her face and she looked pale and frightened.

'Beth, tell me.'

'I don't want you to go away next year.'

'O... K... what's this all about?'

'I... I can't do without you.'

He looked down at his hands, gripping the back of the chair. He didn't know what she meant. Was she having another bad day?

'I don't want you to leave me.'

What was that? Milo looked up from his hands to her face and tried to read it; no, it was no use, he still didn't know what she meant. His heart was thumping and there was a lump in his throat. He felt like crying himself.

Beth spoke again. 'The days when you're with me are good days. And the days when you're not with me are bad days. And... so... I thought... if I saw you every day, then every day would be a good day.'

He let his head drop again. OK. So she did mean that she was having a bad day. She needed him, but only to stop her having a bad day. Well, then. Fine. Not a problem.

'Milo. Do you understand what I'm trying to say to you?'

He nodded. Swallowed the lump in his throat. Concentrated very hard on a knot in the wood on the kitchen table.

'Then ask me,' she said.

'Ask you what?'

She didn't reply for a few seconds. 'Milo, look at me.'

So he did. There was this: she was standing there, in the door frame, her hands clenched by her sides, her face soft and her eyes hoping. Hoping. He saw something different and it gave him hope too. His heart lurched. He didn't dare. Yes he did.

'Do you want me to ask you... if you...' He couldn't say it. Yes he could. 'If you love me?'

She nodded, her eyes shining.

'Do you love me?'

She carried on nodding. He was across the room in three strides and took her head in his hands.

'Really? You really mean it?'

She didn't need to nod. He closed his eyes for a fraction of a second and kissed her very gently, just brushing her lips, they were so soft and warm; he couldn't have imagined anything so warm. In a panic, he pulled away from her and ran his hand through his hair.

'Beth. Shit.' He bit his top lip; this was all too much. He was dizzy and stepped back, and felt the wall near him holding him up. He couldn't touch her.

So she touched him. 'Milo,' she whispered, smiling. 'Stay with me here.'

Her hand was on his shoulder, and she pushed him against the wall and slid her other hand round his back and put both her hands in his back pockets. She was waiting like this, so close, everything touching, looking right into his eyes, waiting for him. He slowly bent his head towards hers and then he kissed her. Properly.

Sometime later, could've been hours later, they had to come up for air. He took her hand, slammed the door with his foot and, still kissing her, led her towards the stairs.

She remembered the party. 'We can't – we've got to go to the pub.'

'I don't want to go to the pub,' he growled, kissing her neck. It tickled and made the hairs stand up. *Party? What party?*

She sat down on the stairs and Milo sat next to her, facing her, his hand on the back of her head, kissing her again until they lay back on the stairs.

'We have to go. Ahhh.' She closed her eyes. 'It's your surprise birthday party.'

'What? Oh no, no. I'm not waiting any longer for you. I've waited so long already. We're not going.'

She tried to be firm. 'We've got to go. Everyone's in the Buck's Head. We'll be late.'

'You're always late. They won't mind. I'm not going anywhere.'

This was true. He was right. It wasn't important. The others could wait. The kissing was becoming quicker now, she couldn't stop, he was turning her into jelly, *Oh God, focus.* She had to focus. She took his face in her hands and pulled her hands through his short curls. *Focus.*

'Milo, there is nothing that I would like more in the world than for you to ravish me here, on the stairs. But we don't have time now. We are going to the pub. There are teachers there. The Tomses are there. You're head boy now. We have to go. We have time for this later.' She was impressed by how responsible she could be.

'Seriously, I don't think I can manage it.'

'You'll never know unless you try.'

Milo groaned and lay back on the stairs, staring at the ceiling. 'This is a very unfair thing of you to do to me. Come here, seduce me, then tell me to stop. This is the worst non-surprise birthday party ever.' He pushed himself up and held out his hand to her. 'How do I look?'

She took his hand and held on to it, looking him up and down. He looked gorgeous. 'Let's see – your hair is a mess. You have some sort of a dirty smudge on your cheek. Your shirt could do with an iron. Your jeans are from the late 1970s. Your shoelaces are undone. Yep, you look quite normal.'

He grinned sheepishly. 'What would you suggest I do about this?' And he pointed at the front of his jeans, which had a bulge in them.

'Oh God. Oh, I don't know. Just think about something really unsexy. Like kissing Margaret Thatcher.'

'I think kissing Margaret Thatcher would be quite sexy.'

'Ugh, you are revolting. Come on, we have to go.' With a degree of strength and maturity she never knew she had, she dragged him to the door.

The rain was still pouring down. He found an umbrella and

held it over the pair of them. *The pair of them.* That sounded good. They walked to the pub together, arm in arm, in comfortable silence, Beth thinking about Milo and Milo thinking about Margaret Thatcher.

'They're coming, they're coming,' shouted Guy, and he ducked under the window frame. 'Everybody ready? Shhh. Stop making noise.'

Everyone – Mr and Mrs Toms, Mr Shepherd, Guy, BJ, Livvy, Tab, Andy and Milo's other friends from the village – sat stifling their giggles and waiting. And waiting. Livvy gestured to Guy that he should look again. He raised his head over the window frame and his eyes widened in shock.

'Holy Mother of Shit.'

'Language please, Mr Revel,' said Mr Toms, who looked out of the window too. 'Bloody hell.'

By now everyone was scrambling to the window, laughing and screaming at the sight of Milo and Beth snogging under the umbrella. Guy knocked on the window and they finally heard the muffled noises. Red in the face, but with ear-to-ear grins, they came into the pub, the door held open by the landlord.

'Would sir and madam be interested in a room?' he enquired.

Everyone was supposed to shout, 'Surprise', but instead there was a long silence, broken by the girls surging forwards to wrench Beth away from Milo. They herded her to a table in the corner, asking her a stream of questions. Beth sat with them, a calm smile on her face, nodding and giggling.

The boys and the teachers watched them for a moment and Mrs Toms said to Milo, 'Happy birthday, dear. Would you like your present?'

'I think he's already had that.' Billy smirked.

'Let's try and keep the level of smut to a minimum, shall we, Mr Rose?'

Mr Toms bought a round of drinks before he and his wife went home. Mr Shepherd followed not long after. The boys drifted over to where Beth and the girls sat, and Livvy made room for Milo. He sat next to Beth and whispered into her ear, 'This is torture.'

At the end of the evening, Livvy, BJ, Guy and Tab said goodbye. They were staying at the Roses' farm overnight. Milo's friends from the village were last seen walking down the road to the chippy, singing *At Last* from *Rain Man*, loudly, out of tune and with slightly less romantic lyrics.

That was the longest evening of Milo's life. Too much talking, not enough kissing Beth. It was impossible to concentrate on what anyone was saying. How did he manage to keep his hands off her? She was sitting next him and even if he didn't look at her, he could smell her and feel the warmth from her.

They sprinted back to the cottage and when he'd closed the door and all the curtains, he turned to her and she was smiling at him like he was mad.

'What are you doing?'

'Umm… closing the curtains. So nobody can see in. I'm quite famous, you know.' *Oh shit, I'm babbling. Stop babbling. Smile, relax, stay cool.*

'Milo, am I making you nervous?'

'N… no.'

'That's the first time you've ever lied to me.'

Busted. OK, well, here goes nothing. He walked over to where she stood. 'I've lied to you before, about the "*love the spring*" flowers.'

'I know.'

'I'll never lie to you again. I am very, very nervous.'

'Don't be.'

'I might be useless.'

'You won't be. Listen, you've already seen me naked, right?'

The pool. Oh yes, how could he ever forget? 'R… right.'

'And you've carried me in your arms.'

'That too.'

'So, let's re-enact those situations.'

'You… want me to carry you upstairs and… take off all your clothes?'

'Something along those lines.'

Right. He was shaking as he took a deep breath. He'd seen this in a film somewhere. It wasn't very smooth but he did his best to sweep her into his arms. Up the stairs, trying to concentrate, one foot in front of the other; not easy when Beth was kissing his neck and biting his shoulder. Somehow they made it upstairs and into Milo's bedroom. The bed. *Beth Atkinson is lying on my bed. With me. This is happening. This is real.*

There was nowhere on earth Beth would rather be than in Milo West's arms. He was delicious and warm and his neck smelt so good, just like she remembered. It was dark in his room, with just the light from a lamp casting shadows on their faces. He pulled his T-shirt over his head and she helped him with his jeans. His arm reached out and undid the buttons on her blouse. One, by one, by one. His eyes were concentrating on those buttons so hard, she thought they might burst into flames. Milo undressed was something she'd seen before, at Greenhill Bridge. But the hairs on his arms, the muscles underneath, every freckle, every skin cell, she drank it in until she was dizzy with him.

Milo kissed her everywhere; he couldn't leave even one part of her unkissed. All he wanted was her skin, her lips, more of her, all of her. He heard her moan, or it could have been him.

Beth moved underneath him and even though they were wrapped around each other, every part of her touching every part of him, it wasn't enough, it wasn't close enough.

They lay together and Milo stroked her hair softly. He traced his fingertips around her face, the scar on her cheek from the broken glass.

'Does it still hurt?'

'Not so much, now,' Beth said. 'I was scared that you didn't like me any more.'

'Are you kidding? Why would you think that?'

'Oh, something about "Why don't you try and stay single next year, blah blah."'

Milo covered his head with his hands. 'What kind of an idiot would have said that?'

'The kind of idiot who sleeps with a girl on the first date.'

'Is this our first date? What about when I fell off the ladder and you saved my life?'

'Doesn't count. A date has to have food or drink involved. Also, both people have to be conscious.'

'The night after the races, then? We had a coffee together. That counts.'

'Then I wasn't conscious.'

Milo rubbed his head. 'Shit. This is our first date. I never knew I was so easy. So, what do we do now? What's going to happen next year? I don't want to be apart from you, not after waiting so long for you to realise you can't live without me.'

'I don't know. It's going to be horrible when you go to Australia.'

'Huh. Australia. Why would I want to go there? They keep beating us at cricket and rugby.'

'What if... I'm at the NFTS and you're in Cambridge? That's not too far away from each other, is it? What is it, about a hundred miles?'

'Sixty-six,' corrected Milo, grinning. 'I measured it on a map. So that's a happy ending, if ever I saw one.'

'I don't like happy endings.'

'Jesus, your films are going to be cheerful. No romantic comedies for you, then?'

'Nope. I was thinking, I'm more of an action kind of girl. Do you think George Lucas would ever hire me to make some more *Star Wars* films?'

Chapter Twenty-Eight

Guy, Livvy, Billy, Jake and Tab drove back to the Roses' and talked about Beth and Milo the whole way.

'I did not see that coming,' said Tab.

'Don't be such an airhead. Everyone could see that coming,' roared Jake, practically dancing in his seat. 'No one can resist the charms of Milo West, his scintillating chat, the unstoppable force of his confabulation. When did you find out about it, little sis?'

'Oh, ages ago, of course. She just wouldn't admit it to herself. But I knew. You too, Guy?' She gave him a pointed look.

'Ah, that is an excellent question, and one that deserves a lengthy answer. Settle down, my friends, for I am the Keeper of All the Secrets of the West, and I will impart them to you and then you will share the wondrous wisdom.

'That cretin has been wetting his pants for her since the first moment he laid his soppy great eyes on her gorgeous arse. I would be willing to bet the lives of my entire family and all my worldly goods, including my Tennis Girl poster and my collection of porn magazines, that it was Ms Atkinson who had to do *all* the running to get him into her pants. Such is the nature of our friend, and always will be. Put on some music, Livs, I'm welling up here.'

So they drove on, into the night, towards their own tomorrows.

Quotes From Existing Works

I've included lots of quotes in this novel that have been nicked from other writers. That's OK – Thomas Hardy did it himself – his title *Far from the Madding Crowd* is from Thomas Gray's *Elegy Written in a Country Churchyard*.

"No man is an island"
from *Meditation 17 - Devotions upon Emergent Occasions* by John Donne.

Various permutations of, quotes and misquotes from *She Walks in Beauty* by Lord Byron.

"The truth will out"
From Shakespeare's *The Merchant of Venice*.

"Love the spring" ("Sweet lovers love the spring")
From Shakespeare's *As You Like It*.

"Ignorance is bliss"
Also from Thomas Gray - *Ode on a Distant Prospect of Eton College*.

Also by F. J. Campbell

No Number Nine

What do you do when your amazing, beloved sister dies?

Hide in your room for two years?
Sleep with a very, very wrong man?
Leave home and start a new life, lying to everyone you meet
including your kind employer, your curious friends
and the man you love?

Pip Mitchell's an expert at making seriously bad decisions. But when her past, present and future collide at the Sydney Olympic Games, she's going to have to decide whose side she's on – or she'll lose everyone she loves.

"This book is in my top 5 surprise books of the year – it gave me a fuzzy feeling in my chest and put a stupid grin on my face. I loved this book, and I can't wait to see what F. J. does next."
Kate Hardy, beautifulbookland.com blogger

"Calling all #hockeyfamily - this book needs to go straight to the top of your summer reading list. Drama, love, laughter, lots of hockey players & hockey club antics we can all relate to."
Helen Richardson-Walsh, GB hockey gold medallist

A novel for anyone who enjoys a well-plotted love story with characters you won't want to say goodbye to – from sweet, confused Pip, to lovable Billy and potty-mouthed Nadine.

No Number Nine is available to buy as an ebook or paperback. To find out more, go to www.fjcampbell.net

Acknowledgements

Although this is my second published novel, it's actually the first one I ever wrote, and as you might imagine, that takes a huge amount of self-delusion and misplaced confidence. My first draft was pretty cringeworthy, and it took another two years after I'd finished that draft to be able to say that I was ready to publish *The Islanders*. But – and this is the awesome bit – some of my friends and family *believed in me*. They told me I could do this – and so I did. Without them, I would never have finished *The Islanders*.

Thanks to Faye Booth, my amazing Editor who kept tabs on where all the horses and the tan marks were supposed to be; and to Joe Shillito and Jonathan White at Troubador Publishing, for whom nothing is too much trouble and no question is too stupid.

Jericho Writers and in particular the Neons (my online writing group) are wonderful and supportive and the *Edit Your Novel* course I did was fantastic, as was the professional critique by Sam Mills. Thank you.

Thanks also to the wonderful author Rachel McIntyre, who mentored me and gave me a big dollop of confidence and some invaluable advice about social media.

Rick, Sarah, Andy, Gretchen and Florence: you read the very first draft and I apologise now for making you do that. I hope your eyes and your brains have recovered. You were so unbelievably nice about it.

Vikki, Lesley, Dorte and Sigrid – thank you for the time you spent reading the book and helping me with your wonderfully kind and honest feedback.

A special mention to the PAF: those long-ago school days and holidays in Cornwall we had together, although not directly described in *The Islanders*, certainly were the inspiration for much of the book.

And last but not least – my favourite three boys in the whole world – Rick, Oliver and Toby. This book (and all my books) are for you.

Last word

The Islanders is an independently published book. So before you close it, sighing wistfully, and return it to your bookshelf, it would be crazily brilliant if you could do me a small(ish) favour.

Tell your friends about *The Islanders* and how much you loved it.

Review it on booksellers' websites (e.g. Troubador, Amazon, Kobo, Wordery, etc), or on book review websites (e.g. Goodreads).

Sign up for my mailing list on www.fjcampbell.net and I'll email you to tell you when my next book's out.

Follow me on social media – like me, share me, retweet me
Twitter @fj_campbell
Facebook FJ_CampbellAuthor/TheIslandersFJC
Instagram fjcampbell_author

The more you do, the more time I have to write my next book – so it's a win-win!